Guilty
Pleasures

Guilty
Pleasures

Deborah
Fletcher
Mello

Kensington Publishing Corp.
http://www.kensingtonbooks.com

DAFINA BOOKS are published by

Kensington Publishing Corp.
119 West 40th Street
New York, NY 10018

All Kensington Titles, Imprints, and Distributed Lines are available at special quantity discounts for bulk purchases for sales promotions, premiums, fund-raising, and educational or institutional use. Special book excerpts or customized printings can also be created to fit specific needs. For details, write or phone the office of the Kensington special sales manager: Kensington Publishing Corp., 119 West 40th Street, New York, NY 10018, attn: Special Sales Department, Phone: 1-800-221-2647.

Dafina and the Dafina logo Reg. U.S. Pat. & TM Off.

ISBN-13: 978-1-4967-0430-6
ISBN-10: 1-4967-0430-4
First mass market printing: April 2016

eISBN-13: 978-1-4967-0431-3
eISBN-10: 1-4967-0431-2
Kensington Electronic Edition: April 2016

10 9 8 7 6 5 4 3 2

Printed in the United States of America

Chapter One

Alexander Barrett grinned as the blond, blue-eyed newscaster slowly brushed a manicured hand across his broad chest, neatening his shirt. The gesture was flirtatious as she batted the length of her false eyelashes at him.

"Can't have you looking shabby, Mr. Barrett," Pam Lawry purred, her deep alto voice dropping to a loud whisper. She tapped her nails against the embroidered logo on his cotton polo.

Alexander laughed. "I appreciate that, Ms. Lawry."

"Would you prefer to be called Alexander or Alex?"

He shrugged. "Alex is fine. You know I don't stand on any formalities."

The woman was smiling from ear to ear as she gestured toward the cameraman, who eyed them both with amusement. "What's my count?" she queried.

"You're live in two minutes," her associate answered.

The woman nodded as she winked an eye in response. She turned her gaze back to Alexander. "Just relax, look directly at me, and smile," she said. "I promise I'll make this as easy as pie."

Alexander laughed. "I guess it's a good thing I like pie."

She laughed with him. "I guess it is!"

The cameraman threw her a count. "Twenty-five seconds."

Pam smoothed the front of her Diane von Furstenberg wrap dress and slid her fingers through the length of her hair. She lifted her microphone between them, then pursed her lips together in an exaggerated kiss before relaxing her face and smiling.

"Five, four, three, two, and we are live!" the cameraman noted.

Pam lifted her chin slightly, tilting her head just so. Her smile blossomed full and wide, her eyes staring into the camera. "Thank you, Stephen! I'm here this morning with former pro basketball phenom Alexander Barrett at the grand opening of his new sports and athletic center! Alex, hello!" she exclaimed as she tilted the microphone toward him.

Alexander took a quick breath. "Hello, Pam! Thank you for being here."

"We wouldn't have missed this! So tell me about Champs," she said, gesturing behind her as the cameraman panned the camera over the new 120,000-square-foot athletic facility. The high-tech glass building sat on twenty-six acres of prime Boulder, Colorado, real estate with a panoramic mountain view in the distance.

Alexander smiled. "Champs is the premier destination for your health and fitness goals. It's been designed to give our members an unparalleled gym experience, supporting all of their health and fitness aspirations."

The camera panned back to the two of them standing side by side.

"It's truly an impressive facility!" Pam exclaimed. "I

was overwhelmed as we took the tour. It looks like you've got something for everyone's fitness level."

Alexander nodded. "It's my dream come true. We offer indoor and outdoor pools, nationally renowned group-fitness instructors and personal trainers, an indoor cycling studio, and cutting-edge fitness equipment. Our programming aims to exceed your expectations, with weight-loss options, yoga, dance, and Pilates classes, indoor-cycling classes, outdoor-cycling rides, and so much more.

"We hope to help organizations, communities, and individuals achieve their total health objectives, athletic aspirations, and fitness goals by engaging in their areas of interest—or discovering new passions with some of our exciting new programs. So, yeah, there's something for everyone!"

Pam nodded. "And the facility will operate twenty-four hours a day, seven days a week, is that correct?"

"That's correct, Pam. Good health doesn't take a holiday."

Pam chuckled as she turned to stare back toward the camera. "Now, everyone here in Boulder knows basketball superstar Alexander Barrett." Her gaze shifted back to stare at him. "We've followed your career faithfully and when your knee injury sidelined you permanently, you built a very successful personal-training business that has been a cornerstone of Boulder's athletic scene. And you've coached talent worldwide, helping some of the biggest names in sports get into shape."

The camera zoomed in on Alexander's face.

"I did, and I'm very proud of that. My education is in sports physiology and I have a master's degree in sports science. I just love what I do and sharing that with others. Champs will now allow me to do that on an even larger scale."

The camera zeroed back in on Pam.

The woman turned her body, looking directly into the lens as she smiled. "Champs is hosting a weekend of free events and hopes that everyone will come out to take a tour of the facility and meet Alexander and his team of trainers. I'm already geared up for a Zumba dance class so I hope you'll come on out and join me. Let's give our hometown champion your support. This is Pam Lawry. Good-day, Boulder!"

There was a moment of pause as she stared, smiling, into the camera, her full grin showcasing picture-perfect veneers.

"And, we are clear!" the cameraman noted. He shifted the camera equipment off his shoulder.

Pam nodded, her television persona morphing back into business mode. "Do me a favor and get some footage of the interior. They're planning on running another segment on the late-night news so we'll be able to cut more detail into the nightly feed."

The man gave her a thumbs-up as he shook Alexander's hand; then he shifted his camera against his shoulder and headed inside.

"Thank you," Alexander said as he extended his own hand to shake Pam's, following the handshake with a loose hug.

"You know I'd do anything for you," she purred, the glint in her eyes reminding him of the one and only date the two had ever had.

Pam Lawry had just gotten the gig at *Good-Day Boulder*, the NBC affiliate's morning news program, and she had hired Alexander to be her personal trainer to get her into shape. She'd been beautiful and available, but he'd known after ten minutes of conversation that she was not the one for him. They'd remained good friends, and he had even attended her wedding to the programming producer who had propelled her journalism career, a man who still sought him out for help with his weight-lifting endeavors.

"So you'll come work out with me?" he asked.

She laughed. "I hate working out, you know that."

"I do, but I promise, we have a new twenty-minute whole-body program that will forever change how you view exercise. It's revolutionary! Besides," he said as he tapped her backside affectionately, "you need to tighten up your assets."

"There is nothing wrong with my assets," Pam said as she gave him a light punch in the arm.

Alexander laughed heartily.

Pam shook her head. "Now, I'll think about your new program but I want something in return."

He shook his head as he gave her a smug smile. "I am not sleeping with you, Pam. I like your husband."

She laughed with him. "I like my husband too! So don't flatter yourself. I want an interview with your brother. An exclusive."

Alexander suddenly bristled. "My brother?"

"Did I stutter?" She laughed again. "Yes, your brother!"

He shook his head. "Well, if he ever comes back to Boulder I'll see what I can do but don't hold your breath."

She smiled. "I won't, but I heard from a reliable source that UFC superstar Zachary Barrett will be moving back to Boulder to begin training for his next title bout. It only seems reasonable that he would train at his twin brother's new gym. Right?"

Alexander's joyous expression had fallen, his mouth

and eyes turned downward in a deep frown. "Who'd you hear that from?"

"You know I can't reveal my sources. So is it true?"

He snapped rudely, "Is what true?"

Pam sighed, her eyebrows lifted as she met his narrowed gaze. "Is it true that your brother is returning to Boulder to train here at Champs?"

"Is this off, or on, the record?"

She shrugged. "If I get my exclusive will it matter?"

He shook his head. "Here's your exclusive and you can quote me. There is no way in hell Zachary Barrett will ever train in any gym I'm affiliated with."

Pam cringed. "Ouch! That sounds like there's some truth to there being problems between the two of you. Do you care to comment?"

He shrugged, his oceanic eyes cold. "Like I said, your source doesn't know what the hell they're talking about. My brother has his own training facility in Thailand, so if you want an interview I suggest you hop on the first flight you can get. That's the best I can do for you."

Pam stood staring at him for a brief moment. She pressed her palm to his chest as she took a step toward him. "Why are you so angry? That's not good for you. You really need to let that go. I don't know what happened between you and your brother but forgiveness is good for the soul. *Your* soul!" There was a moment of pause. "So, do you want to share? Tell me what happened between you and Zachary?" The expression across her face was devious, mischief shimmering in her eyes.

Alexander shook his head. "Pam, you know I love you to death. You've been a good friend. But if we're going to stay friends, we are not going to discuss my brother, or my soul. And we are definitely not going to have that conversation so you can claim some exclusivity over the story."

Pam rolled her eyes as she snapped her fingers, feigning disappointment. "I almost had you!"

"You didn't. Not even close."

Pam nodded, lifting her hands as if in surrender. She gave him a slight shrug of her shoulders, then changed the subject. "So who are you dating these days?"

Taking a deep breath, Alexander forced a smile back to his face. "I'm a man on a mission. I'm building an empire. When do I have time to date?"

She laughed. "Well, plan on having dinner with us sometime soon. There's an adorable new intern I want to fix you up with. Her name's Cookie."

"An intern named Cookie? Really?"

"Really. And she's a sweet Southern girl. You'll like her. You can't stay single forever, good-looking!"

He laughed, his good mood slowly returning. "I can sure as hell try!" he said.

Minutes later Alexander waved his good-byes as Pam and her camera guy pulled out of the parking lot. A nice-size crowd was beginning to gather, early birds coming to witness the official ribbon-cutting ceremony.

The day was going to be the beginning of a new phase in the man's life, and he was both excited and nervous, having achieved one of his biggest life goals. He was kicking his professional career into second gear, and in just a few short minutes they would cut the ribbons to mark the official opening of his new business. The hard work and dedication that had gotten him to this point were exemplified in the massive structure that bore his name, and Alexander Barrett could not have been prouder.

Inside the new health and fitness facility, Alexander stood on the second-floor mezzanine. He spied his parents in conversation with a team of his trainers. He didn't need to hear the conversation to know that Westley and Lynn Barrett were bragging, sharing some story about something he had done back in the day. As he approached, he wasn't surprised to hear his father exclaiming that he always knew Alexander would one day be the proud owner of his own business.

His stepmother pulled him into the conversation, rushing to wrap her thick arms around his waist. She was short, round, and squishy, like soft bread dough. "Here's our man of the hour! How did the television interview go?"

Alexander nodded as he leaned to hug her back. "I think it went well. Pam went easy on me."

"I always did like that young woman," Lynn Barrett said as she nodded her head, her blond Halle Berry wig shaking slightly. "Yes, I did! Just all professional and about her business. I really do like to see that in these young women!"

Westley Barrett nodded in agreement. "She's a sweet girl and she looks as good in person as she does on the television." He winked an eye in his son's direction.

Alexander smiled. He changed the subject. "I need to go check on a few things before the ceremony gets started. Are you two going to be all right?"

His father waved a dismissive hand. The patriarch stood as tall as Alexander, boasting the same burnt umber complexion. It was easy to see where his son had gotten his good looks—Alexander was his spitting image. Even with his snow-white curls and the beginnings of a beer belly, Westley Barrett still turned a few heads. "We're just fine. Having a good time getting to know your staff. You have some good people here. They're going to be good for business."

Alexander nodded as his father patted him on his back. "We still have a few kinks to work out but I'm pretty pleased with how things are progressing thus far."

"Well, your mother and I are very proud of you. You and Zachary have both made us very happy."

At mention of his brother, Alexander rolled his eyes skyward.

Noting his son's glare, Westley shook an index finger at him. "You and Zachary need to squash whatever is going on between you two. You boys are blood and you're all each other has. He's tried to reach out to you and you keep turning your back on him. That's not right, Alex. You need to fix this mess!"

"Pop, I really don't want to talk about your other son. Not today."

"Well, you need to. Especially today. Besides, Zachary's not even married to that woman anymore!"

Alexander eyed his father with a raised brow. "When did that happen?"

"See, if you had been talking with your brother you would have known that."

Alexander shook his head, his eyes closed in frustration as he blew a heavy breath.

His father continued. "Well, today is as good as any other day to end this. In fact, you need to know . . ."

Mama Lynn suddenly rushed between them, her excitement explosive as she interrupted their conversation. "I just saw LeBron James headed toward the basketball court. I think I'm going to go down and see who else is there." The matriarch clapped her hands excitedly. "LeBron James! Alex, do you know if Michael Jordan or Magic Johnson are coming, too? Or that cutie patootie, Stephen Curry?"

Alexander laughed. "No, ma'am. But if any of them are here, they're probably down on the courts trying to get a pickup game going."

"Come on, Westley! Let's go introduce ourselves!" the older woman exclaimed as she pulled on her husband's arm. "Can you believe all the celebrities? Even those Kardashian sisters are here!"

Watching his parents scamper away, Alex thought about his brother, his father's comments resounding through his head. And then he thought about Pam and her tip about his twin planning to return to Boulder. The prospect suddenly had him on edge.

Alexander's kinship to mixed martial artist Zachary "The Hammer" Barrett was well-known in their Boulder community and worldwide with sports enthusiasts. With three world-title belts to his name, Zachary was the poster child for product endorsements and, as the current world heavyweight champion, always in demand. The two were fraternal twins, Zachary older than Alexander by mere minutes. Despite their similar features, telling them apart had been easy, with Alexander's eyes a vibrant shade of ocean blue, his brother's steel gray. Since they'd been knee high, the two had both been highly competitive with each other. It hadn't helped that their father had often pitted one against the other, believing their sibling rivalry was a good thing.

But rivalry had felt like betrayal when Zachary had married Felicia Wells. Felicia had been Alexander's college sweetheart, the woman he had planned to spend forever with. The two had been inseparable, until she met his brother, and then everything between them had changed.

Felicia had fallen for Zachary's bad-boy personality. Zachary was more laid back and impetuous than his brother, trouble following him everywhere he turned. Alexander was the more conservative twin, rarely willing to take any unnecessary risk. His no-nonsense demeanor could be a touch rigid, and he second-guessed each step. Zachary would act on impulse, rarely considering the consequences of his actions. And he hadn't been thinking when he seduced his brother's girlfriend.

The announcement that Zachary and Felicia were engaged came right after graduation. Barely two weeks later the two had walked gleefully down the matrimonial aisle. No one had been more surprised by his brother marrying his girl than Alexander. He'd been devastated, his heart splintered beyond measure. The two brothers hadn't had a full conversation since.

Months later, Zachary and his new bride had moved, with his pursuing the dreams that had eventually made him a household name in the sporting world. The distance between him and his family had only been rivaled by the miles from Colorado to Thailand. Too many years had passed since then. And now someone was saying Zachary was coming back, intent on thrusting himself into Alexander's life.

Alexander shook the thoughts from his head as he focused his attention on the crowd that was beginning to gather in the mezzanine for the ceremony. Colorado's elite, his former teammates, professional and amateur athletes across multiple sports fields, family and friends had all come to support him. The magnitude of that was overwhelming.

His eyes were suddenly drawn to a young Asian woman who stood alone, her hands folded pristinely in front of her. She was a beauty with a head of dark, lush waves that fell to her midback. Her complexion was a few shades warmer than French vanilla, and her cheeks were flushed a pale shade of summer peach. She was petite in stature, and he was suddenly reminded of the tiny Mothra fairies from the classic *Godzilla* movies. But she exuded an air of attitude that made him think what seemed like timidity actually belied her true strength. As if she sensed him staring, she suddenly lifted her eyes, their gazes connecting. She stared, appraising him from head to toe, and when it seemed as if he'd passed her approval, she smiled, the wealth of it shimmering in her dark stare. Alexander felt himself smiling back, his own grin running from ear to ear. Feeling slightly foolish and a tad offsides, he tossed a look over his shoulder and around the room to ensure no one had been watching, and when he did, she laughed.

His curiosity was further piqued when his human resources director moved to her side. There was just a brief moment before she pulled her gaze from his, allowing herself to be drawn into conversation. The two stood engaged for a good few minutes before she finally shook the man's hand and moved off in the opposite direction. Before disappearing, she tossed Alexander one last look over her shoulder, that beautiful smile still lighting up her face.

Intrigued, Alexander took the stairs to the lower level, moving to Dan Winter's side. Tall and buff with a sun-kissed complexion, Dan was a walking advertisement for high-end tanning products. Dan had been a point guard for the Denver Nuggets, and they'd played ball together, both their careers starting at the same time. The two men had been good friends for years. Dan had supported his business venture from the beginning, when Alexander had first voiced the idea.

Dan grinned, his smile spreading from ear to ear as the two bumped shoulders. "You ready to do this, big guy?"

Alexander nodded, his own bright smile filling his face. "I don't think I've been this nervous since the NBA draft."

Dan laughed. "Well, you're in the driver's seat this time. No waiting for a phone call to announce your future. This time you make all the calls."

Alexander blew a heavy sigh as he nodded his head. He changed the subject. "Who was your friend?"

For a brief moment Dan looked confused, his eyes skating back and forth. "My friend?"

"The beautiful woman you were just talking to," Alexander answered, his eyes shifting down the hallway, where she'd disappeared into the restroom.

Dan nodded, understanding washing over his expression. "Actually, she's one of our new hires," he said as he passed Alexander a copy of the woman's résumé from the folder he held in his hand. "Her name's Sarai Montri. *Doctor* Sarai Montri. She's a former Miss Thailand with a doctorate in exercise physiology. She is also a licensed sports therapist and certified clinical nutritionist. She comes with impeccable references. In fact, she has serious managerial skills. I'd like to put her in the office but she wants to train and work with clients. I think she'll be a great asset to the organization."

Alexander scanned the document briefly before passing it back to his friend. "Damn!" he said, shaking his head.

Dan laughed. "She caught your eye, huh?"

Alexander laughed with him. "She did, but now that I know she's an employee I can't go there. Or at least I shouldn't go there!" he said with a deep chuckle.

Dan shook his head. "No, you got it right the first time. You *can't* go there. I would hate for it to get messy after you do a hit and run. First, there's a charge of sexual harassment, then a lot of bad press that makes all us athletes look bad, and then we have to pay her off. And no telling what kind of impact that will have on that squeaky-clean reputation you like to think you have."

A smirk crossed Alexander's face. "Think? I know I have a squeaky-clean reputation. I don't do those kinds of things."

"That's a lie!" Dan exclaimed. "I already know about you and the brunette working the food counter."

Alexander's eyes widened. "I did not hit that. I swear I didn't!" he said, laughing heartily.

"Well, you did something."

"It's more like what she did to me!" Alexander laughed again. "And that was *before* she got hired. I've known her since her days at the Men's Wearhouse. She fitted me for a few suits back in the day."

Dan's head was still waving from side to side as he chuckled under his breath. "Well, I know something happened the way she and the other women around here keep whispering every time you walk into a room."

"Are you sure they're not whispering about you? I didn't do a Colgate commercial, Mr. Man with the Beautiful Smile!"

The two men snickered as only two good friends could do.

Alexander blew a soft sigh. "So, where did you find Dr. Montri?" he asked, curiosity still pulling at him.

"Your father put her in touch with me."

"My father? How does my father know . . . ?"

A rumble of excitement vibrating through the room suddenly stalled Alexander's question. The crowd was jumping with elation, a current of exhilaration sweeping through the space. Women and children screamed, and loud cheers and applause erupted. It started in the parking lot and was rushing with a vengeance into the building. Both men turned at the same time to see what all the commotion was about.

Shock registered on Alexander's face as Zachary "The Hammer" Barrett stepped through the front doors, his arms outstretched as he high-fived the crowd of spectators. The consummate professional, Zachary looked every bit the high-profile athletic machine he professed to be. His shoulders and chest were broad, his hands massive. With his daunting height and size, it wasn't hard to imagine the damage he could inflict on an opponent in the ring. His shoulder-length dreadlocks were pulled into a ponytail at the nape of his thick neck. He wore black denim jeans, a black silk T-shirt, and black Timberlands. His fashion sense was stealth mode with a boatload of *GQ* attitude. His gaze swept through the space until he caught sight of his brother. He pointed an index finger at his twin, then respectfully clapped his palms together in admiration.

As he locked gazes with his brother, Alexander felt himself tense, his fists clenched tightly to his body. His gaze narrowed. He struggled to maintain his welcoming expression, suddenly aware of everyone staring at him. This wasn't how he'd ever imagined he and his brother reuniting. How he was feeling wasn't the expression he wanted showing up in photographs in the blogosphere. Without his realizing, his father had suddenly returned to his side, slapping him against the back. Joy painted the old man's expression, his own excitement palpable.

"Surprise, son!" Westley exclaimed. "Surprise!"

Alexander shot his father a look. "You knew about this?"

The old man grinned. "We wanted to surprise you. Your brother needs to get ready for his next fight and he needed to focus, so I told him to come home. I told him you would help him out."

"You didn't think that was something you needed to speak with me about first? What if I don't want to help him?"

His father bristled. "Don't start. That's your brother," Westley quipped.

His expression was stern, and Alexander suddenly felt like he was six years old again. He heaved a heavy sigh. His stepmother swept in before either man could comment further.

The matriarch jumped excitedly, grabbing both men by their arms. "Isn't this wonderful!" she exclaimed. "All my boys together again. Ain't God good!"

Chapter Two

Minutes after cutting the ribbon and officially welcoming everyone to Champs, Alexander had turned abruptly, moved quickly toward his office. The crowd was still fawning over his brother, everyone's attention diverted long enough for him to make a quick getaway. Not at all impressed with their father's revelation, he needed to find a quiet corner to gather his thoughts.

As he rounded the corner to his office door, he suddenly came face-to-face with the beautiful woman from earlier. Surprise registered across his face, the emotion quickly shifting into anticipation. Sarai Montri stood alone, her cell phone pulled to her ear. He stopped short as their gazes locked for the second time, the woman eyeing him intently.

Sarai was surprised, the nearness of Alexander Barrett unexpected. She would have thought that he would have been out in the crowd with his brother, their excitement to have both men in the same room palpable. She couldn't remember ever being in a space with energy so intense. With everyone's attention focused on the twins, she'd stolen away to return a few phone calls. She'd been listening to her voice mail, hoping that her own family had acknowledged her earlier message that she'd arrived safe and sound in Colorado without mishap. As Alexander stood staring at her, she deleted the few messages that had come in, then dropped the phone back into her purse.

"Mr. Barrett, hello!"

He smiled back. "Hello! You're the new hire, right? How are you?"

"Very well, thank you." She extended her hand. "My name's Sarai. Sarai Montri."

Her hand disappeared beneath his thick fingers. His touch was firm and heated, a nice contrast to her own gentle caress. They both felt a mild quiver of energy shift between them.

Alexander took a deep breath to stall the sudden sensation sweeping up his spine as he squeezed her hand gently. "It's a pleasure to meet you, Dr. Montri."

She shook her head, her smile still bright. "Please, call me Sarai. It's pronounced *Suh-rye. Suh-rye Mon-tree.*"

"My bad," he said with a nod. "It's a beautiful name. I won't mispronounce it again."

She widened her smile, awed as he continued to hold her hand in his. "I'm very excited to be a part of your team. I look forward to working with you," she said softly. There was a warm lilt to her voice, the lyrical timbre soothing to his ear. She had just enough of an inflection in her tone for him to question her origins.

"May I ask where you hail from?" he asked. "You have a beautiful accent."

"It's actually a perverted version of Siamese and French!" she said with a soft chuckle.

Alexander looked confused.

"I was born in Thailand and I went to secondary

school in France," Sarai explained. "English is actually my third language."

Alexander was grinning from ear to ear. "Well, I'm glad you found your way to Boulder. My HR director spoke quite highly of you."

"He was very nice. And I truly appreciate this opportunity."

"Were you really a beauty queen?" he asked.

She laughed, nodding slightly. "I was, but please don't hold that against me."

He laughed with her. "I won't. I promise."

She slowly pulled her hand from his, her palm becoming damp with perspiration. The disconnection was slightly disconcerting. Both stood staring, suddenly at a loss for words as they were reflecting on the rise of tension that billowed between them.

A loud cheer suddenly echoed from the main lobby, the crowd no doubt still excited by something his brother was either doing or saying. For a brief second Alexander imagined the performance Zachary had to be giving, remembering how he was always ready to please an audience. Sarai seemed to read his thoughts, the expression across his face telling.

"Your brother is quite the character. Everybody loves him," she said.

Not everybody, Alexander thought to himself as he shrugged. He nodded slightly as he reached around her to open his office door. "Please, come talk to me," he said, choosing to ignore her comment about his brother.

Curious to know more about the man, Sarai found herself following behind him. She had heard a library's worth of stories about him and his rising success, but there was something about Alexander Barrett that didn't fit the tales of bravado and daring she'd been told. His quiet demeanor seemed to contradict the tall tales she'd been made to believe about his exploits. She found herself excited to discover the man for herself.

The two moved into the room, and he closed the door behind them. He pulled out the leather seat that rested in front of the desk, gesturing for her to sit down. As she did, the sweetest hint of his cologne tickled her nostrils. She closed her eyes and took a deep inhale of air. She reopened them to watch as he moved to the other side of the desk, dropping his body into the leather executive's chair across from her.

There was no denying the shared DNA between the Barrett twins. The two men had the same chiseled cheekbones, broad noses, and full lips. Alexander's hair was cropped low and close, a full fade across a perfectly shaped head. His complexion was chocolate cherry, a warm brown with rich red undertones. His skin was like polished stone, blemish free, and he had the shadow of a perfectly lined mustache and beard.

And his eyes! His eyes were the most magnificent shade of blue, Sarai thought, their color like the ocean waters that kissed the dark sand around the fishing village where she'd been born. There was something hypnotic about his blue gaze, and Sarai imagined that the list of women who'd easily lost themselves in their depths was endless.

"So when do you officially start?" he questioned, shifting the topic of conversation back to her.

"I'll come in next week. I actually just flew into Boulder this morning. I don't even know where I'm staying yet so I need a day or two to get settled in. But

I promise not to take too long! I'm anxious to get started."

"But you do have a place?" A hint of concern washed over his expression.

She nodded, her easy demeanor calming. "I do! I just haven't been there yet. It's somewhere on West Coach Road?"

His eyes shifted back and forth as he tried to recall the neighborhood. Alexander nodded. "Carriage Hills. Very nice. That's not too far from here."

"I'm told it's very close so I'll have no problems getting back and forth to work. I don't like to drive a car if I don't have to so I look forward to walking and riding my bike."

Alexander smiled as he studied her face. Her features were delicate, her almond-shaped eyes like slivered pools of black ice. Her pale complexion was golden, her cheeks tinted warmly with color. She seemed soft and fragile, her feminine air giving him reason to pause. He suddenly wondered if she would allow him to save her if such a thing were ever necessary. And then he imagined Sarai Montri was a woman who would have no problems saving herself.

She smiled. "Well, I should let you get back to your guests. I'm sure people are looking for you."

He shrugged his broad shoulders again. "I doubt it. I trust that everyone is in good hands." There was a momentary pause as his mind shifted back to what might be happening on the other side of the door. The silence was brief as he changed the subject, resuming the conversation. "So how do you know my father? I hear he's responsible for you applying to work here."

Sarai hesitated before responding, her smile widening. "We've actually never met. But he and I share mutual acquaintances. They heard about your venture and were kind enough to tell him about me. He told them you were hiring and that I should apply. So I did."

Alexander nodded. "Well, I'm glad he did. I think you'll fit in well with us here."

Her smile was bright and inviting as her eyes danced eagerly with his. "I'm very excited," she said, her gaze dropping demurely to the floor.

Alexander tried not to stare, but there was no denying that he was captivated. There was something about her presence that filled him, his entire body tingling with delight. He suddenly imagined them naked together, her soft curves pressed against his hardened lines. He bit down against his bottom lip to stall the rise of heat that lengthened the muscles below his waist as he imagined what it might be like to lose himself deep in the valley of her parted legs.

Sarai lifted her eyes back to his, and the look she gave him was searing. He felt himself blush, feeling as if she'd just read every perverse thought that had raced through his mind. And for just a brief moment, he'd definitely been thinking some very X-rated things about the two of them. So much so that heat had exploded with a vengeance through his southern quadrant, and he'd broken out into a sweat, perspiration beading across his brow.

"You're staring, Mr. Barrett!" she said, amusement dancing across her face.

He nodded, a coy smile filling his face. "I was. And I should probably apologize for doing so but I'm really not sorry. You're a very beautiful woman, Dr. Montri."

She smiled. "It's sweet of you to say but I'd prefer we focus on my qualifications."

"Trust me, Dr. Montri, I'm trying. I'm trying very hard. I have no doubts that Mr. Winters is going to give me a very lengthy lecture on how unprofessional I am probably being right now. I'm sure I've broken some serious employer-employee relationship rules. I hope you know though that I'm really not that kind of man. I don't harass my female employees."

"You never gave me that impression. Under the circumstances I think we can overlook any indiscretion," she said, giving him one of her bright smiles and a wink of her eye.

He laughed, his head bobbing as he reveled in the seductive look she was giving him. His eyes danced in perfect harmony with hers, everything between them seeming to sync.

"Did you have a talent?" he suddenly asked, the question coming randomly.

Perplexed, her brow furrowed. "I beg your pardon?"

"That beauty contest. Did you have to have a talent to qualify for Miss Thailand? Did you have to sing, dance, do magic tricks, or something like that?"

Sarai laughed. "No. I was only required to participate in the evening gown and swimsuit competitions. Then there was an interview question-and-answer segment. The contest is more than a beauty pageant. The women aspiring to become Miss Universe must be intelligent, well-mannered, and cultured."

"So you competed in the Miss Universe contest, too?"

"I did. Winning Miss Thailand qualified me for the Miss Universe competition. Unfortunately, the year I competed I was beat by Miss Venezuela. Miss Colombia is the current reigning queen. But I was honored to be the first runner-up. And I am still occasionally obligated to participate in certain pageant-related events. I gave Dan my schedule and I won't let it be a problem. "

"I don't know what the judges had to be thinking," he said, his stare so intense that Sarai suddenly felt as if she'd been stripped naked where she sat. As discreetly as she could manage, she crossed her arms and her legs, needing to stall the quiver of heat that rippled with a vengeance through her sweet spot.

Alexander suddenly shifted forward in his seat. "Would you have dinner with me tonight? I'd really love to talk with you more."

Sarai's eyes widened as his question settled over her. His query was sudden and unexpected, and for a brief moment it threw her. But before she could answer, there was an abrupt knock on the office door. As both shifted their gazes toward the entrance, the door flew open, Zachary sticking his head inside.

"Knock, knock! Am I interrupting?" he questioned, his eyes shifting from one to the other.

As the two men exchanged a look, Alexander moved onto his feet, rising slowly from his chair. Sarai's eyes widened anxiously as her gaze shifted back and forth between them. The air in the room was suddenly strained, and thick with aggression, and Alexander's mild-mannered demeanor was gone. His entire body had stiffened. His jaw was tight, and his eyes had narrowed into venomous slits.

As Zachary moved into the room and closed the door, Alexander eased himself around the desk until they were standing toe-to-toe, neither speaking for minutes. They stood staring at each other, breath rising, heartbeats pounding. The moment was nail-biting, and Sarai fought back the urge to step between them to stop what seemed to be brewing. She gripped the seat cushion beneath her with tightened fists. Zachary broke the uneasy silence.

"It's good to see you again, A," he said, eyeing his twin anxiously as he called him by the pet name only the two of them used for each other.

Alex didn't comment, still standing like stone.

"You're supposed to say, *good to see you too, Z!*" Zachary teased. Nervous anxiety flooded his face, his brow creased as he tried to make light of the situation. He shifted his stare toward Sarai. "A to Z. We were the bad boys of Boulder!" Zach rambled. "Back in the day there was nothing that could stop us! My brother and I were going to conquer the world and we were going to do it together!"

Despite Zachary's best efforts to cajole an ounce of emotion from his twin, Alexander gave him nothing. Not a single muscle twitched in response. Zachary blew a heavy sigh. "I'm sorry," he finally said, once again meeting Alexander's stare evenly. "I'm sorry about everything that happened and for what I did. I was wrong and I promise to spend however long it takes to make amends to you."

The awkward silence refilled the room. It was thick and heavy with regret, and anger. Still getting no reply, Zachary blew another weighted breath, warm air washing over his full lips.

"All right, then." He shifted his eyes back to Sarai. "We should go. The Realtor said she would meet us at the house with the keys," he said as he stole a quick glance toward his wristwatch.

Alexander's head suddenly snapped in Sarai's direction. "You two know each other?" he asked, his question directed at her.

She nodded, the faintest hint of a smile pulling at her thin lips.

Zachary spoke, shifting an affectionate look in her direction. "Sarai's my favorite girl. She's been with me since I moved to Thailand. I don't know what I'd do without her. She helped me get through some tough times."

Sarai's gaze was endearing as she turned her faint smile on Zachary. "Your brother and I are good friends. We will be sharing a house here in Boulder while he trains and I work."

The joyous energy that had shimmered in Alexander's bright blue eyes just minutes earlier suddenly diminished. As he looked from one to the other, a wave of disappointment flushed his face. "It's time for you to leave," he said abruptly.

"Can't we just talk?" Zachary begged.

"Thanks for stopping by," Alexander replied as he moved to the door, brushing past his brother. "But don't make it a habit. I don't want to see you here again."

Zach grabbed him by the arm. "A, please," he started before Alex snatched the limb away.

He glared at the other man, the look laden with venom. "Be gone before I get back. If you're still here I will throw you out." Then with one last glance toward the woman staring at the two of them, he reached for the door handle and exited the room.

Tears misted Zachary's gaze as he stared after his twin, the hurt of his brother's rejection washing over his spirit.

Rising from where she sat, Sarai wrapped her arms around his waist and hugged him. She silently wished her dear friend had been able to tell his beloved brother just how much he had missed him. She sighed softly as he hugged her back.

* * *

The house on West Coach Road wasn't anything Sarai had expected. The custom-built contemporary sat on thirty-four secluded acres in a private gated community. The open design featured a spacious kitchen and family room, formal living and dining rooms, two master bedroom suites, and three additional bedrooms. There was also a walkout lower level with a great room and office and an in-home gym.

Zachary had rented the space fully furnished, the home looking like an interior designer's showcase. With the incredible views and sweeping landscape that surrounded the property, Sarai felt as if she'd been swept into another dimension. It was a far cry from the modest space where she had lived in Thailand or her father's home with its thatched roof and dirt floor.

She stood staring out her bedroom window, overwhelmed by the expanse of pine trees and the mountains that sat in the distance, reaching for the sky. Her luggage still rested on the floor, and she could hear Zachary puttering around in the other master bedroom at the opposite end of the hall. She blew a soft sigh.

He hadn't spoken to her since they'd left the athletic center. His father had been calling repeatedly, and he refused to answer, sending the calls to voice mail. Despite her best efforts, the most she'd gotten from him was a low grunt as he'd carried their bags through the front door. Now he was cussing under his breath, refusing to let her help him decipher the emotion he was feeling. His feelings were hurt and he was angry and his mood swing had taken him to a dark place where she couldn't go. Knowing Zachary's hurt, she could only begin to imagine what Alexander was going through.

She'd been thinking about Alexander since he had stormed out of the room. In that brief moment, she had wanted to hug him too. To offer him the comfort that he seemed to desperately need, because clearly, in that moment, Alexander Barrett was a man who needed someone to assure him that things were going to be all right. But the way he'd looked at her when he discovered that she and his brother were already acquainted had been confusing. There had been something teasing in his stare just minutes before, and then his gaze had gone as cold as the emotion that had spun like a winter blizzard between the two men. Things being right were far from Alexander's mind, and she would have given anything to fix that.

Zachary suddenly interrupted her thoughts. "Hey, are you hungry? I was going to order pizza or something."

She turned to eye him, standing in the doorway of her bedroom. "That's all you have to say to me? Do I want something to eat?"

Contrition painted his expression. "Sorry. My day didn't go the way I wanted it to. But you know that."

"I know that a lot of things didn't go the way people wanted them to go today. It doesn't give you, or them, the right to treat everyone else badly."

He nodded his head, the gesture apologetic. "So, what were you two talking about? You and my brother." He moved into the room and dropped down onto her bed.

She shrugged. "Nothing really. We were just getting acquainted. Then he invited me to dinner."

"Dinner?"

She nodded. "That's when you came through the door and the two of you got into your . . . what did you call it? Your pissing match?"

"You should go to dinner with him," Zachary said, ignoring her comment. "Make friends, soften him up and put in a good word for me. He would listen to you. Everyone listens to you."

She shook her head. "He needs time to adjust. You come back and expect everything to go right back to normal. That doesn't happen. Not after everything that has happened between you two."

Zachary blew a heavy gust of air past his full lips. He looked defeated, his shoulders hunched, his head hanging low as he stared toward the floor. Minutes passed before he finally spoke again. His voice was a low whisper. "I need him, Sarai. I need my brother back in my life. I feel lost without him."

She dropped onto the bed beside him. "I know," she said as she reached for his hand and held it.

The two sat side by side, falling into deep thought. Sarai knew Zachary had been struggling with his feelings for years, even before his relationship with his wife had gone south. Back then, when he was feeling remorseful about the disconnect with his twin and how he'd handled things, Felicia had been there to sway those emotions, insisting that loving her had not been a mistake. He'd fallen for the lies that had convinced him that he neither needed nor wanted his brother in his life. But he couldn't help thinking that loving Felicia had cost him everything, especially after discovering her in bed with an opponent, that other man sweeping her off to the French Riviera with promises of fame and fortune.

Working with him had afforded Sarai opportunities

she couldn't have ever imagined. They'd become fast friends, Zachary often sharing bits and pieces of himself until there was little she didn't know about him. They were friends, feeling like family, and she owed him more than she would ever be able to return in kind. She loved him like a brother, and seeing him in pain actually hurt her heart.

The two sat in silence for a good long while, trying to make sense of their situations. Both wishing they could pull the answers out of thin air. As the sun began to set against the backdrop of mountains outside her window, Sarai turned to look at him, her gaze meeting his.

"What is pizza?" she asked, her dubious expression moving him to smile.

Alexander stood beneath the spray of four bronze-colored showerheads, the hot water like little piercing needles against his skin. His body hurt, and the heated shower massaging his muscles was welcomed. His early morning workout had been a bear, but the exercise was needed to alleviate the anxiety that had been with him since the grand opening of Champs. As he thought about the hard work and effort that had gone into creating and building his dream gym facility, he wanted to smile but didn't have the energy or the wherewithal to make the effort.

He was emotionally exhausted, and if he were honest, he didn't see that changing anytime soon. Thoughts of his brother and the woman who'd called the man her friend flooded his mind. Alexander hadn't been able to stop thinking of either, imagining the unfathomable. How was it possible that his twin had gotten to another woman who'd caught his eye, the two actually living together? For a brief moment he'd been excited at the prospect of taking her to dinner to get to know more about her. There was something about Sarai Montri that he couldn't quite put a name to that had him curious, and Zachary had once again beaten him to the punch. It felt like high school, and college, all over again.

Alexander leaned forward, both hands pressed against the glass tiles that decorated the room. Water washed his face, raining down over his head and his shoulders. He reveled in the moment as the heated spray slowly eased the tension that had knotted his neck and back. When the warm water had begun to chill, he stepped out of the wetness and wrapped a plush white towel around his waist.

An hour later he was dressed and out the door, pulling into the parking lot of his new business. Inside, he greeted the morning employees and patrons cheerfully, excited by the number of people who'd shown up to work out. There was a morning water-aerobics class that had attracted a number of senior citizens, as well as an exercise event for new mothers and their infants. Both were filled to capacity. After passing his briefcase and gym bag to one of his assistants, he moved through the space to ensure that everything was moving smoothly.

He was only slightly surprised to find his brother in the weight room. The man lay supine on a weight bench, doing chest presses with a weighted bar. He stared as Zachary lowered the weight to just below his sternum, then pressed it back up. After a steady procession, his arms began to tremble, and Alexander realized that with the amount of weight his brother was pushing, the movement had quickly become a challenge. He moved to his side, eyeing his twin with a narrowed gaze as he struggled to push out the last couple of reps.

"Flare your elbows out," Alexander commanded. "You need to lock it out more."

Zachary grunted loudly, his arms quivering from exertion. He was at a point of no return, almost dropping the bar across his chest when Alexander reached a hand out to help him set the weight bar back on the rack.

"Why the hell are you in here without a spotter? You could have killed yourself."

Zachary grinned as he sat upright. "You're concerned."

"I don't need you screwing up my insurance rating by being stupid."

Zachary shrugged. "You were always the smart one, not me, remember?"

"Doesn't look like much has changed," Alexander said, his tone dry.

His brother chuckled. "Well, I was just killing time until you got here," Zachary said.

"I told you not to come back."

"But you didn't mean it."

Alexander eyed his twin with a raised brow. "You really don't want to test me," he hissed between clenched teeth.

"I need your help, A!" Zachary responded. "I know you're still mad but I really need us to get past it."

"And what if I don't want to get past it?"

"Then I'm going to lose my next title match."

Alexander rolled his eyes skyward. "You were always so melodramatic!"

"Well, this time I'm dead serious. I barely won my last match and I won't win this one if I don't get your help. My training regime is pure crap. I can't focus and I don't trust half the people I have working for me. No one understands what I need. I have to get back to basics and I only want you to train me."

Alexander stared at his brother. He didn't bother to comment. He turned on his heels and headed back out the door. As he exited the room, he could hear Zachary calling after him, his brother still pleading for his help.

Chapter Three

Alexander paused in the foyer of his family home, eavesdropping on his parents as they sat in the kitchen in conversation. Hearing them talk about his brother and the Asian woman who'd come from Thailand with him had stalled his steps.

"Well, are they dating?" Lynn questioned, a hint of attitude in her tone.

Annoyance tinted his father's words. "Woman, I told you I don't know what's going on with Zachary and that little girl so I don't know why you keep asking me. If you want to know ask Zachary."

"I'm going to ask *her*. That's what I'm going to do."

"That works too."

A cup rattled against the table, someone dropping it heavily against the surface. Alexander took a low breath and held it, still standing like stone in the entranceway.

"Because something must be going on with the two of them," Lynn said emphatically. "He moved her into that house with him. And that's some house! Did you see all that room? Got her living like a queen over there."

Alexander didn't have to see his father to know
that he was shaking his head, his eyes rolling toward
the ceiling.

Lynn continued. "You need to talk to them, Westley. It doesn't make any good sense that they're still
fighting. They're brothers for goodness' sake! And
they used to be so close!"

His father suddenly called Alexander's name.
"How long have you been standing there, son?"

Startled, Alexander jumped slightly, not having
heard his father rise from his seat. He moved to shake
the hand extended toward him.

"Not long. I just got here. I was in the neighborhood and thought I'd stop by to check on you two."

"You need to let people know when you come into
a room. Might hear something you don't want to
hear and get your feelings hurt sneaking around like
that."

Alexander chuckled. "Yes, sir. Sorry about that."

Westley waved his son toward the back of the
home. "We're fine. About to go run a few errands,
then your mother wants to stop by the gym to try out
some dance class."

"It's a step class," Lynn interjected as she moved
onto her feet. She leaned up to kiss Alexander's
cheek. "Hello, baby!"

"Hi, Mama Lynn," he said as he kissed her back.
"You're looking good, girl," he said with a wink of his
eye.

The matriarch giggled. She reached up to touch
her wig of the moment, a burgundy red cascade of
curls that stopped just above her shoulders. "Are you
hungry? Let me fix you some lunch," she said as she
pulled a ceramic plate from a glass-front cabinet.

Before he could respond yea or nay, the matriarch

had overloaded the plate with chicken salad and thick slices of freshly baked sourdough bread. Lynn had been in their lives since he and Zachary had been six years old. She was a woman who firmly believed everything began and ended in her kitchen, always favoring her family with the foods they loved best. Cooking was her passion, and she did it well and often.

Neither he nor Zachary had any memory of their birth mother. If it weren't for the photographs his father kept hidden in a box in the bottom of his closet, they wouldn't even know what she looked like. The boys had only been two years old when Carolyn Barrett had passed away from breast cancer. Everything after that was a blur—until Mama Lynn, who'd successfully turned their harried house into a home by way of her gas oven. Their stepmother had come in loving the twins as if they were her own. And with very little effort on her part, they had loved her back equally as hard.

She was still fussing about Zachary, this time her comments directed at Alexander. "You and your brother really need to sit down and talk, Alexander. This foolishness needs to stop."

He opened his mouth to speak, but she interrupted, leaving him sucking air like a guppy.

"You two love each other. And I don't care what you say," she said, fanning her hand at him. "We're family so you need to fix this."

His father nodded in agreement. "Mama's cooking dinner this Sunday for everyone. It's been two weeks since Zachary got back home and we need to have a family get-together. You need to be here, son. You and your brother really need to talk. It'll be a good time. You both can go sit down in your old bedroom and just air out your differences."

"I don't want . . ." Alexander started.

His father waved his index finger at him. "I don't care. Enough is enough. You'll do it because I said so. You might be grown but I'm still your father and you will do what I say. And I'm saying that this feud is done and finished so get it fixed."

Alexander shot his father a look, the gesture met with raised brows and a tightened jaw. He didn't say anything else, knowing the effort would be futile. He was going to have to talk to his brother whether he wanted to or not.

He shifted his gaze back to his meal. The salad was one of his favorites, Mama Lynn tossing thick chunks of roasted chicken with grapes and pecans. His stepmother made everything from scratch, even the mayonnaise that completed the salad on his plate. Focusing on the food was easier than focusing on the demands his parents were suddenly making.

"What do you know about that pretty little girl?" Lynn suddenly asked, her eyes burrowing into him with curiosity. "The one that came from Thailand with Zachary."

He shook his head as thoughts of Sarai Montri flashed through his mind. "Not a thing," he said after a moment of hesitation.

The older woman blew a heavy sigh. "I just don't understand why you boys never bring home any nice black girls. All the beautiful black women you two could have and you don't seem interested unless they're blond and blue-eyed."

"I have blue eyes," Alexander said smugly.

She cut her gaze in his direction. "And your point?"

He shrugged. "I love black women and I've dated

plenty of sisters. And you know that Zachary and I have both dated women of all races. We're attracted to beautiful, intelligent women and we've never discriminated against any woman because of skin color."

"Well, maybe you should," Mama Lynn quipped.

His father laughed. "Woman, did you forget you're biracial?" He reached for her hand, pointing to her very pale café au lait complexion.

Lynn rolled her eyes. "We're not talking about me. And my father being white doesn't have anything to do with this. When people look at me they see a beautiful black woman and that's how I see myself. I would like my sons to date and marry beautiful black women and give me beautiful grandbabies."

"Our boys are going to have beautiful babies no matter what their mamas look like," Westley said with a slight snap of his head.

Alexander laughed. "Why are we having this conversation?" he asked his father as Mama Lynn excused herself from the table and exited the room.

"Because your mama hates being left out of anything and she wants information on your brother's friend. I don't know why she's so worried though because I'd bet my last dollar that girl would make some pretty brown babies!"

Alexander laughed again, the absurdity of the conversation suddenly lifting his spirit. "So would I!" he responded. "So would I!"

Westley tapped his son on the back as he stood to refill his water glass. As the man sat back down, Alexander shifted forward in his seat. "I was talking to Dan and he said that you referred Zach's friend. Did my brother ask you to do that?"

The older man lifted his eyes to his son's. "No," he said his head waving from side to side. "She called and asked if I could recommend a gym. Yours was opening so it only made sense."

"She called you directly? So you knew about her?"

There was a brief moment of pause as his father took another swig of his beverage and swallowed. He stole a quick glance toward the door before he answered. "Her mother and I were old friends. When your brother moved to Thailand I told him to make contact and he did. Sarai's mother had passed but her father was really helpful to your brother. Referring her to Champs was just my way of returning the favor."

"What kind of friends . . . ?"

"Let it go, son," Westley snapped, eyeing Alexander with a stern stare. "And don't mention it to Mama Lynn. I don't want to hear her fussing about nothing. That was well before her time. Even before your mother. Just something that happened when I was a very young man in the service stationed overseas."

Alexander nodded his understanding, even more curious knowing his father and Sarai's mother had once had a personal connection. He found himself hoping that he could bring the subject up again one day and get a little more information.

The two men talked for another hour, Westley sharing his opinion on the state of the economy, the political climate, and his weariness with race relations around the world. He only briefly questioned Alexander's future intentions regarding his business, offered advice on his lack of a dating life, and suggested his son think about them all taking a family trip once the newness of the gym had worn off and all the employees were settled in. Alexander had been grateful that his father didn't mention his twin, or Sarai, again. Although the elder man knew those were the two topics Alexander didn't have any desire to talk about, he'd already made his pronouncement about them fixing what was broke and didn't feel a need to bring it up again.

When Mama Lynn returned to the kitchen, she'd changed into a jogging suit, running shoes, and a clip-on ponytail that she'd pinned tightly atop her head. "We need to go, Daddy," she admonished as she leaned to kiss Alexander's cheek. "Lock the door if you leave before we get back, baby."

He nodded. "Yes, ma'am."

"Are you going to hang around for a while, son?" Westley asked as he rose from his seat and reached for his jacket.

Alexander shrugged. "Probably not. I need to run a few errands myself, then I need to get back to the gym. I've got new clients coming in this evening."

His father nodded. "Well, I'm sure I'll see you later. We can talk more then."

"Sounds like a plan, Pop."

Walking to the front door, Alexander watched as the couple fussed their way to the car, still bickering as the vehicle rolled out of the driveway. There was much love between them, and he often found himself hoping that he would one day discover what they had. When he was growing up, the two had been a glowing example of a healthy adult relationship for him and his brother to emulate.

The house was suddenly too quiet, the sounds of a faucet dripping and the wall clock ticking the only noises to be heard. Even though he didn't live there anymore, there was something about his parents being gone from the home that left Alexander feeling empty. It had been that way since his brother had moved to Thailand, leaving the three of them behind.

Now that Zachary was back, Alexander couldn't help
but wonder if the feelings of loneliness he often felt
would soon disappear.

Sarai had just finished the last of four employee-
training sessions. For three straight hours, information had been thrown at the new hires, everyone
learning everything they needed to perform the
duties expected of them. With her final paperwork
approved and her employee badge printed and lam-
inated, she was official. Having already memorized
the company's mission statement, she was excited to
finally get started, wanting to prove her worth.

Since that first day, she'd only run into Alexander
twice. Both times he'd ignored her completely, his
dismissive demeanor actually hurting her feelings.
Despite her efforts to draw him into conversation, he
hadn't been interested in talking to her, each time
turning an about-face as he practically ran in the opposite direction. His behavior might have been com-
ical if it didn't have anything to do with her.

"Your brother won't talk to me," she said as she ran
on a treadmill alongside Zachary.

He reduced his speed, slowing his full gallop to a
slow jog. "Welcome to my world!"

"He's my employer. He should at least be able to
speak to me. I didn't do anything to him!"

Zachary shrugged, indifference painting his expression. "He probably thinks I put you up to getting
a job here."

"Well, if he talked to me he'd know that you didn't
have anything to do with me applying for a position.
I just wanted to be able to work with the best in the

industry and he's managed to put together a stellar team for me to learn from."

"I wouldn't worry about it. He's just in his feelings right now. He'll get over it."

"What does that mean? He's in his feelings?"

Zachary pushed the STOP button on the treadmill, coming to a complete halt. "He's just being overly emotional. He's always been that way since we were kids. I'd kill a bug and he'd want to give it a funeral and burial with the wailing and crying. I wasn't that sensitive so kicking it into the dirt was okay with me."

Sarai shook her head. "You can be very cold sometimes. That is not a good thing when you are dealing with people. Especially family."

Zachary shrugged. "Yeah, whatever." There was a lull in their conversation as he pondered her comment. It wasn't the first time he'd heard what she said, all of his friends and family having admonished him at one time or another for the wall he put between himself and others. Especially Alexander. His twin had always been his conscience, that quiet voice over his shoulder, prodding him to do and be better. He sighed.

"I'm sorry," he said. "I really am trying to change."

Sarai stopped her own treadmill. "I know. Hopefully you and your brother will be better with each other soon."

"We're all having dinner together on Sunday. We should be cooking with grease after that," he said, his smile widening.

"That's a good thing. Spending time with your family will help you all heal."

"It will. And Mama Lynn is excited about getting to know you. She's an incredible cook too so the food will be good. We'll have a great time."

Anxiety suddenly flushed Sarai's face. "Me? No! This should just be time for you and your family. I shouldn't be included!"

Zachary grinned. "You're family too, Sarai. You're my family. And I'll talk to my brother about how he's treating you. I'm sure he doesn't mean it. That's not how he is."

Doubt pierced her expression, not wholeheartedly convinced. "He might be a different man since you were married and left Boulder. You've been gone for a long time."

"Trust me. He's not."

Sarai eyed him for a brief moment before turning toward the locker rooms. "I need to take a shower," she said. "I'll meet you after I'm done."

Alexander was standing at the front reception desk when Sarai made her way to the lower lobby. He was joking with two members of his sales team when she entered the space. He watched as she looked quickly about, searching for someone who was nowhere to be found. Her reticence was notable as she slightly waved a hand in his direction before easing off to the side, wanting to avoid any unpleasant encounter between them. He couldn't fault her for the distance since he'd not done much to make her feel welcome. He hadn't wanted to talk to her, and she hadn't forced the issue. He suddenly found himself feeling bad about his shoddy behavior.

There had been no missing her arrival, everything about her presence seeming to tease his sensibilities. She was intoxicatingly beautiful, and there was no way to miss the attention she garnered. When she was near, people turned to look, and despite the interest, she seemed almost oblivious to it. She never gave him any sense that she cared or even noticed the obvious stares.

She'd worked with two new clients and both had asked for her again, which was definitely a positive. People were impressed by her strength, amazed that so much power was packed in such a petite frame. In the gym, she was demanding, and clients seemed to like that too, the standards she set moving them to push past any limits they placed on themselves. She made friends easily, and others on the staff liked working with her. Dan had been right about her being a good fit for the organization. Alexander imagined she was a good fit wherever she went.

He turned, his eyes skating back and forth in search of his brother. He knew that she was probably waiting for Zachary, having no other reason to be standing there by her lonesome. Despite the hostility that still plagued him, Alexander had stopped making an issue of his twin being there at the gym. His brother's money was as good as anyone else's, and since he'd actually purchased a lifetime pass for the privilege of being a member, there wasn't much Alexander could do.

The young woman who'd completed the transaction had been starstruck, not even questioning why the man would need to pay for the privilege of using his twin brother's gymnasium. Despite his anger, the staff seemed completely unaware of the tension between them. For that, Alexander had been grateful. Despite what he was feeling, he really didn't want the negativity to impact his employees or their performance.

Bad business would not serve him well and publicly castigating his brother was seriously bad business.

Taking another look around the room, Alexander excused himself from the conversation he was having and moved in the woman's direction.

"Sarai, hello," Alexander said as he extended his hand to shake hers.

She smiled sweetly. "It's good to see you again, Mr. Barrett."

"Mr. Barrett is my father. Please, call me Alex. We're practically *family*, right?" The question was smug, his top lip twitching with bitterness as he spat the words.

"Alex it is, then," she said with a slight nod, ignoring the tone.

"So, how are you settling in to your position? You're not having any problems that I need to be aware of, are you?"

"No. I'm really enjoying myself. Everyone's been very nice to me."

His mouth lifted in the slightest smile. "I'm glad to hear it. I've been preoccupied lately and I didn't want you to think that I was avoiding you."

This time she smiled brightly. "But you were avoiding me," she said as she crossed her arms over her chest. There was the hint of a challenge in the look she tossed him.

He lifted his eyes to hers, meeting her gaze with one of his own. Amusement danced across her face.

"I guess I was," he said sheepishly, color tinting his cheeks a deep shade of embarrassed. "But you have to admit that our situation is a little unique. Things were just . . . well . . . they were awkward."

"I don't agree," she said softly. "But I do know that

you and your brother are very much alike. He can be a big baby at times, too."

Alexander chuckled. "Baby! That's cute!"

She laughed with him. "Not so much cute coming from grown men."

"I'll take that," he said. "I probably have it coming."

"Yes, you do."

He nodded. "So can we agree to start over and I'll promise to do better? Because despite my bad behavior I really am a pretty nice guy. Most people think so anyway."

There was a moment of pause as she reflected on his comment. Her eyes skated over his profile as she took in the wealth of him. The man was as pretty as his brother. Even more so as he possessed an air of maturity that Zachary often lacked. She found everything about him appealing. Her face glowed as she nodded in agreement. "I look forward to knowing that guy," she said finally.

"Hey, what's up?" Zachary suddenly said, interjecting himself into their conversation. "What are you two up to?"

Both gave the man a look as his gaze darted back and forth between them. Ignoring his brother, Alexander turned his attention back to Sarai. "I'm glad we cleared the air. You have a very good night and I look forward to talking with you again soon," he said.

She smiled back. "Good night, Alex," she said.

There was a moment of pause as if Alexander wanted to say something else, but he didn't, instead turning an about-face and moving in the opposite direction.

"What was . . . ?" Zachary started to question as Sarai suddenly held up her hand to stall his comment.

Sarai took two steps after his brother, calling Alexander's name.

He turned, his eyes wide as she closed the gap between them, coming to a stop when they stood toe-to-toe. "Yes, Sarai?"

"Are you still interested in our having dinner? I don't have any plans tonight if you're free," she said, her expression eager.

The lull in their conversation was thunderous as he stood staring at her, silence sweeping volumi-nously between them. Around him, everything con-tinued like normal, no one else seeming to notice that time had shifted on its axis, leaving him stunned and unsettled. Alexander suddenly felt his head bob-bing against his thick neck, the moment feeling sur-real. "I am," he said, his voice a loud whisper.

She smiled. "Then I would very much like to have dinner with you. We can meet back here, or at the restaurant, whichever you prefer."

"I can pick you up," he said. "If that won't be a problem." He cut an eye at his brother before shift-ing his gaze back to hers.

"It won't be," she replied, tossing Zachary her own look. "Does seven o'clock work for you?"

"Seven is good."

"Do you know where I live?"

He nodded. "My mother says it's a big house." Color suddenly warmed his cheeks as he imagined how foolish that might have sounded.

She smiled sweetly. "I'll be ready when you get there," she said as she turned, heading in the direc-tion of the front door. Without uttering another word, she gestured for Zachary to follow.

The two brothers exchanged one last look. Bemused, Zachary shrugged his shoulders. Alexander gave him a raised brow, his own stare questioning. Neither spoke as Zachary turned, striding quickly to catch up with his friend. Watching the two exit the building, Alexander was flooded with a wealth of emotion, excitement leading the list as he realized he'd just made a date for dinner.

Chapter Four

"And you're having dinner with my brother, why?"

Sarai rolled her eyes skyward. "Because I like him and I would like to get to know him better."

She stood in front of a full-length mirror, modeling one shoe and then another as she debated which to wear with the form-fitting dress that covered her body.

Zachary shook his head. "Wear the black heels. Those are hot!"

She nodded as she tossed the tan pumps aside.

"You like him. What does that mean? Are you interested in him romantically?"

Sarai smiled, her head waving. Amusement danced in her eyes. "Would there be something wrong with that?"

He shrugged his broad shoulders. "You don't think it's a little weird?"

"No."

"But we're best friends and he's my brother."

"We're not dating, have never dated, and will never go there with each other. The same rules don't apply to Alex."

"Is this a transference thing? You can't have me so my twin is the next best thing?"

"I'm not attracted to you, Zachary. Not like that. Your twin is a very different man even if you two do resemble each other. He excites me. You don't."

"I think my feelings are hurt."

She laughed. "You'll get over it."

"Well, I'm leaving before he gets here. Then again, maybe I should stay."

"Please, do not put him in a bad mood before we leave. If you ruin my evening I will not forgive you."

"Then I'm leaving because if he sees me he's going to be in a bad mood. I seem to do that to him. I think I'll go grab a drink with some friends."

"You are not supposed to be drinking, remember? You're in training. Besides, you don't have any friends."

"I have friends. I have lots of friends."

"Do not bring any strange women back to this house, Zachary," Sarai admonished. "I'm warning you now!"

"That's what hotel rooms are for. Make sure you tell my brother that. In case you two get any ideas of your own!" Zachary said with a wry laugh.

"That was so unnecessary!" Sarai shook her head. "Please, leave. Now!"

"I'm going," Zachary said as he stood up, moving toward the door. For a brief moment he stood staring at her, meeting her gaze evenly. "Have fun," he said softly. "And I really mean that."

She smiled. "Thank you."

"And if you get a chance, put in a good word for me," he said. Then with a wink of his eye, he was gone.

* * *

It was only minutes later when the front doorbell chimed through the house, announcing Alexander's arrival. Sarai took one last look at her reflection in the mirror before moving toward the front of the home to greet him.

Pulling the door open, she smiled warmly. "Hello!" she exclaimed, meeting Alexander's nervous gaze.

Alexander wore a casual gray suit, gray leather loafers, and a white dress shirt opened at the neck. He was freshly shaven, and the faintest hint of his cologne scented the air around him. He was a tall, decadent drink of chocolate, and she was suddenly thirsty for something sweet. Sarai's eyes widened in appreciation.

The sight of her instantly eased Alexander's anxiety. She was stunning, and he found himself feeling like he'd hit the jackpot and won the lottery all in the same day. He stepped inside the doorway, the tension lifting from his face as he greeted her with a bright smile. "You look beautiful," he said, his eyes skirting the length of her body.

The dress she wore was a summery shade of peach with a deep V-neck and cap sleeves. The hem stopped just above her knee. It complemented the slight curve of her breasts and hips, and the heels she wore gave her just enough lift to balance her well-toned legs.

"Thank you," she said as she tossed the length of her dark, lush hair over her shoulder.

His cerulean gaze skated around the room behind her, curiosity washing over his expression. His brother was nowhere to be seen, and he found himself thinking that his twin had to be lurking somewhere in the background.

"He's not here," she said, seeming to read his mind.

"Excuse me?"

She eyed him with a raised brow. "Your brother. He's not here."

"Oh, I wasn't . . ."

She held up an index finger, exasperation flushing her face. "Yes, you were."

Alexander flinched. "Sorry. I just wondered . . ." He paused, suddenly unable to explain what he'd been thinking without digging himself into a bigger hole. "I'm sorry!"

Sarai changed the subject. "So, where are we going?"

When it first opened, Radda Trattoria had been named one of the top ten hottest new restaurants by *Bon Appétit* magazine. Time had made it a consistent favorite among the Boulder, Colorado crowd that often frequented the space. Alexander had reserved a quiet table for two, and he and Sarai were seated comfortably by the oversized fireplace that decorated the room.

On the ride over, the two had made small talk, their limited conversation edged in much silence. Both were surprised by the rise of apprehension that seemed to plague their short trip to the downtown area. Once seated, there had been a good ten minutes of focusing on their menus and not each other, both trying to find a semblance of balance.

Alexander sighed heavily, a loud gust of air hissing past his full lips. He found himself apologizing again. "I didn't mean to let my problems with my brother become an issue between us. And I definitely didn't want it to impact our evening! I'm really sorry about that."

Sarai sat back in her seat, dropping her hands into her lap. "Why is it so hard for you to forgive him?"

He met her stare before dropping his gaze to the table. "He betrayed me. He didn't care about my feelings. I trusted him and he stabbed me in the back. I can never trust him again."

She nodded. "He misses you and he wants things between you two to get better."

"I really don't care what he wants." His gaze shifted back to hers, his expression steadfast.

"That's not true. You do care. That's why you're still angry. And it's why you're having such a difficult time now."

He shrugged. "So why is Zachary so important to you? What's your relationship with my brother anyway? Are you two dating?"

She hesitated for a brief second, her eyes skating over his face as she studied his mood. She took a deep inhale of air before finally answering. "Zachary and I are very good friends. He has been very good to me and my father and I owe him my life. I grew up in a very small village outside of Phuket. When your brother moved to Thailand, he hired my father to work for him. They became friends and then he took me under his wing, too. There weren't many opportunities for women there and I didn't have a bright future. My father would have married me off and I would have worked in the fields but your brother arranged for me to go to school in France. He afforded me opportunities that I would never have had access to. And he made it possible for my father to support his family and keep his home."

Alexander nodded, pausing to reflect on her statement. "So you and he have never slept with each other?"

"Never," she said, a hint of annoyance flashing in her eyes. "If I had, this"—she fanned her hand between them—"would never be happening. I'm not Felicia and I would never be with one brother and then move on to the other if things didn't work out. That is just wrong in so many ways!"

"So, you know my brother's wife?" he asked.

"I did. I know that she was not a good person. You should actually thank your brother for saving you from much heartbreak. She used him and she made his life miserable. He still suffers from the hurt of it. She didn't love you and she didn't love him."

"Well, isn't karma a bitch!" he said, his tone dripping with sarcasm.

"Karma is many things and I think it is good karma that has brought you two back to each other. You should follow the spirit and allow what should be to happen."

"I don't know that I agree with you."

"You and your brother are both so stubborn!" She tossed up her hands in frustration.

"I am nothing like my brother," he hissed between clenched teeth.

"You are exactly like your brother!" she hissed back, unmoved by his rancor.

He grunted, frustration furrowing his brow. There was a brief moment of pause as the waiter brought their meals to the table. As the young man stepped away, Alexander resumed the conversation.

"This might be none of my business but what actually happened with Zachary and Felicia? What went wrong?"

Sarai dabbed a cloth napkin against her lips, then folded it on her lap. She took a deep breath and held it for a brief moment as she decided whether or not to make what she knew his business. She blew that breath out slowly before speaking. "Besides her being a bitch? Felicia left him for another man. An expat from Britain who'd come to Thailand to train with your brother. He didn't see it coming and it devastated him. Your brother truly loved her."

"I truly loved her. So now he knows how that felt."

There was an air of satisfaction in his tone that Sarai found off-putting. She pondered on it briefly before responding. She sat forward in her seat, pulling her folded hands to the top of the table as she pushed her plate from her. "You just *thought* you were in love with her. She truly did not have your heart. This has never been about you loving her. It's been about your love for your brother."

"How can you say that?"

"Because you have been bothered more by what he did than you were about her and what she did. You've been so focused on being angry with Zachary that you never considered how *she* betrayed you. In fact, I'm willing to bet that you were never as angry with her as you were with him. You would have forgiven and taken her back but would still have been angry with Zachary."

"And that's not love?"

"That was all ego, feeling like you had to prove you were the better twin."

"I don't agree. I know what I felt was love."

"It was, for Zachary. He's your blood and that tie supersedes all others. Especially since Felicia wasn't a good woman and you knew it. Why would you still want a woman who pursued your brother and tricked him into marrying her, all the time professing how much she loved you?"

"Tricked?"

"Did he ever tell you that she said the two of you really didn't have a relationship? That you were just obsessed with her?"

"He might have but I told him that wasn't true."

"Or that she even accused you of beating her?"

"He knew *that* wasn't true."

"Did he really? Because you do have a bit of a temper. You both do."

He looked at her with a raised brow, then shifted his eyes to stare at the wall. She continued.

"Did you ever stop to think what else Felicia might have been telling him?"

He shrugged his shoulders. "Not really."

"Exactly. She whispered many lies in his ears and he fell for them. Just like you fell for them. She lied that she was pregnant. She said that you didn't want anything to do with her. That's why he married her so quickly. He was devastated to find out she paid a doctor to lie to him about the pregnancy. There had never been any baby."

"He never told me that."

"It's difficult to speak with a man who doesn't want to hear you. And I have been able to see for myself how you push him away. How you don't listen to what he is trying to say to you. You turned a deaf ear to your brother so no matter what he had to say you couldn't hear him."

"You weren't here so you really don't know what you're talking about," he said, an air of attitude ringing in his tone.

"I know that she lied to you too. She even told me

so. She bragged about it! She lied about her family. She lied about accidentally running into you that first time you met. She lied to break you up with the dark-haired girl you were dating back then. Remember her? She lied about being afraid of her ex-boyfriend so that you would want to protect her. She told you many lies and much like your brother you just didn't want to acknowledge them. You still don't. She had you so twisted that you still can't pull your head out of your ass to see straight!"

Alexander suddenly thought about the things between him and Felicia that had never added up. Red flags that had given him fair warning about the kind of woman she had been. And despite the many signs, he'd ignored them, making her the woman he had wanted her to be in his mind. But his relationship with his brother's ex-wife had built like a raging fire, and when the flames had gone out there'd been nothing left but property damage.

Since then he hadn't found a reason to try again. Searching for long-term love seemed hopeless, and he'd adapted to a solitary life that revolved around his business and the hobbies he enjoyed. His failed relationship had made him wary of the hurt and disappointment love left behind. Now Sarai had him considering the source of his heartbreak and considering that perhaps it was as much his fault as anyone else's. The truth of it was painted across his face as Sarai continued.

"I know many things about you, Alexander Barrett. And I know them because your brother opened his heart and shared them with me. I know that you wanted a degree in journalism but did what your father wanted instead, even though it wasn't your first love. I know that you were happier when you were a member of the national ski team because you loved to do that more than play basketball. Zachary encouraged you to follow your heart and instead you focused all your time and attention on helping him discover his passion.

"I know that you would shelter your brother at night when you were boys because he's afraid of the dark. You always kept a flashlight nearby to pacify him. And you would eat his greens and tomatoes when your parents insisted you clean your plates because he hated the vegetables. I know that you told him how to make the moves to get his first kiss before you had even gotten your own." She smiled, the lift to her thin lips returning to her face. She continued.

"The things I know, that your brother has shared, tell me that you love your brother very much. And I know firsthand how much he loves you. You're angry with him because you do care. And now, you are letting him be an issue between us because you truly miss him and I am the closest thing to him that you have right now."

Hot saline simmered behind Alexander's eyelids. He refused to meet the woman's intense stare, fearing the tears might actually fall if he looked at her. There was much truth to what she said and even more that he needed to reflect on.

Still looking at the space over her shoulder, he took a deep breath and spoke. "Why did you agree to have dinner with me? Was it just to plead my brother's case?"

"What you should be asking is what motivated you to invite me to dinner. If I'm not mistaken you didn't know about my relationship with your brother when you first asked me to go out with you. Did you?"

He finally dropped his eyes back to hers. "No, I didn't. I asked you out because I liked you and I thought we'd made a connection."

She met his stare, her own eyes shimmering with life. "Thought or knew? Because I didn't have any doubts."

A quick smirk crossed his face. "I didn't have any doubts either. I *knew* something had clicked between us and I was excited to see where that might go."

"And I accepted because I liked you, too. And I wanted to get to know you for myself. Because from everything your brother has told me and everything I've read about you, and what your friends and family have had to say, it would seem that you're an incredible man. Respected, trusted, honorable, talented, spiritual, the list is endless. If I were to believe it all, you're damn near perfect." Her words were soft and seductive, her slight smile teasing. "But, truth be told, I'm not convinced," she concluded, "even if you do have the most beautiful eyes."

A smile pulled at his full lips, drawing his mouth into a half-moon. His tone softened. "So where do we go from here? How do I convince you that I really am one of the good guys?"

She paused momentarily before answering. "I guess that will depend on where you would like us to go. And whether or not you can resolve things with your brother. Because he's my friend and I want to see you both happy."

"And if he and I can't fix things?"

"I trust that you will. You will do it for you and you will also do it for me. Your brother has earned my friendship so he will always have my loyalty. You and I are just beginning to know each other. You still have some work to do. But I assure you I am well worth the effort. But hopefully you'll want to get to know me and discover that for yourself."

Alexander grinned. "And how does Zachary feel about our getting to know each other?"

"Zachary is my friend. He is *not* my father. But he cares about me and I know that he only wants the best for both of us."

Alexander took a bite of the steak on his plate, allowing everything she'd said to settle in his mind. The small talk continued as they enjoyed the meal, still working to find balance with each other.

"Would you be willing to give me a do-over?" he said as he pushed his empty plate away.

"A do-over? What is that?"

He chuckled softly. "It's where you let me make this evening up to you. Would you let me take you to dinner again? And this time I promise not to spend the whole night obsessing about my brother."

Sarai smiled, joy shimmering in her dark eyes. "I would *love* to have dinner with you again."

Sarai could hear Zachary before she saw him. He lay stretched out across the living-room sofa, snoring loudly as the television played in the background. Three empty beer bottles resting on the coffee table made her frown. He needed to be in training mode, but there were too many things on his mind holding him back. Sarai had been concerned before, but now she was starting to seriously worry. He was less than eight months from his next title bout, and that time would come and go before he realized it. His being fit for everyday activity was a far cry from his being fit to get back into the ring. She cleared the table, taking the trash to the garbage can in the kitchen.

Moving back into the living room, she laid a cashmere blanket gently over his large body. He shifted beneath the covering, rolling until his face was pressed into the plush pillow, muffling his snores. Sarai tiptoed to the television set and muted the volume. With one last look in his direction, she turned and headed toward her own room.

Inside, she stripped out of her clothes and into her nightgown. In the adjoining bathroom, she washed the makeup from her face and moisturized her skin. She whispered a quick prayer for protection before sliding between the cool sheets and pulling the blankets up to her chin.

Reaching beneath the spare pillows, she pulled a framed photograph from its hiding spot. An image of Alexander and Zachary in their early teens stared back at her. Their father stood between them, his arms draped around their shoulders. Their stepmother sat in a chair in front of the three and a lit Christmas tree appeared to twinkle in the background. The old photograph had once been a holiday card addressed to her own beloved mother.

The day it had arrived there had been an air of sadness over the older woman as she'd sat staring at it, and then she'd smiled brightly when Sarai had wanted to see, the matriarch excited to show off her friends from America. Sarai had been smitten from the moment she'd laid eyes on that Christmas greeting. There was no mistaking that the two boys were twins. They had stood like matching statues in the same ill-fitting suits. Zachary had made a face at the camera, the moment capturing that devil-may-care attitude of his. Alexander's expression had been more stoic, his smile slight. But there had been something in his deep blue gaze that had captured Sarai's attention and was still holding it tightly.

Back then she could never have imagined either one of them ever crossing her path. So Alexander had become a beautiful fantasy for her to hold tight to, imagining herself sharing her life with such a beautiful man. When her mother had died, she'd felt alone and abandoned, her fantasies seeming even less attainable. When everything had felt hopeless, the beginnings of a downhill spiral taking hold, Zachary had swooped in to save her, her dreams coming true in a way she would never have fathomed. There was nothing she wouldn't do to repay him for everything he'd done. The love and friendship he'd given so readily had been a lifeline that had kept her afloat, and she had needed it more than she could have ever imagined. And now Alexander was in her life, wanting to also be her friend.

The smile that pulled at her mouth twisted to a full grin. Heat rippled through her core, tiny currents of electricity piercing her feminine spirit. She bit down against her bottom lip as she curled her body against the mattress, drawing her knees to her chest. Staring at the photo for a minute longer, she pressed her lips to the glass and blew Alexander a good-night kiss. One day, she thought, she would tell him about the photo and her daydream-fueled fantasies. One day. Tucking the image back beneath the pillow, she soon drifted off to sleep, thoughts of the blue-eyed man billowing through her dreams.

The items and mementos that lay across Alexander's childhood bed had filled a plastic shoebox.

The shoebox had always been hidden beneath the floorboards of his father's closet. He and Zachary had found the secret hiding place when they'd been boys, playing hide-and-seek. For them it had been a gold mine full of wondrous treasures, a looking glass into a time neither boy had any memory of. There had been many times that Alexander had "borrowed" the box, always putting it back where he'd found it when he'd satisfied his need to reminisce.

He held up a photo of his parents, both looking like they were barely out of their teens. Their smiles were bright, something decadent shimmering in their gazes as they stared at each other and not the camera. There was another of the young couple holding their infant sons, both beaming with joy. Their mother had been a beautiful woman. Mocha skin, shoulder-length hair, and the bright blue eyes that he'd inherited.

Searching through the old photos, the military pins, ticket stubs, and other assorted memorabilia that his father held near and dear to his heart, Alexander hoped to find something that might tell him more about the man's relationship to Sarai's mother and to Sarai herself. Finding nothing he hadn't seen many times before, he repacked everything neatly, then tiptoed into his parents' bedroom to return the box to its resting spot. Although his father always knew when he went thumbing through those old photos, Alexander never made a production of it, not wanting Mama Lynn to be upset by him revisiting a time in their lives that didn't include her.

Downstairs he could hear his stepmother fussing as she put the finishing touches on the Sunday meal. His parents were excited at the prospect of having both their sons at their dining table after so many years of their being apart. The playful sparring between the couple brought a smile to Alexander's face.

When he'd risen that morning, he'd been reluctant to come for their family reunion, but the prospect of seeing Sarai again had been just enough motivation to pull him out of his bed and point him in the direction of his parents' home.

He and Sarai had talked for a good long while during their first dinner date, the event one comment shy of being a total disaster. In all honesty, believing she and his brother were a couple, Alexander had only gone hoping to piss Zachary off, and when she'd called him on it, he'd felt like a complete idiot. Because truth be told, he liked Sarai. He liked her a lot, and she had deserved better from him.

The young woman had been opinionated about everything, beginning with him and his relationship with his twin. He hadn't been prepared to hear what she'd had to say, but she'd broken it down in no uncertain terms, not caring whether or not he'd been ready. In that moment he realized that Sarai Montri was a woman to be reckoned with. She didn't mince words, nor did she shy away from things that were difficult. She also liked him and wanted to know what kind of man he was instead of believing what she might have been told. From start to finish, though, he hadn't made a very good first impression, and he was hoping to change that around.

Since then things between them had gotten easier. He enjoyed the brief moments they shared when their paths crossed at the gym. They'd fallen into a comfortable routine, and he looked forward to those moments in his day when they could share a few moments in time. Conversation was no longer awkward, and he enjoyed her humor and her flirtatious spirit.

As Alexander sat on the edge of his parents' king-size bed, losing himself in reflection, everything was beginning to feel right again. He felt as if he were getting a second chance, and he was determined to make the most of it. And then the doorbell rang through the house, announcing his brother's return to their childhood home.

Chapter Five

The result of hours of labor in the kitchen was splayed out across the formal dining-room table. Mama Lynn had prepared a smorgasbord of their favorite foods, the quantity as if she were planning to feed two armies and an entire nation.

Alexander laughed heartily. "Mama Lynn, did you forget that he's supposed to be in training and that I make a living telling people *not* to eat this way?"

The older woman fanned a hand in his direction. "One day isn't going to hurt you or anyone else," she said as she passed him a platter of fried chicken. "I soaked that bird in buttermilk and garlic all night just like you like it. That breast meat will melt like butter in your mouth!"

Zachary pulled a forkful of barbecued pork past his lips. "This is definitely not good for me," he mumbled, "but I sure missed it!"

"It's all so good!" Sarai exclaimed as she reached for another serving of the matriarch's infamous macaroni and cheese. "I'll have to work out twice as hard this week, though."

"We all will," Alexander said, tossing the woman a slight smile.

Mama Lynn's gaze skated around the table as she eyed her two boys and their new friend. Tears misted her eyes, and she jumped, turning toward the kitchen abruptly so that no one could see her struggling not to cry. "Save room for dessert!" she exclaimed, her voice cracking ever so slightly. "I made chocolate pie for you, Zachary, and fried apple pies for you, Alexander!"

Westley chuckled softly. "Your mama's about to bust she's so happy to have you boys back home," he said, his voice dropping to a loud whisper.

The brothers exchanged a look, neither commenting. Zachary refilled his plate with collard greens as Alexander took a bite from the drumstick he'd grabbed, both refocusing on the food.

"Should I go check on her?" Sarai asked, concern washing over her expression. She looked around the table at each of the men.

Westley shook his head. "She'll be fine. She's a tough cookie! She'll be even better once these two fix what they need to fix," he said.

Sarai nodded, eyeing one brother and then the other. Her gaze shifted back to their father, who was staring at her intently. She smiled, her own eyes dropping to the table.

"Young lady, you look just like your mother," Westley said, his tone dropping an octave. "I was very sorry to hear about her passing. She was an incredible woman and a very good friend."

The young woman smiled. "Thank you for saying so, Mr. Barrett. How well did you know my mother?"

Westley cut an eye at both of his sons, who were

eyeing him curiously. "I imagine you must miss her very much," he said and then he deflected the conversation.

"So Alexander, what's this I hear about you doing a golf training program with Tiger Woods?" he asked as he took another bite of his candied yams.

Minutes later Mama Lynn returned to the table, her smile bright and full. "Your daddy probably thinks I forgot all about him with you boys being home." She reached for her husband's hand and gave it a squeeze. "I made you two honey bun cakes, Mr. Barrett!"

Westley laughed. "That's what I'm talking about and I don't care if I work it off or not!"

The family all laughed with him. The dinner conversation was light and easy, each of them taking many trips down memory lane. Lynn and Westley were kind and generous as they tried to make Sarai feel welcome, pulling her into their conversations. Both asked a ton of questions about her home and family, as curious about her as she was about them. On the outside looking in, no one would have ever imagined any of them not getting along.

As Westley finished the last of his cake and the sliver of chocolate pie his wife had placed on his dessert plate, he leaned back in his seat, folding his hands together in his lap. For a brief moment he seemed to drift off into thought. As his family caught him staring into space, their conversation came to an abrupt halt, everyone turning to stare. He suddenly lifted his gaze, observing them all one by one. He rested his eyes on his sons but directed his conversation toward the women.

"Sarai, I know you're a guest but if you don't mind I would really appreciate it if you would give Mama Lynn a hand with the dishes while these two go handle their business. I have some light reading I'd like to catch up on."

The young woman nodded. Her voice was soft as she answered. "Of course, Mr. Barrett. That's not a problem at all."

Alexander felt himself bristle, every muscle in his body tensing. Zachary's discomfort was suddenly as palpable as his own. He took a deep breath and held it as he and his brother locked gazes. Their father continued.

"You two need to go on up to your old room and hash out your differences. Don't come back down until you're best friends again. Is that clear?" He fixed his gaze on Alexander.

Knowing that there was no need to respond, the brothers both stood at the same time. Heading out the room, Zachary stopped at the oak buffet and reached for a bottle of scotch that rested against the cabinet's top.

Following on his brother's heels, Alexander grabbed two highball glasses. Tossing Sarai a quick glance over his shoulder, Alexander disappeared from sight, the two men bounding up the stairs together.

When the bedroom door slammed closed, everyone sitting at the table released a collective sigh. Lynn and Westley exchanged a look, a silent conversation playing between them. Sarai's gaze skated back and forth before finally dropping to the floor, for the first time feeling like she didn't belong. Her own anxiety level rose tenfold.

Mama Lynn patted her on the back. "Don't you worry, dear! Everything's going to be fine."

Sarai reached for the empty plates, helping to clear the table. "This will be good for them," she said softly.

The older woman nodded in agreement. "So tell me, Sarai, how long have you and my son Zachary been a thing?"

The silence was uncomfortable. Neither man spoke. Alexander took a seat on his mattress, dropping the two glasses in his hand to the nightstand that separated the two twin beds. Zachary sat on his own bed as he popped the cap on that bottle of scotch, filling the two tumblers with the amber-colored fluid. He passed one glass to his twin, then lifted the other in a mock toast. Alexander watched as his twin guzzled the warm drink; then he did the same, the scotch burning his throat as he swallowed it down. He slapped the glass back onto the nightstand, and Zachary refilled it with another shot of booze. Half the bottle was gone before either man said a word.

"So, what now?" Zachary asked. "What do I need to do or say to make things right with you?" Contrition seeped from his stare, his left eye twitching nervously. His brow was lifted, his expression questioning.

"I don't know if there's anything you can say or do," Alexander answered honestly. "Things will never be the same between us, so does it really matter?"

Zachary heaved a deep breath, sucking warm air into his lungs. "It matters to me. And things might not be the same but I really want them to be better. I miss you, A. You were my best friend."

Alexander jumped abruptly, pointing a finger in his brother's direction. "Your best friend? If what you did is how you treat your best friend I'd hate to see what you'd do to an enemy!" He found himself shouting, his tone harsh.

Zachary jumped with him, the two men standing toe-to-toe. "But you weren't my enemy, you were my brother!"

"Then you should have acted like it!" Alexander screamed. There was a brief moment of hesitation as his rage rose to a crescendo, and then with nothing but revenge in his heart, he threw the first punch, his fist connecting with Zachary's jaw.

The punch to his face threw Zachary's head back, everything about the punch unexpected. He stumbled; then his body instinctively shifted into defense mode. Reflex tensed every muscle, and before he realized it, he'd lifted his hands, balled his own fists, and threw a punch back, connecting with his brother's eye. Before either could rationalize what they were doing, they were suddenly rolling around the room, their fight a knock-down, drag-out brawl.

Below, the family all lifted their eyes to the ceiling at the same time. The noise coming from above was thunderous. Sarai held her breath, the anxiety sweeping through her like a bad virus. She tossed the two parents a look, the couple exchanging their own stares.

"They are tearing that room up!" Mama Lynn admonished, her head waving from side to side.

Westley shrugged his shoulders, his expression indifferent. "If they break it they'll fix it," he said nonchalantly. He went back to reading the magazine that had held his attention before the interruption.

"Just doesn't make any sense," the older woman muttered. She reached for her teapot and refilled Sarai's cup with the warm brew. "They've been fighting like that since they were little boys. One would get angry, then they would hit and punch each other for an hour. Ten minutes later they'd hug and make up like nothing happened."

"That's what we want," her husband interjected. "They need to get it out of their system, then get to the hug and make-up part." His graying head bounced up and down as if unhinged.

Mama Lynn rolled her eyes skyward. "Grown-ass men acting like they're two years old. Don't make no kind of sense! Time for this nonsense to stop!"

Sarai smiled, amusement painting her expression.

The noise from the second floor continued for a good few minutes, bodies sounding like they were being slammed against the floorboards. The walls shook, and muffled grunts and curses echoed in the air.

Back in the bedroom, the two men finally came to a halt, their fight stopping as quickly as it started. Both men were breathing heavily, air coming in deep gasps. Alexander slid his buttocks across the floor, backing himself against the twin bed. Zachary retreated to the space across from him. They sat in the quiet that followed, the wealth of it feeling like a healing balm.

Zachary took another breath, words returning. "You and I had been dating the same women since we started dating. Why was this different?"

"You always *chased* after the women I dated!"

"And you were guilty of doing the same thing! You were never serious about any of them, so what did it matter? It's not like you ever really cared!"

"I cared about Felicia!"

"Before I married her or only after?"

"I loved Felicia!"

"I didn't know that."

"How could you not know? You were my brother. You knew she was the only woman I was seeing."

There was a moment of pause as the two stared at each other. Alexander pulled his knees to his chest, wrapping his arms around his legs.

"And what about Stacy?" Zachary asked, his tone accusing.

"Stacy? Who's Stacy?"

"She worked at the hotdog place. The cheerleader with the big . . ." Zachary's comment stalled as he gestured with his hands, the appendages waving over his chest.

Alexander blinked. "What does she have to do with anything?"

"If you were so in love with Felicia, why did you sleep with Stacy?"

"I didn't sleep with Stacy!"

"It was the night after midterm exams. You and Felicia had been fighting and you drove Stacy home. She says you slept together. She told everyone, including me and Felicia, how you two had something going on."

"I . . . we . . . well," Alexander stammered, trying to remember a time in their lives that had come and gone. Then the memory hit him. He locked gazes with his brother as he tried to explain himself. "Felicia and I were on a break. We had needed to take some time apart."

"Exactly."

"But . . ."

"But nothing. You dated someone else and Felicia did too. It just happened that she dated me."

"But we were trying to make things work when you turned around and married her!"

"I fell in love with her! And I thought she loved me."

Zachary's voice cracked, and there was no missing the hurt that simmered in his tone.

"She married you, didn't she?" Alexander said, no longer yelling.

His brother shrugged. "She did but she didn't love me. She only married me for the image she had for her life."

"And she didn't see that with me?"

"You weren't interested in playing ball back then. This was well before you were thinking about going pro. Back then you wanted the two-point-three kids, the picket fence, and the dog. You would have been happy being a high-school English teacher."

"And Felicia really wanted to be with a baller. Or a rapper!" The comment was clearly a statement and not a question, Alexander knowing the answer as he remembered back to that time and the woman he and his brother had allowed to come between them. This time he took a deep breath before he continued. "Why didn't you at least talk to me? We had never done anything that we didn't talk about first. But you actually married her and never said anything to me."

Zachary's gaze drifted into thought as he pondered his brother's question. "You would have stopped me," he finally answered, his eyes reconnecting with Alexander's stare. "And back then I really thought it was time I did something on my own without you being a part of it. Or at least that was what Felicia had me thinking."

"She didn't want me to stop you either. She thought she was going to lose her meal ticket!"

Zachary laughed, and the faintest hint of a smile lifted his brother's lips.

Another blanket of silence dropped down between them, the two falling into their own thoughts.

Suddenly everything that had been their past seemed irrelevant.

"I'm sorry," Zachary said. "I'm sorry because I did need you. I never should have let her convince me that not having you in my life was better for me. Because it wasn't. It's the worst thing that could have happened to me."

"Yeah, you were wrong. And you hurt my damn feelings."

His brother nodded. "I hate that it happened but I swear, I'll do whatever it takes to make things good with us again. I love you, A." He swiped a heavy hand across his eyes, moisture pooling behind his lids.

Alexander reached for the scotch bottle that had fallen to the floor and the glass that had rolled beneath the bed. He started to pour them both another shot, then stopped, lifting the last of the bottle to his own lips instead.

"I thought we were making up? Now you're not even going to share?" Zachary said, his eyes wide as he held out his empty glass.

Alexander shook his head. "You're supposed to be in training. If you're going to attach my name to how you do your business, then you're going to follow my rules. And rule number one is no drinking. Tomorrow we're turning that diet of yours around, too. Today, though, I'm going to let you have one more slice of Mama Lynn's pie."

Zachary grinned. "So we're good, A?"

His twin shrugged. "We're getting there."

"I'll take that," Zachary said. "I'll definitely take that."

* * *

Sarai pressed an ice pack to the side of Alexander's face and over his eye. Her touch was anything but gentle, and he winced from the pain that shot through his head. "That hurts!" he hissed, leaning away from her heavy hand. "Don't be so rough!"

She shook her head as she flipped her eyes at Zachary. "You should both be ashamed of yourselves," she said as she cut her gaze back toward Alexander.

Zachary laughed, his wide grin like a beacon in the center of his face. "We've done worse." He sat with a bag of frozen peas against his bottom lip as Mama Lynn bandaged a gash across his forehead.

Alexander nodded. "We have," he said, shooting Sarai a look out of the corner of his eye. "This really wasn't bad at all. Zachary's gone soft."

"Soft! That black eye you're sporting shows just how soft I am!"

"This black eye was a lucky punch. There's no way the world heavyweight UFC champion could have been beaten by an amateur if he wasn't soft."

"I didn't get beat."

"No, you got slaughtered! By an ex–professional basketball player, no less!"

Zachary rolled his eyes skyward.

"Well, I don't know who beat who," Mama Lynn said, "but I do know you tore that spare room apart. Just made a holy mess up there!"

"Zach has to replace the chair," Alexander said.

"You have to buy a lamp!"

"You both will have to replace that closet door," Westley said.

"Well, I don't care who fixes that big hole in the wall," Mama Lynn interjected, "but I definitely want that fixed!"

The two men pointed at each other, both laughing.

Sarai slapped Alexander against the back of his head with the flat of her palm.

"Ouch!" he snapped, drawing his hand against the new spot that suddenly stung.

She crossed the room toward the sink, pausing only briefly to give Zachary a swift punch in his arm as she passed by him.

"What did I do?" he said, rubbing at the offending bruise.

She tossed him a narrowed gaze, but she said nothing as she dampened a bath cloth with warm water. She moved back to Alexander's side. She gently dabbed at the dried blood that had crusted beneath his nose and on his face.

"Don't say I didn't warn you," Zachary said, meeting the look his brother was giving him, "but she has a mean streak. Do not let that demure appearance fool you!"

The look Sarai gave her friend was cutting, her eyes thin slits of displeasure. She bit back the comment that pulled at the tip of her tongue, instead turning her attention back to Alexander, who was smiling at her with amusement. He took her hand in his and squeezed it gently, giving her a wink of his eye. The gesture moved her to smile, a glint of light shimmering in her eyes.

Zachary sat, staring at the two of them. Sarai stood leaning into Alexander's body as she gently nursed his bruises. They were so close that had his brother turned his head, he would have planted his face right between her small breasts. She drew a slow hand across his back, and under different circumstances, the gesture could have been seen as salacious. But there was something in how Sarai interacted with his twin that was new to Zachary, her gentle mutterings so loving in nature that they surprised him, and only because he'd never heard such a thing from her before. It didn't go unnoticed, despite what she or Alexander might have thought.

"You should probably go have that hand looked at," Westley suddenly said, interrupting Zachary's thoughts.

He dropped his gaze down to his fingers, then shrugged his broad shoulders. "It'll be fine. They're just going to tell me I have some hairline fractures. It happens all the time." He winced as he squeezed a fist and then relaxed it.

Mama Lynn sucked her teeth in frustration. "I don't know why you two couldn't have studied law or medicine or something easier on your bodies. And my nerves!"

Minutes later, with both men cleaned up and bandaged, the family sat back down at the dining table for the second round of dessert. Laughter was abundant as they shared stories and caught up on the time they'd missed being together. The oversized clock that decorated the living room wall chimed on the midnight hour before the brothers stood up again to leave. Hugs and kisses were exchanged as the family wished each other a good night.

As the door closed behind her family, Mama Lynn shook her head. She turned to meet her husband's stare.

"What's wrong?" Westley asked as the woman moved past him to clear the last of the dirty dishes away.

Mama Lynn shook her head. "I'm glad the boys were able to put all their mess behind them, but I swear, it didn't take no time at all for another woman to get between them."

"What do you mean?"

"I know Sarai said she and Zachary are just friends, but you wouldn't have known it by the way he was watching her and Alexander. And how could you miss how Alexander and that girl were making eyes at each other? It's bound to be a problem. Sooner or later she's bound to be a problem between them."

Westley shook his head. He wrapped his arms around the woman's waist and hugged her warmly. "Stop worrying about them boys. They'll figure out things with that little girl all on their own."

Chapter Six

Still hyped on adrenaline, the twins and Sarai moved their reunion from the Barrett home to the Denny's on Baseline Road. The clientele in the twenty-four-hour eatery was minimal, and they had their pick of tables.

Sarai took the inside seat in one of the rear booths. Zachary slid into the cushioned seat across from her, and after a brief moment of hesitation, Alexander sat on the seat by the young woman's side.

"Does it hurt?" she asked, the pads of her fingers gently tracing the outline of his bruised eye.

Alexander shrugged, a slight smile spreading across his face. "I'll pop a Tylenol before I go to bed. It'll be better in the morning," he answered.

"Oh, please," Zachary quipped. "I think that first punch he threw broke my nose and you don't see me complaining. And I use this face to help build my brand!"

Sarai stared at him, tilting her head left, then right, concern washing across her face as she shook her head.

"What?" Zachary asked anxiously. He sat forward

in his seat, trying to see his reflection in the glass windows. His eyes were wide as he tapped at the bridge of his nose with his fingers. "Does it look bad?"

Alexander laughed. "There is nothing wrong with your nose. Sarai's just messing with you!"

Sarai giggled, mischief shimmering in her dark eyes. "Your brother doesn't want to hurt your feelings," she said teasingly.

"Hahaha, you are so funny," Zachary jeered. "You don't see me cracking jokes about your breasts . . . or lack thereof . . . do you?"

She gave him a sneer, her expression smug. "Yeah, they're small. I can't help it if I'm still waiting patiently for puberty to fully kick in," she joked. "But you don't have an excuse for that football sitting in the center of your face."

Alexander laughed at the two of them. "Are you two always this entertaining to be around?"

Zachary grinned. "We have our moments."

Sarai rolled her eyes.

Before she could comment, the waitress came to take their order. The woman was long and lean, with skin the color of black licorice, and a Kewpie-doll pout. Her hair was braided in an intricate updo that flattered her profile.

"I'll just have coffee," Alexander said. "Black."

"I want scrambled eggs with whole wheat toast, please," Sarai said.

The waitress turned her attention to Zachary. "And, what can I get you, good-looking?" she grinned, her expression showing her rising interest.

Zachary grinned back. "What's sweet, besides you, beautiful?"

The woman leaned forward, lightly licking her

lips. "I'm the sweetest thing you'll get here, Hammer. And I'm off the clock at four."

Alexander laughed. "So, you know who he is?" he asked, pointing at Zachary.

She nodded. "I know who you both are, Mr. Barrett. I'm a big fan!"

Sarai rolled her eyes skyward.

The flirtatious banter continued between them until Zachary finally ordered a slice of peach pie with ice cream and a side of country linked sausage. Admiring the expanse of her assets, both men watched with appreciation as the young woman walked away.

Sarai cleared her throat, her gaze shifting back and forth between the two men. "You, too?" she questioned, her eyes resting on Alexander.

"What?"

"I'm used to your brother staring at other women's asses. I didn't expect it from you."

He laughed. "I wasn't staring at that woman's ass!"

"Yes, you were!"

Zachary chuckled with the two of them. "She's just upset because she doesn't have any ass either. She's still waiting for puberty to bring that, too!"

Alexander tried not to laugh at his brother's joke, but the exchange was too funny, their playful razzing overly amusing. He waved a dismissive hand. "Don't listen to him, Sarai. You have a very nice ass! Even if it is a little small!"

"It's not as . . . how do you say it, Zach? It's not as *thick* as the women's here in the United States but it's firm. I work very hard to get this bubble!"

"Yes, you do," Zachary said, his smile filling his face. "Most Thai women aren't known for their curves. It's their petite, slender figures that men are drawn to. I talked to a lot of guys who visit Thailand who say that

Western women have become too masculine-like with their muscular bodies."

Sarai nodded. "The European men who visit Thailand just think we are submissive and nonconfrontational. That's what they're drawn to!"

"Clearly, they haven't met you!" Zachary said. "Or any of the women in Thailand that I thought about dating."

Alexander looked at him with a raised eye.

"It was all fantasy. I've sworn off women so I haven't been dating anyone," Zachary added with a soft chuckle.

His brother turned his attention back to Sarai and continued the conversation. "But most of that is just individuals perpetuating the stereotypes," Alexander interjected. "It's no different from people saying all black women have attitudes and are bitter and angry. Or that blond and blue-eyed women are every man's ideal. They're generalizations, not fact."

She nodded. "That's true but it still amazes me that there are so many men who think all Thai women are just sexual kittens for them to play with."

"I'm sure it's not that bad," Alexander said. He chuckled softly.

She laughed. "Do you know how many times I've had men say, *fucky sucky five dolla'* to me? It's really insulting!"

Alexander laughed, amused by how her Asian accent had thickened with the comment.

"Don't waste your breath," Zachary said as he licked the sugar from his fingers. "I've argued this with her more times than I care to count."

Sarai tossed him a look. "Because you know I'm right. It's been one extreme or the other. Here in the States, more people are surprised that I actually have a college degree and don't work in a nail salon than not. It's bad."

Zachary shrugged. "Like my brother said, I know that it's just people being stupid about stereotypes. No one makes any effort anymore to get to know someone who is not like them."

Alexander threw an arm across the back of the booth, turning in his seat to face her. "So, tell me again how you two met?" He looked from her to his brother and back.

Zachary popped a sausage link into his mouth, holding up a hand as he chewed. "Pop gave me her mother's contact information when I moved to Thailand."

Sarai nodded. "My mother had died a few months earlier. So, when he called he got me and my father instead."

"Her father came to work for me. He taught me the lay of the land. Helped me get acclimated. And he watched my back."

"Your brother was a big help to us. My father has great respect for him." The woman smiled.

"Sarai was a real pain back then. She should have been in school but she had to work in the rice paddies to help support the home. It was either that or prostitution."

"And *that* was not an option for me," Sarai said emphatically.

"Anyway, I had a friend associated with a boarding school in Paris. He pulled some strings to get her in and the rest is history."

Alexander smiled. "So what was the deal with your mother and our father? Do you know?"

"I want to know that too!" Zachary interjected. "I just thought they were casual friends but now I'm not so sure!" He sat forward in his seat, leaning over the table in anticipation.

Sarai dropped into a moment of reflection as she thought about her mother. Khim Montri had been a beautiful woman, and there had been stories about the men who had fawned over her, lavishing her family with gifts in hopes of garnering her attention. Khim's father had been overly protective, banishing most of her suitors away. When Sarai had asked about the men who'd come calling, her mother had only spoken of one, Sarai's father, the farmer with the shy smile who'd become her husband. But even as a little girl, Sarai had known there was something, or someone, her mother had kept secret, taking that tale to her grave.

The two brothers sat staring at her, waiting for an answer. She blew a soft sigh before lifting her gaze. "I think . . . I think they were in love once."

"How do you know that?" Alexander asked.

Sarai smiled. "Because when my mother would talk about your father she would get the same look in her eyes that your Mama Lynn gets when she talks about him now."

The two brothers exchanged a look, both reflecting for a brief moment on her comment.

"Pop was a playa!" Zachary suddenly laughed, his tone teasing.

Alexander laughed with him. "I think Pop put the *p* in playa!"

Sarai shook her head at the two of them.

Minutes later exhaustion settled over the three of them with a vengeance.

"I need to go get some sleep," Zachary said as he tossed a twenty-dollar bill onto the table. He yawned, throwing his whole body into the gesture.

Alexander added additional currency to the pile. "Yeah, we're starting bright and early," he said. "We need to get right to work on your training program."

He extended a hand toward his brother as both men stood up. Zachary shook it gladly. The gesture led to a shoulder bump, and then the moment turned awkward as they stood staring at each other.

"Thanks, A!" Zachary said, his voice dropping to a loud whisper. "I appreciate you giving me a second chance."

Alexander nodded. "It's cool, Z. We're good."

Sarai smiled, the endearing moment making her teary.

Zach met her stare. "Are you riding home with me, or what?" He cut an eye at Alexander, then shifted his eyes back toward her.

A blush of color tinted her cheeks a shade of crimson. Her eyes widened, annoyance creasing her brow.

Zach lifted his hands as if he were surrendering. "I had to check. You never know these days. I don't know what's going on with you two, so I didn't want to make any assumptions."

"You are such an idiot," Sarai said, biting back the curses she really wanted to bless him with.

She dropped a warm hand against Alexander's forearm and leaned to kiss his cheek. Her touch was heated, and the kiss ignited a flicker of current between them. He took a swift inhale of air and held it.

"Thank you," Sarai whispered softly. "I had a very nice time."

He blew out that breath as she eased out of the booth. He wrapped an arm around her shoulder and hugged her gently. The scent of jasmine and lavender perfumed the air around her, the subtle aroma teasing.

"Dinner tomorrow?" he asked, his voice dropping to a whisper meant only for her ears.

She nodded her head yes. "I'd like that."

"Can I come?" Zachary asked, interrupting the moment. He looked at his brother, then her, and back.

The couple exchanged a look, delight dancing in both their stares. Sarai and Alexander both answered at the same time. A resounding "No!" echoed through the room.

"How do I look?"

Sarai spun herself in a slow circle, looking for Zachary's approval.

"You look fine," he muttered, never once looking up from the video he was watching.

Sarai dropped a hand to her hip. She stood staring at the big-screen television for a good minute or two. "What are you watching?" she questioned, cutting her eyes in his direction.

"My opponent's last fight. Alex told me to study it. This kid's got a mean roundhouse kick! You have to watch that elbow of his, too. He also likes to attack from the left and that's my blind side." He rubbed a heavy hand across his face, something like fear piercing his eyes. "I don't know if I can beat this kid," he said, looking up at her for the first time since she'd entered the room. Meeting the look she was giving him, he pushed the PAUSE button on the remote he'd been holding in his hand.

"Then you've already lost," she said matter-of-factly. "You might as well give up now if you plan to have a defeatist attitude. If you want the win, then claim the win. Isn't that what you tell the guys you train?"

His gaze tripped up and down her body, taking in

the low-slung denim jeans and white tank top that she'd paired with thigh-high black leather boots and a black leather bomber jacket.

He changed the subject. "You look really good," he said. "Where are you going?"

"Out to dinner, remember? Your brother told me to dress casually."

Zachary gave her a thumbs-up. "I remember now."

The two stared at each other for a brief moment before either said another word. Something in the air suddenly felt awkward between them, and Sarai found it disconcerting.

"Are you going to be okay?" she asked, concern washing over her expression.

Zachary shrugged his broad shoulders. "Yeah. I'm good! I'm going to finish these tapes, then I plan to go for a run. After that I will eat that meal my brother had delivered. I'll probably be in bed when you get back. We're starting before daybreak tomorrow."

"Alex had food delivered?"

"Yeah, some food service company that's going to prep all my meals for me. They deliver every two days or something like that."

"So things are good with you two?"

Zachary took a quick moment to reflect on her question. The day had started well. He and his brother had met earlier that morning. Alexander had gone right to laying out a game plan for working him back into shape. He'd been the epitome of professional, his straightforward, no-nonsense demeanor everything Zachary knew he needed. Alexander had made it crystal clear that if they were going to work together, Zachary would have to abide by every one of his rules—and the list had been lengthy. Those few hours had reminded them both of their best days together, and it had felt good, Zachary feeling as if they were once again in sync.

"I think so," he finally answered. "I think Alex and I are off to a good start. We actually had a conversation today that didn't feel hostile."

"Just remember what I told you, it might take some time, so baby steps. But it will all work out," Sarai said confidently.

Zachary nodded in agreement. "Is Alexander picking you up?"

Sarai shook her head. "Not this time. I'm meeting him." She stole a quick glance at the watch on her slim wrist. "I should be going," she said, "or I'll be late."

"Have fun," he said, "and I promise to work on that attitude of mine."

With a smile, Sarai leaned to kiss his forehead, her hand gently squeezing his shoulder. She turned to leave, excitement leading her steps. There was no missing the eagerness that fueled her spirit. The prospect of seeing Alexander had her brimming with joy.

As she moved in the direction of the door, Zachary pushed PLAY, the video resuming. On the screen the two martial artists were going at it, arms flailing as both men threw blow after blow. He glanced at the scene briefly, then shifted his eyes back toward her. With a slight wave of her hand, Sarai disappeared down the hall and out the front door. Zachary continued to stare until he heard the entrance close behind her. Turning back to the television, he tried to focus, but failed, consumed instead with processing the feelings of jealousy that had suddenly taken hold of him.

Alexander took one last look around his home, ensuring everything was in place. He studied the table settings on the dining-room table before lighting a display of pillar candles that decorated the room. In his kitchen the aroma of comfort food scented the air, the house smelling like stewed chicken and sweet cake. When everything was to his satisfaction, he moved to the front of the home to peer out the window. He was excited for Sarai's arrival, and the waiting had him on edge, every one of his nerve endings firing with anticipation.

Standing in front of the massive bay windows, he was surprised by the anxiety sweeping through him. But he had never invited any woman to his home before, and his desire for everything to be perfect for Sarai was compelling. He took another glance around the luxurious log home. The stunning Boulder mountain estate had been designed to showcase the breathtaking views of the city and the awe-inspiring mountains from every room. Before Champs, the sixty-five-hundred-square-foot home had been his single greatest investment, and as he stood staring out at the lights flickering across the city, he had no regrets, hoping she would love his home as much as he did.

He blew a low sigh as he found himself chewing nervously at his fingernails, something he hadn't done since he was a teenager, hoping to get laid before senior prom and high-school graduation. Back then, despite his best efforts, he hadn't been able to convince Cynthia Montgomery to drop her panties, the young girl having taken a vow of chastity until marriage. This time, getting laid wasn't on his radar, but making a great impression on the beautiful woman was.

* * *

Sarai pulled into his driveway at the stroke of seven. The home's proximity to downtown Boulder had made it easy to find, and she hadn't had any problems following Alexander's directions. Stepping out of her car, she took a deep inhale of air to quiet her nerves. The evening air had a hint of chill to it, and the oxygen filling her lungs felt good.

Since she'd left her home, she hadn't been able to suppress her excitement, practically jumping out of her skin to get to Alexander. Just the prospect of spending some alone time with him had sent waves of exhilaration through to her core. She took another deep inhale of air, swallowing hard to stop the shaking that had every muscle in her body tense.

Looking out over the landscape, she was in awe of the view of downtown Boulder. The evening sky had turned a murky shade of silver gray, the early day striations of blue spattered with white clouds disappearing with the setting sun. But the bright lights flickering like abundant stars made the growing darkness look like fantasy land. A smile crept across Sarai's face as she took it all in.

Turning toward the house, she stopped abruptly. Alexander stood in the window, watching her. As their gazes connected, the look he was giving caused a ripple of electricity to shoot deep into the pit of her abdomen. She inhaled swiftly, drawing one hand to her stomach as she waved at him with the other. He waved back, his own smile filling his face as he gestured for her to come inside.

He met her at the entrance, his own enthusiasm merging with hers as he threw the door open. "You found the place!" he cheered, eagerness ringing in his tone.

"I did," she answered as she stepped over the threshold. "You gave perfect directions."

"Let me take your coat," he said as he reached to help her take the garment off. His hand brushed against her shoulder, the touch teasing to them both.

Sarai cut her eye at him, biting down against her bottom lip to halt the quiver of heat as his fingertips grazed her neck and down the length of her arm. "Thank you."

She looked around the dramatic two-story foyer that led into an oversized great room. The décor was rustic, everything in place to highlight the large hand-hewn logs. The structure was grand and impressive. "This is beautiful!" she exclaimed.

He smiled. "Thank you. It's still a work in progress but it's my home! It's my favorite place to be when I'm not down at the gym."

"And I bet you also have a gym here, right?"

"You know I do. I'd love to give you a tour after dinner," he said as he took her hand and pulled her along beside him. "Right now, though, I hope you're hungry because I'm starved!"

"I am. And it smells so good in here. What are we eating?"

Alexander led her to the dining room, pulling out a chair at the head of the table. "We're having Tuscan lemon chicken, Spanish rice with roasted tomatoes, and pound cake with mixed berries for dessert."

"I'm impressed! You outdid yourself." She pulled her chair up close to the table. "I didn't know what to expect when you said you wanted to cook for me. It would seem that you're a man of many talents, Alex."

He chuckled as he poured wine into two crystal goblets. "I have to be honest. I didn't actually *cook* the food myself. I had a little help."

Sarai laughed with him. "Really?"

He grinned. "Yeah, Mama Lynn's been here all afternoon. I didn't want to risk your running off because the food was bad."

"I don't think you have anything to worry about," she said, their gazes locking tightly. "I don't think there's anything that could run me off."

There was a moment of pause. Alexander's eyes narrowed, his gaze seductive as he reflected on her comment. He grinned brightly. "I should get the food," he said as he gestured toward the kitchen.

Sarai laughed warmly. "You should."

Minutes later, their plates were filled and the conversation was flowing easily. They talked about everything, no topic left untouched. Sarai found him totally engaging as he told his side of the stories she'd heard from his brother about their exploits when they'd been younger. Together they laughed, and the laughter was like the sweetest balm. By the time they'd finished their cake, licking the last of the berries from their fingers, it felt as if they'd been the best of friends their entire lives.

"It really was not that funny," Alexander said. "And we both got a beating for it!"

"You should have," Sarai laughed. "It was horrible of you two!"

"It was only concrete. How did we know we couldn't make a mold of the toilet without clogging up the plumbing? When you're seven years old, stupidity actually makes sense!"

Sarai giggled, her head waving from side to side. She swiped a cloth napkin across her lips. "That was delicious. Thank you and you have to thank your mother for me. She is such a good cook!"

He nodded. "She's too good. It's hard to stay in

shape the way she cooks. I keep trying to get her to change her ways but she refuses."

"It's actually a nice reprieve from the salads and greens we constantly eat. Healthy eating is a science and sometimes you just want to enjoy the food for the sake of enjoying the food. When I'm teaching nutrition I try to show people how to balance the two."

Alexander nodded but said nothing, suddenly delighting in the light that gleamed from her eyes and the glow that shimmered across her face. Everything about her spirit warmed his. Her openness and honesty were heartfelt, and he found everything about her to be absolutely genuine.

A pregnant pause grew full and large between them. Sarai stared as his eyes danced with hers. He smiled, and she couldn't stop herself from smiling with him. But there was something heated in his gaze, temptation weeping from the oceanic orbs. Her breath caught deep in her chest, a light gasp falling past her thin lips. Moisture suddenly puddled in all of her creases. She pressed her knees tightly together to stall the rising desire suddenly sweeping through her with a vengeance.

Their casual conversation gave way to something else, words that held more meaning to them both as Alex shifted the conversation.

"I'm really glad you came, Sarai," he said, reaching across the table for her hand. His touch was gentle as he entwined his fingers between hers. He sat, playing with her fingers, slowly caressing their length as he teased her palm. His eyes were focused on memorizing each dent and dimple. When he lifted his eyes back to hers, she snatched her stare toward the other side of the room, suddenly riddled with anxiety.

When she finally responded, her voice was a loud

whisper. "I am too, but it's getting late and I know you have a full day tomorrow. I hate to eat and run but I should probably let you get some rest," she said as she slowly pulled her hand from his, needing to stall the heat rising swiftly between them.

Alexander tilted his head, drawing her gaze back to his. "But I promised you a tour." He pushed himself up from the table. "Let me clear the dishes; then I'll show you around before you take off," he said as he lifted the dirty plates from where they rested.

Sarai nodded. "Let me help," she said as she stood up with him.

Together, they loaded his dishwasher and sealed the leftover food in plastic Tupperware containers. After wiping down the counters and moving the last remnants of their meal to the refrigerator, they stood in the center of the room staring at each other.

"That wasn't too bad," he said.

"Not bad at all. We work well together."

"Yes, we do," he answered, grinning foolishly. "So, now that you've seen my kitchen, how about the rest of that tour that I promised you?"

Chapter Seven

"It's so big!" Sarai exclaimed as they moved from room to room. There were three bedroom suites on the second floor, a third-floor loft area that had been decorated as a reading room, a finished basement complete with a sauna, a fully equipped exercise room, and an enormous recreation space. "Why do you need so much room when it's just you?" she asked.

"I wasn't planning on it always just being me. I planned on having a family and I'd hoped that one day I'd have a wife and we'd have children that we would raise together in this home."

"So what happened? Because I'm sure there have been women in your life who would have gladly done just that. Why aren't you married already?"

He turned, sauntering slowly toward the other end of the home. Sarai followed behind him. There was an amused smirk lurking across his face.

"Finding the right woman proved to be more of a challenge than I anticipated," he answered. "There have been plenty of contenders but none ever measured up."

"Well, let's hope I can change that," Sarai said

smugly, meeting his stare as he tossed her a look over his shoulder.

He laughed heartily, her daring surprising him. "You're funny," he said, his smile wide.

She laughed with him. "I have my moments."

Alexander stepped into the master suite, the last room on his tour. "And this is my sanctuary," he said as he pointed out the adjoining private sunroom, two walk-in closets, and the connecting bathroom with the whirlpool tub, double sinks, and oversized shower.

Sarai strode through the space slowly, admiring the heavily carved furniture and king-size bed. The décor was simple, the neutral colors calming. Two original pieces of art hung on the wall over the bed, framed charcoal sketches, one of a nude male and one of a nude female. The work was a stroke shy of being primitive, but made a bold artistic impression. She stood staring at the pair, impressed by their simplicity.

"Do you like them?" Alexander asked, pointing in their direction.

"I do," she answered, her head bobbing.

"Thank you. They were my first attempt at figurative work."

"You did them?"

He nodded. "I like to paint and draw."

"I'm even more impressed then. Something I didn't know about you, Alex."

He smiled, pride puffing his chest ever so slightly.

She rounded the side of the bed. The pillows were abundant, the bedding in varying shades of brown against a cream-colored comforter. A mandarin-orange accent throw lay folded at the foot of the mattress. On the nightstand was a picture of his family, the exact same image that had graced that holiday card her mother had received so many years ago. Sarai pulled the framed photo into her hand. The memories made her smile.

"What?" he asked, eyeing her curiously.

She paused as she thought about it being the first time she would ever reveal her secret to anyone, most especially him. She looked at Alexander, and he was still staring at her, the question hovering in his expression. "I have this picture. Your father sent it in a card to my mother one Christmas when I was a little girl. I kept it all these years, fantasizing about you. Wondering what kind of boys you and your brother were. What kind of men you would grow up to be. Sometimes I would pretend that we were all family or that you were my boyfriend. Is that weird?"

Alexander's eyes were wide. He nodded. "It's a little weird."

Sarai shrugged. "Maybe, but I'm not a stalker or anything like that so please don't get the wrong impression. I just didn't have much else to entertain myself with back then."

His smile was full. "I was actually thinking that it was kind of sweet. In a weird sort of way." He chuckled softly.

She continued as she placed the photo back on the nightstand. "My mother would sometimes cry when she looked at that picture."

His brow creased slightly. "I'm sorry."

Sarai shrugged her narrow shoulders a second time. "You have no reason to apologize. My mother once said that sometimes love isn't what we hope it will be, but a love that lasts a lifetime can sometimes be everything we need it to be. And now that I know more about your father, I think I understand."

"I wouldn't know. According to you I've never been in love, remember?"

She laughed. "I don't recall saying that."

"No, that's exactly what you said about my feelings for Felicia."

"Felicia wasn't the right woman for you."

"And you know this because . . . ?"

"Because I am nothing like Felicia."

Alexander took a seat on the foot of the bed, his hands folded together in his lap. He stared at her, the smirk across her face teasing his senses. He knew enough about Sarai to know that she didn't make those left-handed comments without wanting to prove a point. And if he were honest with himself, he seriously liked the point she seemed to be trying to make.

"We don't know each other well yet, Dr. Montri, but I'm very attracted to you," he said. "You are truly a breath of fresh air!"

There was the faintest air of nervousness billowing in the space around her. Her lips were parted ever so slightly, and he suddenly wondered what they would feel like pressed against his own. He found himself imagining the sweetest sensations sweeping between them, and then he was unable to contain the surge of nature that had risen with a vengeance. He crossed his legs, one over the other, hoping to stall his hardening manhood. The moment was pressing, and he reached behind his back for a pillow, dropping it into his lap.

Sarai laughed. "I like you too," she said. "I like you very much." She moved slowly to his side, coming to stand by the foot of the bed.

Desire was suddenly orchestrating the moment, raw passion the guiding emotion. Alexander eased his arm around her slim waist and gently pulled her toward him until she stood between his legs. He stared into her eyes, and her gaze was full of trust and need, with a hint of apprehension flickering in the dark orbs. He could feel her warm breath on his face, sweet, soft moist air tinged with the scent of lemon and vanilla against his skin. The moment swept a shiver of emotion up his spine. And then, without giving it a second thought, he kissed her.

It was the barest touch of his lips against hers, warm flesh against warm flesh, as they both fell into the sensation and the intimacy of such a simple act. Alexander couldn't remember ever being kissed so exquisitely. Her reaction was spontaneous, her lips parting slightly as she pulled in a bit of air. He let his own lips part as well so he could feel the hot, soft steam of the breath they shared. His mind went completely blank as he focused solely on the sparks of need and the crackle of raw sexual electricity passing between them.

Sarai leaned into him. She grabbed the pillow with a tight fist and purposely slid it from his lap to the floor. She nestled herself deep between his spread legs, pressing her pelvis against his hardened member. Her body was telegraphing a need for more, even though neither was truly sure what more was at that point. He encircled her completely, one hand gently caressing the back of her head as his fingers tangled in the length of her hair. The other circled her waist, drawing her even closer to him. She suddenly drew back, gasping lightly as she worked to catch her breath. Desire danced in her eyes, hinting at something secret and sensuous.

Alexander pressed his mouth back to hers, capturing her lips more firmly against his own. He let the tip of his tongue trace the outline of her mouth, teasing the outer rim. She whimpered softly, and he felt her entire body relax, her torso going slack as she swooned in his arms. He savored the taste of her, his touch butterfly soft as she gave in to the slow, sensual sizzle building with a vengeance between them.

He made love to her mouth with his tongue, lapping at her gently, letting it slide slowly between her parted lips. Inside the hot wetness, he found her tongue waiting eagerly. As he teased the tip, she shivered, then purred, the sound a soft, quiet uttering that melted his heart and caused his dick to throb painfully for attention.

He thrust his tongue deeper into the cavity, tickling the roof of her mouth as he slid over the smoothness of her teeth, no dip or crevice left untouched as she pushed back against his tongue with her own. Returning his touch she sucked his tongue gently past the line of her teeth, demanding, controlling, and eager to pleasure him as he was pleasuring her.

Alexander pulled back, his excitement monumental. It took every ounce of his fortitude not to take her right then, wanting to lose himself in the most intimate connection he knew they could share. Instead, he planted a rash of damp kisses across her face, letting her feel his hot breath on her cheek and her chin.

Sarai pressed her palms against his chest, the heat from her fingers searing. As if she could read his mind, she took a step back. She lifted her eyes to his, panting as she struggled to catch her breath. "That was very nice," she whispered softly.

He nodded, his own breath coming in short, clipped gasps as he fought to fill his own lungs with air.

"But I think I should be going," she murmured, her body shivering as she tried to shake the sensation of his hands and mouth. "Before this goes any further."

"Would that be a bad thing?" he asked, still holding tightly to her, his hands skating across her back.

She shook her head. "I imagine it will be a very good thing when it happens. But it just can't happen right now. Not tonight." She brushed a soft hand along the curve of his cheek.

Alexander's eyes skated across her face as he studied her expression. There was something in her eyes that pulled at his heartstrings, but he couldn't put his finger on what it was. "Are you okay, Sarai?"

She smiled, nodding her head yes, but her body language said something else. She shifted her eyes, fighting to avoid his gaze.

"Then stay," he said, his head shifting slowly from side to side as he stared at her.

Tears suddenly misted her gaze, her glossy stare concerning to him. She shook her head, her whole body beginning to shake ever so slightly. She whispered, "I can't. I really do have to go."

Alexander responded by recapturing the pout of her lower lip between his teeth and lips. He tenderly sucked and nibbled on her mouth. But before they became lost in the flowing sensations, the oral exploration exquisitely magical, he took a swift inhale of air and pulled himself from her. With his hands on her shoulders, he pushed her gently as he stood up, and she took two steps back, a cool breeze billowing between them. He didn't bother to adjust the bulge in his pants.

Grabbing her hand, he entwined her fingers between his own and guided her out of the room and back to the foyer of his home. They stood in the quiet of the moment as he wrapped his arms around her and hugged her close. She fit nicely in his arms, the top of her head stopping just beneath his chin. He pressed his face into her hair and inhaled the soft floral scent of her shampoo and conditioner. The thick waves tickled his nose and face and made him smile. He drew back, then leaned to kiss her forehead, his full lips caressing. "I had a great time tonight," he said, his smile endearing. "Thank you for coming."

"Thank you for having me," she whispered again, the tingling through her body causing her voice to quiver ever so slightly.

"Are you sure you're okay, Sarai? I didn't do or say something to upset you, did I?"

Her head waved from side to side for the umpteenth time. "No!" she exclaimed. "It's not you. It's nothing. I'm fine. Really!"

He stared at her, still not convinced but he kept the opinion to himself. "Call me when you get home, please, so I know you got there safely."

Sarai nodded, and with one last kiss to his cheek, her lips lingering briefly, she disappeared out the front door, leaving Alexander to wonder what had gone wrong between them.

Zachary was still planted in front of the television when Sarai returned home. As she moved into the room, he sat forward, pushing the PAUSE button on the remote. "Hey, how was your *date*?" he asked, more emphasis on the word than necessary.

"I had a very nice time," Sarai said.

He nodded. "I was just about to make some popcorn and find a movie to watch. You want to hang out for a minute?"

She shook her head. "I thought you had to be in bed early? Or did you forget about your training already?"

"No, I just . . . well . . ." he shrugged, biting back

any comment as he took in the narrowed gaze she was giving him.

Sarai shook her head. "Go to bed, Zach. You're back to your old tricks and bad behavior and it hasn't even been forty-eight hours yet."

"So, you're not going to tell me about your *date*? Did you get a good-night kiss at least?"

She rolled her eyes skyward. "We actually had wild, passionate sex on the dining-room table. It was a really good time," she said facetiously.

His face was stone as he stared at her, his lids blinking rapidly. "You had sex? At the restaurant?"

"We didn't go to a restaurant. Alex cooked dinner for us at his house."

"Alex invited you over to his *house*?"

"Why do you say it like that? You sound surprised."

Zachary shrugged his shoulders. "I am actually. We've always had this unwritten rule that you don't invite women to the crib. Keeps them from getting so attached."

"Clearly, Alexander is following a different set of rules," she said as she turned an about-face.

"So no movie?"

She shook her head. "I'm exhausted. I think I'm going to turn in. You have a good night."

As she reached the doorway, Zachary called her name.

"Yes, Zach?"

"You really didn't have sex with him, did you? That was a joke, right?"

For a split second Sarai stood staring at her friend, disbelief shining in her eyes. She shook her head. "No, we didn't have sex," she finally answered as she turned back out the door. She tossed him one last look over her shoulder. "Your brother and I made love. Sweet, beautiful, passionate love!"

Sleep eluded her. She'd been tossing and turning for over an hour, unable to will herself into dreamland. Sarai rolled onto her back, drawing an arm up and over her head. She couldn't stop thinking about Alexander, wishing she had stayed to spend the night in his bed. Then she thought about Zachary and his game of twenty questions with an air of attitude that had made her uncomfortable. There was so much on her mind that sleep didn't stand a chance of getting in to lay claim to her.

Sarai had wanted more. And wanting more had surprised her. Alexander's touch had been like the sweetest drug imaginable, and she was hooked. But she'd been afraid that he might have looked at her unfavorably, thinking that she might be a woman who was fast and loose with all the men who showed her attention and fed her dinner twice. She blew a soft sigh.

Dating had always been a challenge for her. Western ways were not Thai ways. As a little girl it was expected that a man would court her when she grew up. They would have become friends first and there would have been no touching of any kind and definitely no kisses like the kiss she and Alexander had shared. Any public displays of affection would have had people seeing her as easy or, worse, a prostitute. Any traditional, well-educated Thai girl would have been devastated to be thought of so lowly. And a Thai man would not have wanted to marry a girl of such low class. Sex would only have come after a lengthy engagement and parental approval of the union.

Europeans who visited Thailand came seeking wives and viewed Thai women as submissive and accommodating, with magical vaginas. They wanted female partners who bowed down to the patriarchy, knew a woman's place, and had no opinion that contradicted their own. Wives who would conform to the stereotype without any deviation and provide them with unspeakable sexual pleasure.

In France she was thought to be a nerd, socially segregated because all Asians were only good at math. She'd been seen as sexually modest, a china doll that might break if touched inappropriately. Her intellect had been allowed to flourish, her sexuality not nearly as much. The varying sexual mores only served to wreak havoc on her self-esteem as she came into herself, discovering everything there was to know about being female.

Her friendship with Zachary had opened her eyes to men who fully appreciated a woman who embraced her sexuality. His honesty and openness had been enlightening, and she'd come to appreciate his views about relationships, even if she didn't always agree with him. The devastation that had been his marriage had cued her to a man's vulnerability, and hours of conversation had helped her to put it all into perspective, as she came to believe that having her own wants and desires was a very good thing.

But the nearness of Alexander and the wealth of emotion that had accompanied his touch had actually frightened her, and despite her best efforts, she'd not been able to hide that fear as well as she would have liked. She wanted it to be perfect for them both, because if she were honest with herself, and with him, Sarai wanted Alexander to love her as much as she had imagined herself loving him. And she didn't think love had anything to do with what he'd been feeling for her.

She rolled against the mattress as she drew her legs to her chest. She wished that Zachary had been in a different frame of mind because she really could have used a friend to help her figure it all out. But she instinctively knew that sharing her feelings about his brother was no longer a good thing. They'd been friends for so long that Sarai had grown accustomed to his mood swings. But this time there was something about his renewed interest in her relationship with his twin that felt very different.

Blowing another low sigh, Sarai rolled to the other side of the bed and closed her eyes. Despite her love for her dear friend, she didn't have the energy to worry about Zachary and his feelings. She needed every ounce of fortitude she could muster to handle her own feelings and what was, or wasn't, happening between her and Alexander.

Alexander had been pacing the floor of his bedroom since Sarai's departure. Despite what he felt had been a great evening, he was now feeling like they'd left each other with something unsaid, and the unspoken words suddenly felt like a growing chasm in his head, and his heart. The memory of that look that had crossed her face, a wave of panic dancing in her eyes, was haunting.

He couldn't stop thinking about her. Every time they were in each other's presence, he found himself wanting to spend more time with her. He loved to hear her laugh, the musical lilt to her tone, which was one of the sweetest sounds. He enjoyed wallowing in that light in her eyes, that dark shimmer making him feel like they were the only two people in the room. It had been a long time since he'd felt that way about any woman, and it was a feeling he intended to hold tight to for as long as he could.

He moved to the side of his bed and sat down. Reaching for his cell phone, he contemplated giving Sarai a call. Despite the late hour, he reasoned that she could still be up and thinking about him, like he was thinking about her. If she were, she might welcome hearing from him. That's what he wanted to believe. He eyed the digital clock on the nightstand, and when he realized just how late it was he changed his mind. He imagined that she was probably sound asleep, and he had no desire to disturb her rest.

Realizing that he was only a few short hours away from the start of his own new day, he lay down across his bed. They had tomorrow, he thought, as he reached for the light on the nightstand, sending the room into darkness. And tomorrow he was going to ensure they cleared the air and said whatever it was that needed to be said. Because the next time he kissed her, Alexander thought, he had no intentions of letting her slip out of his arms.

Chapter Eight

By nine o'clock the next morning Zachary had already run his first ten miles for the day. He'd spent an hour in the gym, working on his chest and triceps with a weight trainer handpicked by his brother, and was walking on a treadmill when Sarai came into the room. She had a client with her, and she stopped for only a quick minute to say good morning before moving off to the other side of the gym.

When Alexander entered the space and moved to his brother's side, she was already a good twenty minutes into putting the tall redhead through her paces. He waved in her direction, his smile wide; then he moved to the empty treadmill beside his brother and engaged the unit to a modest run. His friend Dan joined them.

"We need to get your endurance up and work on your core. You've gotten spongy around the middle."

"Spongy? Maybe a little soft but I'm definitely not spongy!" Zachary laughed.

"Says you," his brother quipped. "You're starting to look like your father around your midsection. Both of you look like you're about to deliver any day now."

Dan laughed heartily.

Zachary chuckled with them. "Your father's been pregnant for a while now. I don't plan to get that bad!"

"Then you better increase the speed on that treadmill because you've got a good ways to go!"

The three men all increased their speed, their low jog shifting to a moderate run. Dan changed the conversation. "I'm hearing good things about Dr. Montri. She's becoming very popular around here."

The two brothers both looked in her direction. Sarai was laughing, her head tossed back over her shoulders at something the other woman had just said.

Alexander nodded. "She is impressive. Beautiful and intelligent."

Zachary snorted. He cut an eye in his brother's direction. "So what's going on with you two? How'd your date go?"

Dan tossed a glance toward Alexander. "Really? You took her on a date? Did we not have a conversation about you dating her? Specifically about you *not* doing that!"

Zachary leaned forward to stare at the man. "He cooked her dinner at his house!"

Dan shook his head. "I don't know what we're going to do with you. I swear!"

Alexander shook his head. "It's not like that. Sarai and I have great chemistry. I really like her."

"Don't you have rules about dating your employees?" Zachary questioned, his breath coming in short pants.

"Yes!" Dan interjected. "We have rules!"

Alexander chuckled. "And because everyone knew I would break those rules is why I set up the hierarchy such that I have no influence over hiring or firing."

"I know that's right!" Dan said. "We already risk being sued with some of your brother's stunts. There's no way the advisory board would let him have control over personnel too. That would have been like throwing lighter fluid on a fire."

"You say that like I have no moral compass or self-control."

"He says it like he knows you," Zachary joked.

Dan nodded. "So how did it go?"

"What?"

"Your date."

"Oh," Alexander smiled. "We had a really nice time. She's really something special."

There was a moment of pause. For a split second Alexander could almost see his brother's mind shifting into overdrive. He met the look his twin was giving him. "What?"

"Sarai is special so don't you forget it. If you're looking to hit it and quit it she's not the one."

"Is that what you think of me?" Alexander asked. "You actually think that's the only reason I'm interested in her?"

His brother shrugged his broad shoulders. "How would I know what to think? You've been chasing after her since you found out she and I were friends. For all I know you might just be chasing after her to get even with me."

Alexander pushed the STOP button on his machine and came to an abrupt halt. He turned to give Zachary his full attention. "You really don't want to go there with me. If anything I've been chasing her since she walked through the door, *before* I knew you two were acquainted. And I have never been that kind of man. I would never mistreat her or any other woman."

"I'm just saying," Zachary continued. "She's my

best friend and I won't see her hurt by you or anyone else."

"You don't want to see who hurt?" Sarai suddenly asked, having snuck up on the conversation. Her presence startled both men, the tension between them wafting aimlessly with nowhere to go.

Zachary tossed his brother a look before lifting his eyes in her direction. "Me. Alexander is trying to work me to death and I don't want to hurt anything. I was saying I don't want to see me get hurt."

She looked from one brother to the other, knowing a little white lie when she heard it. Whatever the two had been discussing had left them both twitchy. "Is that all?"

Alexander shrugged his broad shoulders, his expression smug. "Yeah, really, it was nothing."

Sarai shook her head. "Are you free for lunch, Mr. Barrett?" she asked.

Alexander grinned. "I am, Dr. Montri. In fact, I kept my calendar open hoping you'd have time to spend with me."

"Can I come?" Zachary asked.

Sarai tossed him a look. "You're on a special diet, remember? They've got your meal prepped and ready for you in the cafeteria."

"You're going to do me like that?" Zachary pouted.

Dan laughed. "Dr. Montri, I'm going to need to see you in my office later. I really need you to sign some release forms absolving us of any liability should things between you and Mr. Barrett go south. I'm sure our attorneys would insist on it."

Sarai looked from him to Alexander.

Color flushed his face as he gave her another shrug of his shoulders. "He's joking," Alexander said to her as he moved to her side. He tossed a look over his shoulder, he and his twin exchanging gazes one last time. "We can revisit our conversation about *your pain* later," he said.

Zachary nodded his agreement, his eyes narrowed, his brow furrowed. He watched as Alexander grabbed Sarai's hand and pulled her toward the exit door. He and Dan had come to a stop. Dan shook his head as they cut an eye at each other.

"I really wasn't joking," Dan muttered.

"I don't think Dan was joking," Sarai said. She lifted a forkful of lobster ravioli in a sage butter sauce past her thin lips. "Have any other women at the gym had to sign disclaimers to date you?"

Alexander gave her a wry smile. "I haven't dated any of the women at the gym."

"Not even the brunette at the concession stand?"

He laughed. "I don't know how that rumor got started! But no, I have never dated her."

"To hear her tell it you two are well acquainted."

"Don't pay any attention to what she tells you. I assure you much of it has been greatly embellished."

Sarai grinned. "How greatly? Because she spoke quite favorably about you." She gestured with both her hands, holding them about a foot apart. Her eyebrows were raised. Her expression was teasing.

Alexander laughed heartily, a gut-deep rumble that brought tears to his eyes. When he finally caught his breath, his head waved from side to side. "Do you women really sit around talking about us men like that?"

"Women talk the same way men talk. And you know how you men do sometimes."

He nodded, his grin still canyon deep. "I personally

don't do those kinds of things but I know some men who do."

She giggled. "Okay, if you say so!"

His eyes danced across her face. "I was worried about us," he said, his tone dropping an octave. "I thought I'd done something last night that might have upset or offended you. You seemed out of sorts when you left my house."

Sarai sat back in her seat, folding her hands atop the table. "You had me out of sorts. I had to wrap my mind around what I was feeling."

"And what were you feeling?"

She hesitated for a quick moment, her eyes skating back and forth as she stared down at her plate. She hadn't anticipated his questions, and the moment suddenly had her nervous. When she lifted her gaze back to his face, he was studying her intently, anxiously awaiting her response.

She took a deep inhale of air and blew the warm breath out slowly. She chose her words carefully. "You had me excited, Alex. When you kissed me I hadn't expected to feel as intensely about you as I found myself feeling. I wanted to stay. I wanted to make love to you and if I had, I know that it would have been an incredible night."

"And that would have been a *bad* thing?"

"It wouldn't have been the *right* thing. I don't want just one night of great sex. I really don't do hookups. And you and I still don't know each other well enough yet for it to be anything more than that. But I want more," she said as she met his gaze evenly.

Still staring at her, Alexander reflected on her statement. *I want more.* When he'd repeated every word she'd spoken in his head at least a dozen times, he finally nodded his understanding. *I want more.*

Sarai took a deep breath, her eyes connecting again with his. "There's something you should know also," she said, her voice dropping to a loud whisper. She wrung her hands together in her lap.

His brow lifted, and his expression was curious.

Her gaze fell as she continued. "I have been with other men. Well, *one* other man. I am not a virgin."

The comment surprised him, his eyes widening. His head bobbed up and down slowly, amusement dancing over his face. "I have been with other women. *Many* other women. I'm not a virgin either."

Sarai shifted a quick look in his direction. "I didn't know if . . ."

He forestalled her comment. "We're adults. We both have history. I don't need or want any details of your past unless it's just something you feel a need to share and I don't think you want details about mine. But if you ask I will be honest."

Sarai smiled, looking as if a weight had been lifted off her shoulders.

"Do you hike?" he suddenly questioned.

His swift subject change and question threw her. "Excuse me?"

"I'd like to take you hiking. It's one of my favorite things to do when I have some downtime."

"In Thailand they sometimes take the tourists trekking. I think it's much the same but I've never been hiking."

"Great! Then I look forward to sharing your first time with you."

She smiled, the light shining through the window shimmering in her eyes.

He continued. "Do you cook? I mean . . . can you cook Thai food?"

She tilted her head slightly. "I can cook, yes."

"I've never eaten authentic Thai food before. It's something I'd really like to try."

"Then I would like to cook for you."

"Then it's a date. The minute we both have some free time we'll go hiking, then we can go back to my place and you can cook. Unless you'd rather do something else?"

She shook her head. "No, that sounds like it would be a lot of fun."

"Good. I think so too. Let's push for this weekend or definitely sometime next week." He reached across the table and dropped his large palm against the back of her hand. His fingertips teased her flesh. The look he gave her was soul deep, causing her to take a swift inhale, holding the air deep in her lungs.

"We can take this as slow, or as fast, as you want, Sarai. And when we make love you won't have to worry about it only being a one-night thing. Because I want more too. I think what you're feeling is what I'm feeling and I really want to see where we go with it. I really hope that's what you want too."

There was a soft lull in the conversation as she reflected on his comment. Sarai hadn't held back to prove any point. She didn't subscribe to a ninety-day rule nor was she holding out because of any sexual reservations or prudishness. For her, taking things slow was more about building a level of trust and comfort between them. A mutual respect that went both ways. Emotion that was between the two of them and had nothing else to do with his brother, or his family, or anyone else who had an opinion about them. She said so, her explanation moving him to pause as they strengthened the foundation they were building on.

When everything was said, Sarai's expression was

light filled, joy shimmering out of every pore. She
nodded as she released that breath she'd been holding. "So, now will you tell me what Zachary was saying
to you earlier before I interrupted?"

Alex chuckled. "He doesn't want to see you hurt
and he just wanted to make sure my intentions were
honorable."

She blew a sigh. "He shouldn't have done that. He
should not have said anything to you."

"Yes, he should have. He's your friend. And he
loves you. And if there is ever a time that I can't protect you I need to trust that my brother will."

The comment widened Sarai's eyes and lifted her
lips in the faintest of smiles. She watched as he took
a bite of his own food. The slow side-to-side gyration
of his mouth and his tongue peeking past his lips
fired a low flame deep in the pit of her midsection.
She laid her own fork against her plate, her hand beginning to quiver.

For another hour the two talked, still sharing information. She learned that he liked to read, and he ad-
mitted to enjoying a good romance novel as long as it
had a hint of suspense or mystery to it.

"That's going to be our secret," he said, chuckling
softly. "How would it look if a stud like me was caught
with a Harlequin under his pillow?"

She laughed with him. "You keep them hidden
under your pillow?"

"No, I mean . . . well . . . you know what I mean! If
anyone found out I'd lose my Boys Club card over some
mess like that!" His smile was warm and endearing.

"Yes, but it would definitely garner you points in
the Girls Club. We love men who are both rugged
and in touch with their emotional sides."

"I'm very in touch with all of myself," he said. He

leaned forward in his seat. "So I can trust you to keep my secret?"

She giggled. "I don't know anything," she said. "At least not until I publish my memoirs!"

The laughter between them was abundant, and Alexander liked how her eyes narrowed and her top lip quivered when he teased her. He enjoyed learning her likes and dislikes as they languished easily together, the conversation consuming.

"So, bugs don't bother you but you're afraid of birds?"

"Not afraid. They just give me the creeps."

"All birds or just select breeds?"

"All of them, especially those beady-eyed crows. They make my skin crawl!"

"I like birds!"

"I like cats!"

"I'm not a cat guy. They're too sneaky. You can't trust anything that won't let you pet it."

"You can pet a cat."

"On its terms. And they're temperamental. You can't trust any animal that will hiss at you when you're trying to be nice to it. Dogs don't hiss. Give me a dog over a cat any day."

They were so enjoying their time together that Alexander had insisted they stay for dessert, ordering a slice of chocolate strawberry cheesecake for them to share. Their waitress delivered the decadent treat with two utensils. He tossed one spoon to the side as he picked up the other. Sarai smiled as he began to feed her, passing her one bite and then taking another for himself.

She hummed softly. "Ummm! This is divine!"

He nodded. "It's good. It's really good."

"I wish I could eat like this every day."

"You could as long as you're burning off the calories."

"Is that your professional advice?"

"We're not having a professional moment. This"— he waved the spoon from side to side—"this is very personal. This is you and I having a very personal exchange."

She smiled. "I like personal," she said as she gently cupped her hand around his when he slid the spoon to her lips to savor the last bite of cheesecake.

Alexander leaned forward to press an easy kiss to her mouth, lightly licking at a drop of chocolate that clung to her bottom lip. "I'm liking it too!"

Back at the gym Sarai completed a stack of client assessments, delivered them to the office, then headed to the weight room. Inside, Zachary was in the newly constructed elevated competition cage, his hands taped as he sparred with someone she didn't recognize. He was throwing good punches, a level of comfort returning as he dominated his opponent. Alexander peered through the side fencing, his arms crossed over his chest as he assessed his brother's abilities. He was nodding his head approvingly, sometimes leaning forward to get a better view of the two men in a clinch. He would occasionally shout out a suggestion, but for the most part he was there as an observer, allowing his twin to do what he did best.

She watched as Alexander signaled for the two men to come to a halt. He moved up the short length of steps into the cage, going to stand before Zachary. He gripped him by the wrists, the duo in intense conversation. As he stepped back out, signaling for the two to go again, he caught her eye. His smile was slight as he gave her a quick nod of his head and an eye-wink just before turning his attention back to the brawl in the fight ring.

Sarai stood watching for a few more minutes before easing her way back out of the gym area. She headed to the employee room, grabbed her bag out of her locker, and ended her workday by punching the time clock. Minutes later she was still thinking about Alexander as she found her way back to the luxury neighborhood and the space she'd come to call home.

Everything about Alexander Barrett made her heart sing. He was her dream come true, and she imagined that any other time, in any other universe, it would all come to an abrupt end if she pinched herself. She was grateful that the stars had aligned in her favor. She turned on the sound system that had become one of her favorite amenities in the home. The sound track from the Broadway production of *The Lion King* swept through each room. The joyful beat of "I Just Can't Wait to Be King" made her smile. It was one of Zachary's favorites, and he played it over and over. Loving musical sound tracks was Zachary's secret that she'd sworn to never tell.

She closed her eyes and inhaled the music for a moment. It had been a good long while since all felt well in her small world. For over a year she'd watched in frustration as Zachary had tried to self-destruct, heartbreak fueling a wealth of hurt. He'd pulled away from everyone who cared about him, none of their friends or family able to turn things around. Convincing him to return back to his roots had taken months of begging and pleading, and for the first time it seemed as if her efforts hadn't been futile. The bond between the brothers was proving to be a new lifeline for her as much as for the two of them.

Inside her bedroom she changed into a pair of casual sweatpants and an oversized T-shirt. Pulling back the bedclothes, she slid the Barrett family photo from its hiding spot. Staring at the image, she couldn't help but think that the two boys she'd fantasized about for so many years didn't come close to measuring up to the two men she'd actually come to know.

With the framed image in hand, she moved down the hallway to Zachary's room. The closed door hid the explosion of clothes and junk that littered the space, every surface covered with something out of place. She shook her head, making a mental note to call for the cleaning service he'd been promising to contact.

Weaving her way through the mess, she moved to the unmade bed and the nightstand cluttered with empty paper cups and well-worn magazines. She cleared enough space to prop the photo atop the wooden surface. Satisfied, she backed her way out and closed the door behind her. Halfway down the hall, she heard her cell phone chime. By the time she made it back to her room and the device resting on the bed, the image of Alexander had faded, replaced by the missed call sign.

She was just a fingertip away from pushing the REDIAL button when Zachary burst through the front door, calling her name. His exuberance echoed in the volume of his tone as he made his way to her room, his large body lumbering in the entranceway.

"Hey! Why'd you leave? Did you see me?"

She smiled. "You looked good. Your punches were strong."

"My brother is a beast! He even got in the ring and sparred with me. I busted up his lip good!" Zachary laughed heartily.

"Why would you do that?" Concern washed across her expression.

"It was an accident. I didn't do it on purpose. I caught him with a roundhouse kick. He didn't duck in time. He took it well, though. Came back at me with a series of uppercuts that stung like hell! He was actually better than I thought he would be."

She shook her head, her tone admonishing. "I really wish you'd stop messing up his face. I love your brother's face and I really love it without the bruises."

Her comment hit a nerve, his good mood seeping like air from a deflating balloon. Zachary cut an eye at her. "Can we spend one night not talking about how much you like my brother?"

She gave him an eye roll, her dark gaze spinning skyward. "What's gotten into you lately? Why are you suddenly having issues with me and your brother?"

"I'm not having issues," Zachary snapped. "I just don't need to hear how special you think he is every ten seconds. I didn't bring you here to be fawning all over him like some lovesick puppy."

Sarai stared at the man, her expression stunned. His comment was off-putting, leaving her with a bad taste. She snapped back, "You didn't bring me here, so don't get it twisted, Zachary Barrett. If anything, you tagged along with me."

"You threatened to come get my brother and bring him back to Thailand. So what?"

"And the minute I booked the flight you suddenly

had a change of heart. You couldn't wait to get on the plane with me. I didn't ask you to come!"

There was a moment of pause. Zachary took a deep breath before he spoke again. "I don't want to argue with you," he said, his voice dropping back to a normal tone.

"Then don't," Sarai answered. "I didn't start this. You did."

Zachary moved into the room, easing to her side. He slid a heavy hand around her waist and drew her close against him. Sarai bristled, his touch unexpected, and unwanted.

"What . . . what are you . . . what are you doing?" she stammered. She pressed both of her palms to his chest, pushing him from her.

"I love you, Sarai, and I don't want us to be at each other's throats. You're my best friend and well . . . I think you and I could really be good together. So I get a little crazy sometimes when all you do is talk about my brother." He pulled her back to him, wanting to eliminate the air that filled the space between their two bodies.

This time Sarai gave him a harsh punch to his chest as she wrenched herself from his grasp. "Are you serious right now?"

Zachary looked confused. "Why wouldn't I be?"

"Because you know there will never be anything romantic between us. Kissing you would be like kissing my father. It should turn your stomach as much as the thought turns mine. Did you fall down and bump your head while you were in the ring?"

Zachary sighed, then moved to the bedside and dropped down onto the mattress. His upper body fell forward as he leaned his elbows against his thighs. He blew another gust of air past his lips. "You and I were always so good together. What's happened?"

Sarai took a seat beside him. "We're still good together when you aren't trying to pick an argument for no reason. Or do something stupid like that stunt you just pulled!"

"So, why didn't you fall for my charming good looks? My brother and I almost look alike. I just happen to be more handsome than he is!"

Sarai laughed. "You and I would never work, Zachary. From the beginning you've been like a big brother to me. I'm indebted to you for everything you've ever done to help me and my father. You single-handedly kept me from a life of servitude. I have a college degree because of your support and generosity. Because of you I can support my father in his old age. There is absolutely nothing that I wouldn't do for you but I will not allow you to think that we would be good together because you know it wouldn't work. We'd kill each other after the first week. Then we'd break each other's hearts and it would ruin our friendship."

She took a deep breath before she continued. "I've worked very hard to make you proud of me, Zachary. I would never want to do anything to disappoint you. But I can't pretend that I don't care about your brother when I do. I love you but how I love you isn't like how I'm growing to love Alexander."

"Isn't it a little early for you to be professing your feelings like that? You don't know him well enough to be in love with him."

Sarai rolled her eyes. "I didn't say I was in love with him. I said that I had love for him but that it's very different from the love I have for you. You're the one twisting my words."

Zachary turned his head to stare at her. His hands were clasped together, and he wrung them awkwardly. "You're right," he finally answered. "And I know you're right but I can wish, can't I?"

"You can't wish that and definitely not about me and you together." She skewed her face, her nose twisted as if something smelled bad. "That's just so wrong."

"Like you didn't get excited that time you saw me naked."

She laughed. "Trust me, I didn't. It was actually embarrassing. Especially for you." She eyed him with a raised brow, her gaze teasing.

"I was cold," he said, color warming his cheeks. "You had the heat turned off and I'd just gotten out of the shower!"

"You don't need to explain it to me," Sarai said with a warm laugh.

He eyed her as if he were unconvinced, their gazes locking for a quick minute. He finally nodded as he jumped onto his feet.

"The food service sent enough dinner for both of us. I can have it heated in ten minutes and we can eat and watch a movie together. Unless you have other plans?"

She shook her head. "No, I think I'm in for the night."

"Good, because I miss just hanging out with you." He held up both hands as if surrendering. "And I promise no more wild fantasies about the two of us. We're just friends. I guess I was just missing my BFF."

"Don't say BFF. It just sounds all kinds of wrong!"

He laughed. "Okay, I was just missing my homie!"

"That's not better." She shook her head.

"You pick the movie. Something with some killing in it!" he said as he headed out of the room. "Or maybe some zombies." As he moved out of sight, he was still chattering easily.

With the conversation leading them, Sarai followed on his heels, relief flooding her spirit. It would be an hour or so later when she'd remember that she hadn't returned Alexander's last call.

Alexander looked at his cell phone for the umpteenth time. Sarai hadn't acknowledged his message, not bothering to return his call. He'd thought about calling her again but had talked himself out of it. He didn't want to seem pushy, figuring that if it was important to her, she'd make an effort to call him.

He shifted a fresh ice pack against his lower lip. The bruises to his face were just enough to make his blood boil every time he looked at his reflection in the mirror. He hadn't intended to get into the ring with Zachary. He knew that sparring with his brother was best left to amateurs interested in chasing after his sibling's title. His brother was the best in the industry, and it took a fool to think they could outmaneuver, outbox, or outfight him. The more intelligent fools demanded a percentage of the net purse and their names on the fight roster. The others were willing to step into the ring for free. Alexander wasn't either kind of a fool.

But Zachary had wheedled and nagged, then dared him. His taunts had been reminiscent of when they'd been in their teens, determined to best the other at everything they attempted. The challenge had come with much instigating from Dan, their father, and everyone else standing around the gym watching. Not wanting to seem weak, or scared, he'd wrapped his hands, donned a pair of leather gloves, and stepped into the cage. He'd been that kind of a fool.

He'd actually impressed himself with how well he'd been able to hold his own against Zachary's skills. He'd successfully blocked and had thrown some serious punches. Even his twin had been surprised. But Zachary's legs were steel-infused appendages, his kicks connecting like a concrete hammer. Zachary had nailed him good when the top of his foot had connected with Alexander's face, kicking the protective head gear clear to the other side of the cage. The follow-up kick had nailed him in the ribs, knocking the breath from his lungs and his legs from under him. But he'd come back swinging, getting in a few good licks that had backed his brother up and given him pause.

Ice was now the only thing keeping the swelling at bay. Without it, he would probably look more like Quasimodo, everything hurting so badly that standing hunched over was the only thing keeping the pain to a minimum. And now, to add insult to injury, his girl was home with his brother, not answering his calls. Alexander would have rolled his eyes if they didn't hurt too.

His doorbell ringing surprised him. He stole a quick glance at the time. It was after ten o'clock, and he couldn't begin to imagine who was stopping by for a visit at such a late hour. Moving onto his feet, he eased his way from the family room to the front foyer. As he stared out the oversized bay windows, a wide smile pulled across his heart. The energy in his step increased tenfold as he threw the door open, Sarai standing on the other side.

Chapter Nine

"You didn't call me," Alexander mumbled, his bruised lip making it difficult to speak.

She giggled, the soft lull teasing to his ears. "You mad? Do you want me to leave?" she said, motioning as if she intended to turn around.

He grabbed her arm to stop her, his head waving from side to side. "Of course I don't want you to leave. Come inside," he said as he pulled her through the entrance.

"Good, because from the looks of things you look like you could use some help." She held up a red canvas shopping bag, shaking it about.

"You still didn't call me back," he mumbled as he closed the oversized door, securing it behind them.

Sarai nodded. "I apologize. It's why I came over. I got distracted and the time got away from me. And since I wanted to check on you I figured coming over to lay eyes on you was the best way." She eased her fingers against the side of his face. "That really looks like it hurts!"

"He nailed me good! I hate to see what he'd do to some stranger he's never known."

"Your brother is the best for a reason. I've seen him demolish men who were bigger and thought they were better. The fact that you went up against him is impressive."

They had moved back into his family room, setting themselves comfortably on the chenille sofa. Alexander leaned his body against hers, allowing his arm and shoulder to brush against her arm and shoulder.

"When we were boys we were obsessed with wrestling. We'd watch WWE on television for hours! Then we'd move all the furniture in the living room and try the moves on each other. We both hated to lose and we became obsessive about competing with each other."

She shook her head. The look she gave him was chastising.

"I know. I know. It's well past time we grew out of that."

"Acknowledging that you have a problem is the first step."

He nodded as he laughed, amused by her tone. "So what was so distracting that you didn't call me back?"

She chuckled. "Your brother and I had a moment." She paused for a quick second, then continued. "After we made up we ate dinner and watched a movie. Then my father called and after I talked with him, I came to see you."

Alexander cut an eye at her. "Is my brother going to be a problem? I mean . . . is there something else between you two that I should know about?"

For a brief moment Sarai had thought about spilling the details of all that had happened between her and his twin, but she changed her mind. What she and Zachary needed to get past didn't need to brew stagnant between the two brothers. It was done and finished and best left unsaid.

Her smile was the sweetest as she met his gaze. "He's working through some things but it's all good," she said as she leaned to kiss his cheek.

Alexander winced, a hint of hurt twisting the nerves in his face and coursing from his head down through the rest of his body. He blew a slow hiss of air through clenched teeth.

Sarai laughed. "I need to fix you," she said. She moved onto her feet, reaching for that red bag. "Give me ten minutes, then come up to your bathroom."

"What are you . . . ?"

"Just do it," she said sternly, stalling his question.

Fifteen minutes later Alexander lay in a tub of hot water that smelled of lavender, rosemary, and juniper. He was still dressed in his briefs, submerged up to his shoulders, the whirlpool jets on high. He was lost in a moment of quiet bliss, his muscles finally beginning to feel new again, when Sarai stepped back into the bathroom. She carried an oversized glass of tea-colored drink over cubes of ice.

"You need to drink this," she said. "It will make you feel better."

He reclosed his eyes as she rested the glass on the tub's edge. "Soaking in this bath is working miracles. What did you put in the water? Some kind of Thai home remedy?"

She laughed. "Epsom salt and some essential oils."

Alexander opened one eye and looked at her. "Seriously?"

Sarai nodded. "Tried and true, a cup or two of Epsom salt dissolved in a warm tub of water works wonders for aching muscles. You need to make sure you don't have any other health conditions, such as heart problems, high blood pressure, or diabetes, though. Then it's not so good."

"And that's because . . . ?"

"Epsom salts are made up of magnesium sulfate. Magnesium is a natural muscle relaxant and as a salt it helps to pull excess fluids out of the tissues to reduce swelling. That salt isn't good if you have any other health issues. But you knew that."

"Just testing you," he said teasingly. He took a sip of the beverage. "This isn't bad. It's not good but it's not bad. What is it?"

"It's a blend of apple cider vinegar, water, molasses, honey, and ginger. It will help with healing from the inside out. And as soon as the water cools I'm going to give you a massage. Tomorrow you'll be back to your old self."

Alexander sat forward ever so slightly. "A massage?" There was a flash of something wicked in his blue eyes.

Sarai laughed. "Not that kind of massage!" She grinned brightly. She crossed to the counter, pulling a plush white towel into her hands. Moving back to his side, she rested it beside him. "When you're ready I'll be in the other room."

"You're not going to stay here with me?"

"I have to get some things ready," she said, her smile teasing. "You'll be okay."

Alexander tossed her a look that made her laugh. "I promise," she said, "I'm not going anywhere until I know you're feeling better."

As she stepped out of the room, she paused for a brief moment, turning to eye him with a narrowed gaze. The look was soft and seductive and caused an erection to suddenly swell full and large. He palmed the wealth of flesh with a heavy hand, a shiver of energy coursing up his spine and deep into the pit of

his stomach. He inhaled, taking deep breaths of air
to try to stall the rising sensation.

Pulling himself upright, he sat for a few more minutes in the cooling water until the matter pressing between his legs eased, the throbbing pulse reduced to
the faintest of beats. Lifting himself from the water,
he stepped out of his briefs, kicking them to the opposite end of the bathtub. He turned on the shower
and allowed the spray of cold water to wash over him.
When he finally felt more in control, he stepped from
the shower and reached for the towel to dry the moisture from his skin.

Moving into the bedroom, Alexander found Sarai
sitting on the edge of his bed. She held a bowl and a
spoon in her hand, stirring something in a slow rota-
tion. The candles in the room were lit, and she had
turned the lights down low. The gas fireplace was
turned on, flames dancing in brilliant shades of
orange and red. He stood staring at her for a brief
moment, in awe of how the light reflected across her
face, highlighting the fine lines of her profile. She
was exquisite, every dip and curve of her features
picture perfect, if such a thing was possible. But more
than her physical beauty, she exuded a level of warmth
and an energy that lifted his spirit to new heights. He
cleared his throat to announce his entrance.

Sarai lifted her gaze to his, pausing to stare at the
man. He stood with that white towel wrapped around
his waist. His bare chest was broad, his skin like decadent chocolate. Every muscle rippled, the sinewy
threads evidence of much hard work in the gym.
The sight of him took her breath away. She smiled as
she moved onto her feet and gestured for him to lie
across the bed.

"Are you feeling any better?" she questioned.

He nodded. "I really do. I'm still a little sore but not nearly as much as before." He crawled up onto the mattress, resting on his hands and knees before he slid onto his stomach, his arms outstretched over his head. He glanced back at her over his shoulder. "What's in the bowl?"

"It's a restorative blend of coconut oil, ground cloves, helichrysum, peppermint, and wintergreen. My father swears by it."

Alexander lay his head back down as he watched her kick off her shoes. She also undid the buttons to the white cotton blouse she was wearing, exposing a lace-edged tank top beneath. She folded the garment carefully and laid it atop the nightstand. As she climbed onto the bed to join him, he bit down against his bottom lip, fighting the constriction of muscle that pulled taut for the second time.

Straddling his body, she sat with her buttocks against his, her knees pressed against his sides. His white towel and her Lycra leggings lay between them. She rested the bowl of massage oils to the side, dipping her fingers into the mixture.

"You need to take slow, deep breaths," she said, her voice a loud whisper. "And relax."

He chuckled. "That might be a little hard," he whispered back.

"Why is that?"

"Because I'm a little hard, if you get my drift." He lifted himself up on his elbows, turning slightly as he tossed her another look. He was amused by the color that suddenly tinted her cheeks. "Are you blushing?"

Sarai gave him a slight eye roll.

"I'm sorry, I maybe should not have said that."

A wry smile pulled at her thin lips. "When I'm done you won't even notice that anymore," she said.

Her gaze danced with his as they stared at each other for a brief moment.

He laughed, resuming his prone position. He closed his eyes as he took one deep breath and then another.

The first pass of her hands across his bare shoulders made him shudder. The sweeping sensation was unexpected as it sucked the breath from his lungs. He gasped loudly. Her touch was heated as she kneaded the melting oils into his skin. On the second and third pass, he heard himself moan. The guttural sound was deep, an expulsion of breath and voice that sounded foreign to his ears. Each stroke of her palm and fingers manipulating his flesh was firm, and teasing, everything about Sarai's touch mesmerizing.

"Breathe," she whispered softly, the word a soft brush of air against his ear. "You have to breathe!"

Alexander hadn't even realized he was holding his breath until she said so, pointing out that he'd been holding air in his lungs for longer than he'd imagined. He took a deep inhale of oxygen just as her fingers inched into his lower back, the pressure instantly relaxing the tightened muscles.

Sarai found herself wishing she'd come earlier. Wishing she had forgone dinner and a movie with Zachary. Wishing she'd laid hands on the beautiful man beneath her well before the moment they were sharing. Being with Alexander had her wishing all kinds of things for the two of them, and not all of it was G-rated.

His skin was heated from the bath and her touch, and caressing him felt like the most natural thing in the world. She kneaded his shoulders until the tightened knots beneath his skin and along the line of his neck were gone. Her hands danced the length of his back,

pushing and pressing until she felt the tension give
way. When she reached his lower back, lifting her
body enough to hover slightly above him, she pressed
and rolled the palm of her hand until she felt him
collapse fully, his body deflating every ounce of
anxiety and tension that had plagued him.

Alexander snored softly, slipping into the deepest
sleep. Easing off to his side, she lay beside him and
watched him for another hour, unable to fathom how
she'd been so blessed. Each exhale of air came with
the slightest whistle, the sound moving her to smile.
He needed the rest, sleep the best healing balm for
all his hurts.

Easing her body from his, Sarai slid off the bed,
being careful not to disrupt his sleep. She reached for
the coconut oil and with the tip of her finger gently
brushed a layer of the moisturizing seal across his
bruised lip. Leaning, she allowed her cheek to glide
against his just briefly before leaving him with the
gentlest of kisses against his cheek and lips.

Moving around the room, she blew out all the
candles and extinguished the light. She left the fireplace burning, the glow of logs warming the room.
Hours later, when Alexander woke from the best night's
rest he'd had in ages, Sarai was gone, slumbering comfortably in her own bed across town.

Alexander literally skipped into work. He was
amazed at how he felt, not an ounce of pain in any of
his steps. The crew at the front desk greeted him
warmly, one of the assistants passing him a stack of
messages that had come in the early morning.

"Have you seen Dr. Montri?" he asked, eyeing each
of the staff members preparing for their day.

One young woman nodded. "She's with a client. I think they were headed toward the cardio room."

"Thank you," he said, his bright white smile gleaming.

As he headed in the direction of the gym, he actually kicked up his heels, his excitement palpable. Sarai stood jotting notes into a three-ring binder as her client, a middle-aged woman with two spare tires around her midsection, walked the treadmill. The woman was sweating profusely, but her smile was eager as Sarai periodically looked up to give her a few words of encouragement.

Alexander stood in the doorway, watching as Sarai moved her from the treadmill to the exercise bike, making the appropriate adjustments to her routine and the equipment before promising to come right back

"I need to run these papers over to the office. You need to ride the bike for twenty minutes. No stopping, Mrs. Woodman!"

"I promise."

"You're doing really well. I'm so excited by your progress!"

"I couldn't have done it without you, Sarai. You've been a lifesaver!" The woman named Mrs. Woodman clapped her hands.

Sarai smiled. "Thank you. I'll only be a quick minute," she concluded as she turned an about-face, moving toward the door.

Alexander's standing there surprised her, her smile widening as he lifted his hand in a slight wave. "Good morning!" he exclaimed as she moved to his side. He slid his hand into her hair as he leaned to kiss her lips. His touch was heated and possessive, the intensity of it causing her knees to shake with excitement.

"Good morning," she said, as she took a swift inhale

of air to stall the quiver of energy that surged through her body. She skirted her gaze from side to side, suddenly conscious of the people who were watching them curiously.

As if reading her mind, he grabbed her hand and pulled her into the hallway outside the gym area. Tossing a look in one direction and then in another, he led her to a quiet corner near a utility-room door, where they were out of sight of prying eyes.

"You left!" he exclaimed, a hint of attitude in his tone. He took a step toward her, easing her against the eggshell-colored wall.

She laughed, grateful for the support against her back that kept her standing. "You fell asleep!"

Alexander pressed his left palm to the wall above her head, leaning his body into hers. He rested his right hand against the curve of her hip, drawing her body to his. His cologne mingled with the light aroma of her perfume. His voice was low and deep, a loud whisper of air teasing her ear. "You should have woken me up. Even better, you should have spent the night and woken up beside me."

"You needed your rest," she muttered. She pressed her palm to the side of his face, her thumb gliding lightly over his lips. "It's still a little swollen but it looks much better than it did last night."

"It feels better and I feel great! You've got some serious skills, woman!"

She giggled again. "It helps that you're in good shape overall."

Someone moving down the hall caught her attention. Sarai shot Alexander a look just as he tossed a glance over his shoulder to stare where she stared. If she'd been able to take a step back, she probably would have. Since she couldn't, she slid back into the heat of his body instead. Whoever was passing didn't bother to look in their direction. He turned his attention back to her, his fingers still teasing the side of her waist.

"I actually had a great time last night," he whispered softly. "I'm really glad you came over. Although, I have to admit you had me nervous at first."

Sarai giggled. "Nervous? About what?"

"I thought you might have been trying to work some witchcraft or voodoo on me. I almost didn't get into that tub!"

"You're silly!" She brushed her palm across his broad chest, her fingertips tapping at the fabric of his T-shirt.

"But I really wish you'd gotten into the tub with me. That's what I really wish."

She giggled again as he leaned to nuzzle his face into her neck, leaving a trail of damp kisses across her jawline. When he pulled back, she pressed her own lips to his and kissed him warmly.

"I need to get back to work," she said, blowing a soft sigh. "Will I see you later?"

Alexander leaned to kiss her mouth one more time. "You'd better see me later!"

The twins stood toe-to-toe as Alexander wrapped his brother's hands in gauze tape. He was painstakingly meticulous with the over-and-under, round-and-round covering that would afford his twin a semblance of protection from the elements in the ring. Zachary's eyes skipped from his sibling's face to the process and back again.

"You sure you don't want to get back into the ring with me?"

"I'm sure."

"You didn't do too badly yesterday. I need competition like that."

"You need to focus more. I got in way too many hits. That kid's going to be punching harder and faster when you get in the ring with him."

Zachary nodded. "I hit hard too! Ask your face," he said with a low chuckle.

Alexander grinned. "You did that on purpose. Just jealous that I'm prettier than you."

"Says you."

"Says everyone."

Alexander tied on the first of the gloves, ensuring that it fit properly, with no slipping and sliding over his brother's hand. When he was satisfied, he did the other. "You're only boxing this afternoon. Keep your feet on the floor and your eyes on your opponent, please."

Zachary eyed the young man who stood ready in the ring. He was punching his two gloves together, his expression stern as he tried to appear intimidating. "I swear," he said, his head waving from side to side. "They keep getting younger and younger, don't they?"

Alexander cast his eyes toward where his brother stared. He shrugged his own broad shoulders. "It just looks that way because we're getting older, Z."

The two men exchanged a look.

"How are things going with you and my girl?" Zachary asked, changing the subject.

Alexander smiled. "How does she say it's going?"

"She likes you. She likes you a lot."

"Then it's all good. We're still getting to know each other and . . . well . . . I like her a lot, too."

There was a moment of pause as Zachary seemed

to drift off into thought. He shifted his gaze back toward his brother. "So, there's something I need to tell you."

Alexander was adjusting the last tie on his brother's glove. "What?" He lifted his eyes to meet the look Zachary was giving him. His brother's expression was sheepish, something like regret seeping from his gray eyes. Alexander rolled his own eyes skyward. "What the hell did you do this time?"

Zachary shrugged. "I made a pass at Sarai."

Alexander bristled. His jaw tightened, and his eyes narrowed. He dropped his hands to his sides, curling them into tight fists.

Zachary held up his gloved hands. "Before you go crazy, it was a mistake and she shut me down hard. And I mean really hard! I just wanted to apologize to you because I know I was wrong."

His brother took a deep breath, his eyes still locked with his twin's. "Why would you do that?"

Zachary shrugged, his shoulders jutting skyward before his whole upper body dropped from the weight that burdened him. He took a step closer to his twin's side, his voice dropping to a whisper. "I was jealous."

Alexander took a step back, the tension through his torso easing ever so slightly. "She didn't say anything to me about that."

"And she won't. She doesn't want us to go back to fighting and not talking. But trust me, she handled it."

There was a momentary pause that grew full between them.

"Just how hard did she shut you down?" Alexander widened his stance as he crossed his arms over his chest.

Zachary grinned. "I'm still bruised. She seriously hurt my feelings. But I was wrong and I should never have done that to her. Or you. I just lost my head for a minute."

"Is there anything else you need to tell me?"

"No. But I can assure you that I was stupid once. I won't be stupid twice. I just . . . well . . ."

"What?"

Zachary took a second to gather his thoughts, a wealth of weight seeming to drop across his shoulders. "I'm just having a hard time getting it all to make sense. It's why I needed to come back home. And it's why I need you."

Alexander took a quick moment to reflect on his brother's words. In the ring, the young boxer was jumping up and down on his toes, anxious to get started. Zachary looked like he was ready to give it all up without fighting at all. His brother's somber expression pulled hard at his heartstrings. He nodded. "Just keep your hands off my girl."

"You just remember what I told you. If you hurt her you'll have to deal with me. I wasn't kidding about that."

Alexander laughed. "That goes both ways. You remember that too and we'll all be good."

Zachary smiled. "Personally, I don't know what she sees in you. You're not that good-looking, not that smart, and definitely not that rich. She could do better."

Alexander pondered the comment briefly. His expression was smug as he responded, "She probably could. I'm glad she doesn't want to. Now get your ass in that cage!"

Across the room Sarai stood watching, her mouth easing into a warm smile. The brothers were laughing, both looking completely at ease with each other. Their joking back and forth together was a sign that things had changed between them. They were better together, and she imagined from this point forward there would be nothing they couldn't accomplish together.

As Zachary stepped into the ring, everyone in the room stopped talking. The quiet lull rippled heavily through the space, and then he threw his first punch. The harshness of it echoed in the warm air. Alexander's deep voice calling out instructions was the only other sound to vibrate through the space.

Minutes later the young man who'd been eager to spar with the champion stepped out of the cage, looking like he'd gone up against something demonic. The color had drained from his face, sweat poured from his body, and the areas where the blows had connected with his flesh were starting to swell black and blue. He was visibly shaking, and Sarai actually felt sorry for the young man. Over all the years she'd known him, Zachary had broken many an aspiring fighter, their dreams crushed after sparring with the man for ten minutes. As she watched Alexander pull the kid aside, the conversation between them for his ears only, she was grateful that for once, there was someone to build them, and their hopes, back up.

She had punched out and was just minutes from her home when her cell phone rang. She pushed the button for the car's Bluetooth and engaged the unit.

"Hello?"

"You left. And you didn't say good-bye."

She laughed. "Why are you always fussing at me, Alexander?"

"I wasn't fussing. I was stating fact."

"Well, you were busy and I didn't want to interrupt."

"You can always interrupt me. And you should. I

hate it when you leave me and don't say good-bye. I'm really starting to have issues with it."

There was a thick pause, only the exhalations of their deep breaths cutting through the quiet.

"Are you still there?"

She nodded as if he could see her. She'd pulled into the home's driveway and had shut down her car. His comment had her thinking, and she hadn't been sure how to respond. "I am," she said finally, her tone soft. She hesitated a second time before voicing her thoughts. "Aren't you concerned about what people might say? They already whisper about you and the women they think you're seeing. I wouldn't want them saying anything bad about you and me. Doesn't it worry you?"

She could hear him take a deep breath on the other end of the line before he responded.

"I don't give a damn what people whisper. As long as you and I know what's true and what's not. I think we have something special that we're building together. That's what's important to me. You, Sarai, are important to me. So let me tell you how this works. You come first. If you need me, want me, whatever, all you have to do is say it and I'll be there. As long as you're my woman, no one and nothing will ever come before you and your needs. But with that I have expectations. I expect that I will also come first with you. I expect that you will care about my needs and wants as much as I do yours. If Zachary or any other man makes a pass at you again, I expect you to tell me. And I don't want you ever leaving me again without saying good-bye!"

Sarai smiled into the phone line. "Is that everything?"

"Probably not. I'm demanding, Sarai, but I'm never unreasonable."

"Okay," she said. "I promise it won't ever happen again."

She could feel him smiling back.

"I have to get back to my brother. He's going through sparring partners like water."

Sarai chuckled. "Take the gloves off him. He really needs to work on his holds. He folds in a clench and forgets how to use his body for leverage."

"Good to know," Alexander said as he laughed with her. "I'll call you back as soon as I'm done here."

After saying good-bye and disconnecting the call, Sarai sat in her car for a few good minutes. Alexander had claimed her. He had called her "his" woman. She liked that he had staked his territory. She liked it very much.

Chapter Ten

The Boulder area was a hiker's dream come true. Already many feet above sea level, some in-town trails climbed thousands of feet higher. Between the prairie grasslands in the east, the foothills and canyons in the west, and the high mountains, there was something for everyone.

Alexander had chosen the challenging Mesa Trail for them to follow. Stretching some seven miles from end to end, it was a good two- to three-hour adventure through the arid high-desert environment, thick forest, and incredible rock formations. Sarai had never seen the likes of such beauty.

Their morning had started at the southern end of the trail at the South Mesa Trailhead, where they'd left his car for the return home. Together they'd driven in her car to the northern end, at the Chautauqua Trailhead. The early morning air had been crisp, the gentlest of breezes blowing about. Alexander had packed a backpack for them: a map and compass, sunscreen and lip balm, a flashlight and first aid kit, a knife and multitool, bottles of water, energy bars, and a few pieces of fruit.

"I didn't know how ambitious you were feeling," he said, "so we'll only walk it one way. Next time, though, we'll hike it both ways. That's a good fourteen-mile workout!"

Sarai laughed. "You don't even know if I like hiking yet."

He wrapped an arm around her shoulder and hugged her close. "You will *love* hiking!" he said as he grabbed her hand and pulled her along to the start of the trail. From the parking lot, they followed the sign that read BLUEBELL TRAIL, a detour that promised to be more scenic as well as more strenuous. For the first thirty minutes Alexander teased and cajoled as he guided her along. They walked slowly, enjoying the cool breezes. The conversation between them was easy, filled with much laughter. They debated everything from politics and international relationships to old-school versus new-school rap music. What Alexander quickly discovered was that Sarai was not only opinionated but always ready to argue her point.

"But you can't talk about hip-hop and rap without discussing the contributions of Kurtis Blow, Run-DMC, the Sugarhill Gang, and Grandmaster Flash. And definitely Afrika Bambaataa! They all defined rap music. They were the fathers of rap music."

"I don't disagree," Sarai responded, "but I think Wu-Tang, Biggie, Tupac, Snoop, and Eminem also gave rap music definition. You have to credit their contributions as well."

"You did not just say Eminem!"

"I did. You can't discredit his accomplishments. His *Slim Shady* album put him on the map."

"Eminem was a white boy in a black medium. He spit profanity-fueled lyrics that had nothing to do with the black experience."

"Are you saying that just because he was white means his life perspective had no validity? He rapped about lower economic situations and lives filled with rage and little hope. It sounded a lot like life in Thailand for many of us and many of the black experiences I've read and heard about."

Alexander tossed her a look. "That's not what I'm saying."

"That's what it sounds like. And I suppose you also have issues with the women in the game as well? What about Missy Elliott, Lil' Kim, Remy Ma, Rah Digga and their contributions to the rap game?"

"I don't have any issues with them at all. In fact, I think Missy Elliott is in a league of her own. That needs to be recognized first and foremost. You can't compare the others to what she's brought to the game."

"What about the new-school girls, Nicki Minaj, Iggy Azalea . . . ?"

"Ohhh!" Alexander winced. "Iggy Azalea? Really?"

Sarai laughed. "You're killing me!" She stepped over a fallen log, navigating herself carefully over the steep terrain before she continued. "I agree with you that new-school rap has become very generic and invariable. The same stanza over and over again. Old-school rappers brought a certain je ne sais quoi that these younger rappers know nothing about."

"Exactly! Back in the day rappers put more thought into the rhymes they wrote. They wanted their music to mean something. It was rich and raw and it had serious flavor!"

"You'll get no argument from me there."

"How do you know so much? Did they even play rap in Thailand?"

She laughed. "You'd be surprised what gets played

in Thailand. All kinds of foreign influences. But it was your brother who introduced me to Nas, 50 Cent, Soulja Boy, and some others. The rest I researched on my own."

Alexander stopped to take a swig of water from one of the bottles in his backpack. He passed the drink to Sarai, who followed his lead.

"You need to stay hydrated."

She nodded. "It's starting to get really warm."

"It's only going to get hotter. We'll be exiting the forest soon and then there won't be much shade. We'll have some cloud coverage but that sun is still bright."

Turning back to the trail, Sarai led the way, mindful of each step she took. Watching her walk away made Alexander smile. She'd worn form-fitting athletic pants with a matching sweat top. The pants fit what little curve she had nicely, giving him a pleasant rear view. She stomped through the underbrush in a pair of waterproof hiking boots that had lace ties and a rubber toe protector that came in a shade of fuchsia and gray, with neon-yellow lugs. She was absolutely adorable, and it took everything he had to keep his hands to himself. Fighting the desire to undress her with his eyes, he shifted his gaze back to the trail and the small signs pointing them in the right direction.

Their walk and talk continued for the last three miles. As they stepped off the trail back into the parking lot, Sarai fell forward at the waist. Stretching her body down to the ground she pressed her palms to the space between her feet. Her flexibility was impressive. The view she was giving him even more so. Unable to resist, he tapped her backside with a wide palm, his hand gently caressing the supple tissue of each butt cheek.

She snapped back up, grinning at his brazenness.

Her hands fell to her hips, amusement shining in her eyes as she looked at him. "I beg your pardon!"

Alexander laughed. "Sorry about that. I couldn't resist!"

She shook her head as she eased into his arms, sliding into a deep bear hug.

He kissed her forehead. "You did such a great job. I wanted to give you a pat on the back. I'm really impressed that you were able to keep up with me."

She laughed with him, the lilt of her voice sounding like a gentle wind chime. "I'm sure that any woman with you, Alex, has to keep up if she wants to *stay* with you."

They made a quick stop at Lucky's Market on Broadway so that Sarai could purchase the ingredients she needed for their meal. Her shopping list included a host of organic produce, and she delighted at the quality. Alexander was bemused by her enthusiasm. When she'd found everything she needed, they headed toward his home.

The ride was quiet, both comfortable in the silence. A Taylor Swift song played on the radio, followed by Bruno Mars, and then the crooner Sam Smith. The music had them both bobbing their heads up and down, occasionally singing along. As they pulled into the driveway of his home, both sighed collectively, the hint of fatigue beginning to settle into their muscles.

"Are you hungry?" Sarai asked as they stepped through the front door, Alexander closing it behind them.

He shook his head. "Not really. I need a hot shower before I can even think about food."

"I could really use one of those myself," Sarai said with a nod. "I can cook for us after."

"That sounds like a plan," he said as she picked up her athletic bag from the tiled floor.

Alexander grabbed her free hand and pulled her up the stairs to the second floor. Stopping in the hallway, he took a towel and bath cloth from the linen closet. He pointed her in the direction of the spare bedroom.

"There's plenty of hot water. I'll give you some privacy and if you want to lie down for a minute the mattress on that bed is very comfortable."

She smiled sweetly. "Thank you."

He hesitated for a brief second as if there was more he wanted to say, but there were no words. Finally, he pointed toward the master bedroom door. "I'll be in my room if you need me," he whispered softly. He leaned to kiss her cheek, and as she turned he gave her another tap on her backside.

Tossing a quick gaze over her shoulder, Sarai smiled again, amusement shifting across her expression. As she disappeared into the second bedroom, closing the door between them, he was smiling back.

In his own bedroom Alexander threw his sweat-stained clothes into the clothes hamper. Sauntering naked over to the sound system, he turned it on, flooding the entire house with the sounds of Nina Simone. It was her greatest-hits album, and the woman's eclectic tone was haunting as it painted the walls in varying shades of emotion. Moving from the bedroom into the bathroom, Alexander turned on the shower. Waiting for the water to warm, he allowed the music to draw him in as he thought about Sarai down at the other end of the hallway.

It had been a good day. Being with Sarai felt all

kinds of right, and he relished the time they shared. As he reflected on their hike, it dawned on him that he hadn't thought about the gym once that whole day. It was the first in many years that he hadn't obsessed about business. He'd been able to relax completely, and he fathomed such was a very good thing. Stepping into the shower, he closed his eyes and ducked his head beneath the spray of hot water. It trickled over his face and down his wide back. He clenched and released his pecs, his broad chest dancing beneath the wetness as it seeped to the floor between his toes.

The bathroom door's opening surprised him. He turned abruptly as the glass shower door slid to the side. His eyes were wide as Sarai stepped into the shower with him. She stood staring at him, her gaze locking with his. Neither said a word as she eased her lithe body against him.

The moment Alexander touched her, Sarai knew deep in her heart that in his arms was where she was supposed to be. As she had stripped out of her clothes, standing in the other room, she found herself longing to be back with him. Everything about their day together had been perfect. He had been engaging and attentive. He made her laugh, and being with him was everything she had ever imagined it to be. In that moment, as the subtlety of blues swept through the air, all she wanted was him. That wanting had fueled each of her steps as she'd found her way to his room and his shower.

Sarai fell into his embrace. His arms were like anchors and she held on easily. Pressing her naked self against him felt like she had reconnected with something that had been lost. Everything about Alexander felt like home.

He captured her mouth with his own, his lips frenzied as they skated above hers. Everything about Sarai was beautiful. Her body was toned like a runner's. Her breasts were just a handful of orange-sized tissue, full and firm. Her waist was paper thin, the faintest hint of her abdominal muscles peeking beneath skin. Despite her short stature, her legs made her seem like she was model tall. Her half-moon eyes were closed, her lengthy lashes batting against her pale skin. She was exquisite, and in that moment she was completely his.

Alexander wrapped his arms around her waist as he lifted her off her feet. She weighed next to nothing, and he was surprised by how light she was in his arms. As he held her close, she wrapped her legs around his waist, her buttocks hovering above his pelvis. She snaked her arms around his neck, her fingers caressing and teasing the edge of his hairline, brushing at the slightest baby hairs that curled there.

Neither had broken the kiss, tongues tangled as they clutched at each other hungrily. They savored the taste of each other, lips gliding like silk against silk. Alexander's hands were like hot coals rolling across her back as he clutched the round of her backside, holding her tightly to him. Heat surged with a vengeance between his legs, his cock a bulging rod of bone and steel.

Pulling herself from him, Sarai gasped for air, her lungs burning with the heat that coursed like a firestorm throughout her body. She unlatched her legs, wiggling until he set her back onto her feet. She reached for the bar of shea butter soap, the light scent of sandalwood teasing her nostrils. Soon she was lost in the rhythm of lathering his shoulders, back, and arms. Her hands glided up the inside of his legs, kneading his hamstrings and inner thighs. She massaged his hips, tipped her pinkie into his belly button, and brushed her palms over his broad chest. She worked her fingers easily across every inch of his body as the suds covered his dark skin. She wove a slow, circular path around him, and with each pass of her hand his hardened member bounced eagerly for attention.

When she finally reached between them to grasp him in her palm, Alexander tensed, every muscle in his body constricting. He was hard and dripping, and as she slowly stroked him with her fingers and palm, he felt like he was about to burst, his whole body ready to combust from the inside out.

She massaged the thick muscle below his testicles and slid her fingers up and down his shaft. She stroked him slowly, long, gentle passes that had his knees shaking. He pushed his hips forward, and they fell into a smooth rhythm, the give and take a sensuous exchange. His breathing quickened, and he suddenly tensed, fighting the surge of energy that threatened to send him over the edge. Sarai released the hold she had on him, dropping her hands back to her sides. Turning her back to him, she leaned into the spray of water that rained over their heads and washed her own body.

Regaining a semblance of control, Alexander dropped his hands to her hips and pulled her against him. He nuzzled his face into her neck, lightly biting at the soft flesh before whispering in her ear, "Let's move this party to my bed."

With a teasing smile, Sarai reached to shut off the water, then turned into his chest. Alexander lifted her into his arms and carried her from the shower into the bedroom. He snatched the bedspread to the floor and lay her on the cool sheets. He hovered over her, kissing his way slowly up her body. His fingers led where his lips followed. She shivered, his touch the sweetest sensation she had ever experienced. Their gazes locked for a brief moment, and then he plunged his mouth back to hers, his tongue like a piston reaching for the back of her throat. His kisses were wet and deep, and she responded by caressing his tongue with her own. Weak with love and desire, her body writhed, unable to contain her own excitement.

He kissed her eyes, her nose, licking a slow, damp trail to her ears and along her jawline. She reached between them to grab his cock, and he was hard and throbbing. She exhaled swiftly when he suddenly lifted himself from her and reached into the nightstand for a condom. Before she could blink, Alexander had sheathed himself and dropped his body back against hers. The desire that raged between them was magnanimous, the wanting so intense that it was consuming. Sarai parted her legs, opening herself to him. She inhaled swiftly, holding her breath as he used his hand to slowly drag his erection across her swollen slit. He teased her unmercifully, and she heard herself whimper, her need thick and abundant.

"Open your eyes," Alexander demanded, his voice coming in a throaty whisper. When she did, their gazes locking, he slid himself easily into her. He plunged his body into hers with one swift push, then held her tightly, allowing them both to savor the moment. Sarai wrapped her legs around his back, locking her ankles above his buttocks. She wanted him like she had never wanted any man before him.

She clung to him as he began to thrust himself in and out of her, their bodies moving in perfect sync. And then she lost total control. Sarai called his name over and over again.

Alexander pushed and pulled, the connection so sweet that tears puddled behind his eyelids. And then he slammed forward sharply and froze as his body spasmed with quick, heavy pulses. He orgasmed, his explosion igniting hers as they fell off the edge of ecstasy together. The moment was earth-shattering. Sight and sound were sheer bliss, their screams muffled beneath another deep tongue-entwined kiss. Her body shook, quivering with his. Ripples of pleasure connected them, and then with the last shudder, they both fell into the sweetest glow.

Alexander woke with a start. For a brief moment he was disoriented, having no idea how long he'd been asleep or the time of day. His bed was empty, Sarai nowhere to be found. For a brief moment he imagined that he'd been dreaming as Nina Simone claimed to have put a spell on him. Coming to his senses, he turned to eye the alarm clock on the nightstand, noting the early evening hour. Sleep had only lasted a good two hours.

He sat upright and called out her name. When he got no response, he threw his legs off the side of the bed. Outside, it had started to darken, the last rays of the daytime sun beginning to disappear over the horizon. He swiped a heavy hand over his face, then lifted his naked frame from the bed and moved to the closed bedroom door. As he threw it open, the decadent aroma of food cooking greeted him from the floor below, wafting up from the kitchen. He was suddenly hungry, his stomach rumbling with anticipation.

He called Sarai's name a second time.

She called back from the bottom of the stairwell. "Hi, sleepyhead. You're finally up!"

"I thought you'd gone."

"And not say good-bye?" She laughed easily. "I wouldn't end our perfect day with a fight."

"We wouldn't fight. I'd be mad but we definitely wouldn't fight."

She giggled again. "Come on down. Dinner's ready."

Down in the kitchen, Alexander found Sarai dressed in one of his T-shirts, the oversized garment like a short minidress. As he leaned to kiss her mouth, he slid a slow hand beneath the top, gently caressing her upper thigh and buttock. He was delighted to find her naked beneath, the discovery causing his manhood to quiver.

Sarai giggled as she pushed his hand away. She grabbed his face between her palms and kissed him again. "I thought you were hungry?" she questioned.

Alexander laughed with her. "I was just thinking about dessert."

She gestured toward the table. "Well, let me feed you first. We need to get your energy back up."

"I'm already back up," he teased as he copped another feel of her backside, caressing each cheek with a heavy hand.

Slipping out of his grasp, Sarai laughed heartily as she grabbed a bowl from the counter and headed to the table.

"It really smells good in here," he said as he took a deep inhale of air.

"I know how finicky you are about your diet so I hope it tastes as good as it smells."

He took a seat at the table as she set plates of food before him. He was impressed as she pointed out what each dish was. There was soft tofu that had been floured and deep-fried and was served with a soy glaze. She followed that with a refreshing cucumber salad in a light vinaigrette, garnished with sesame seeds. And then the entrée, a stir-fry consisting of chicken, cashews, pineapple chunks, bell peppers, bamboo shoots, baby corn, celery, and onions, served in spicy garlic sauce with brown rice. It was all good, and he said so.

"You really can cook!" he said as he swallowed his last bite of chicken. "This was incredible!"

Sarai smiled. "You had doubts?"

He shrugged. "You never know. I dated a woman once who swore she was a master chef. Then I discovered she was ordering food from a local restaurant and having it delivered before I got to her house."

Sarai laughed. "Well, my mother taught me how to cook. When she died I had to take over cooking for my father."

"I can't wait to meet your father."

A wave of sadness suddenly crossed Sarai's face. Her eyes dropped to the table. She spoke to her father regularly, and each time he admonished her for some of her choices, it hurt her feelings. It upset him that she was not married and that she had left home to follow dreams he had no understanding of. He wanted her back in Thailand and regularly said so.

"What did I say?" Alexander questioned, concern rising in his tone.

She shook her head. "I just miss my father, that's all." She lifted her mouth into a slight smile. "I'll see him again soon, though."

Alexander nodded. He extended his hand, pressing his palm to the side of her face. "Don't be sad."

She pressed her hand to his. "I'm not sad. You make me happy." She lifted her mouth to his and kissed his lips lightly.

"Why don't you go up and relax," Alexander said. "I'll do the dishes."

Sarai grinned. "Are you sure?"

He nodded as he gave her a wink of his eye. "Positive. And when I'm done, I'll bring you some of that dessert."

Chapter Eleven

For weeks Sarai and Alexander had been inseparable. They were tied at the hip, with work the only time that the two found themselves apart. The duo had fallen into an easy routine with each other, and it all felt good. Hiking had become their second-favorite pastime. Sarai had fallen in love with the natural waterfalls that spanned the area and the trails that took them past the spectacular water sights. She'd been excited to drag him to the annual Colorado Shakespeare festival, and despite his reservations, he'd actually enjoyed the theater production of *Othello*. She motivated him to do and experience things he'd never considered before.

He and his brother had also fallen into a comfortable routine with each other. Fully focused on his training, Zachary barely missed her presence when he'd find his way home to fall into his bed. Alexander had put him on a strict regime, and he was so intent on following it to the letter that he didn't have time to focus on anything, or anyone, else.

Alexander let himself into his brother's home, calling out the man's name. He found Zachary slumbering heavily on the living-room sofa. He snored loudly, a low rumble of air echoing around the room. Staring down at him, Alexander couldn't help but smile. Zachary was working hard, and everything had improved since he had shown up on his doorstep. Knowing how hard his brother was working, he almost hated having to wake him from his deep sleep. Almost. He swatted a pillow at his twin's head, smacking him in the face—hard.

Zachary jumped, his eyes wide. "What the . . . ?"

Alexander laughed. "Wake up. It's just me."

His twin shot him a look through narrowed eyes, not at all amused. He stretched his body upward and yawned. "What time is it?"

"Time to get a good run in before we head to the gym."

"Why didn't you just call me?"

Alexander shrugged. "Does it matter?"

Zachary yawned again. "I guess not." He looked around the room. "Where's Sarai?"

"My place. She was still sleeping when I left."

"Lucky girl. I wish I was still asleep."

"Sarai's not in training. Now get up," Alexander said, casting a glance down to his wristwatch. "We're already thirty minutes behind schedule."

Zachary nodded. He eased his legs off the side of the sofa and sat up. Rising from his seat, he moved to the bathroom to wash his face and rinse his mouth.

Alexander wandered through the house as he waited. The space was oversized and lavish, but it felt cold, nothing about it feeling like a home. The last weeks had found Sarai at his home more than not. He had convinced her to move her stuff, giving her a key and unfettered access to every aspect of his life.

He sensed that with her gone, the house was now just a house and little more.

Standing in the doorway of Sarai's room, he saw that the space no longer showed any evidence of her previous presence. Zachary seemed to read his brother's mind as he came out of his own bedroom, pulling a long-sleeved cotton T-shirt over his head. "It's quiet since she left. It doesn't even feel the same."

Alexander nodded. "Do you miss her?"

The two men exchanged gazes.

His brother shrugged. "Not really. It's not like I don't still see her every day. And we still talk. It's just different."

Minutes later the two were running through the streets of Boulder. There was a distinctive chill to the air, the start of winter beginning to settle in. The pace was enough to get their heart rates up but not so much that they couldn't continue their conversation.

"I think you should move in with us," Alexander said, his eyes staring at the landscape before them. "Into my house."

Zachary's head snapped toward the man. "Excuse me?"

"Even though you're in training you still need to be close to family and friends. It's not good for you to cut yourself off from people. Dad and Mama Lynn barely hear from you anymore and the only time we talk it's always about your training regime. Your emotional health is as important as your physical health. You sitting around here by yourself all depressed and lonely isn't good. So I think you need to move into my home."

"Who says I'm depressed?"

"You always look depressed."

There was a moment of quiet as Zachary pondered his brother's offer. "I don't want to be a third wheel between you and my girl. That would definitely depress me. Besides, things are good with you two right now. I wouldn't want to mess that up."

"Things are *great* with Sarai and me right now and there's *nothing* you could do to mess that up. But you're my brother and she's your best friend so you wouldn't be a third wheel. It'll be good for all of us and it'll save you some money on that rent you're paying. That place has to be costing you a fortune."

The two men finished another half mile before Zachary answered. "I'll think about it. No promises but I will give it some thought."

"That's not a problem. Whenever you're ready," Alexander replied.

Zachary shot his brother another look. "Thank you," he said, and then he picked up the pace, leaving Alexander close on his heels, trying to keep up.

Sarai marveled at the sensations sweeping through her. Alexander had her feeling some kind of way. No words in any of the languages she spoke could describe the emotions flooding her spirit. As she lay on her stomach, his hands glided lightly over her entire body, a thin layer of lavender-scented massage oil moisturizing her skin.

His first touches were warming as he established a sensuous connection. He gently massaged her head, her neck, her shoulders, back, arms, and legs. His strokes were hard and soft, then fast and slow. He worked each muscle with firm, teasing passes that dissolved every ounce of tension and relaxed her into a gelatinous mess. When he reached her butt cheeks, he massaged each slowly and deeply. He used his forearms against her lower back, her bottom, and down her hamstrings, and then he reversed the process.

He rubbed her feet, kneading the length of her legs up to her inner thighs. She opened her legs further with each long, hard stroke, and he teased her inner groin with his thumbs. He had caressed her entire body from head to foot when he told her to turn over.

As she rolled, a smile pulled full across her face. Her nipples were hard, and her neatly trimmed pubic hair glistened with her wetness. Alexander continued, massaging her face and neck, then focusing his full attention on her breasts. He caressed her nipples, rolling the hardened buds between his thumb and forefinger. Her skin was heated, her pale complexion flush with color. He caressed her rib cage and kneaded her arms, and her hands. His strokes lengthened and slowed as he moved his hands up the insides of her legs to her thighs.

Sarai's parted legs fell open with complete abandon, exposing the folds of her labia. His fingers teased her, his nails lightly grazing the skin until she quivered unabashedly. She opened her eyes as he taunted her private parts, his own soldier at full attention. And then he stroked her clit, tapping gently at the swollen nub. She gasped and moaned loudly as she threw her head back against her shoulders, arching her back off the mattress. She was wet and throbbing, her intimate juices coating his fingers.

Sarai was completely gone when Alexander pushed her legs out, guiding her knees toward her shoulders. Crawling onto the bed, he dropped his mouth to her

most intimate spot and he licked her hard. His tongue
dived deep into the folds, gliding back and forth. His
mouth trailed, slithering across her ass and back. Her
feminine nectar flowed in abundance as she writhed
and twisted, her hands pressing against the back of
his head. As he sucked at her core, her hips began to
buck and she pushed herself against his mouth over
and over again. Sarai suddenly raised her hips high
and froze. Then she collapsed and squeezed her
thighs around his head. Her inner lining contracted
as she came, the hard pulses energized by her deep,
throaty moans. She gushed into his mouth, and he
continued to lap at her greedily until there was nothing left in her inner fountain for him to drink.

Alexander continued to sex her slowly, his touch
possessive. Need and desire fueled their bond as they
made love over and over again. He fell deep and hard
into the intimate connection, and time stood still,
nothing and no one between them. They loved each
other from one side of the bed to the other, their
antics moving over every square inch of the home.
And when they rested in the aftermath, cradled
tightly against each other, neither had any doubts
that the bond between them would last well past their
lifetimes.

Despite their best efforts, Zachary was finding it
difficult to find a level of comfort in his new home.
The decision to move in with his twin and his friend
had come with some reservations, but he'd been
missing them both and was hoping they could all re-
connect on a whole other level.

He could hear them in the kitchen, giggling together. It had been a good long while since he'd seen

Sarai so happy. There was no denying the joy his brother brought to her life, the love they shared irrefutable. Because he loved them both so much, it made his heart sing to see them together. But as he watched them basking in the newness of their relationship, trading easy caresses each and every time they were near each other, he felt an emptiness that was both awkward and debilitating.

Sarai had proclaimed it movie night, and the smell of freshly popped popcorn scented the air. The two had been debating an action film versus a drama, and then they'd called his name, proclaiming that he would have to make the final decision. As he stepped into the kitchen, Sarai stood against his brother, her petite frame lost within his thick arms. Alexander was kissing her passionately, the two so lost in their love for each other that nothing else mattered.

Zachary cleared his throat. "You two really need to get a room."

Alexander broke the kiss and grinned. "That's why I own my own home."

Sarai giggled. "What took you so long? Your brother was just about to make me watch some stupid Jean-Claude Van Damme movie!"

"I like Jean-Claude Van Damme," Zachary said as he leaned across the kitchen counter.

Alexander gave his twin a high five. "Brilliant minds think alike," he said.

She rolled her eyes skyward. "Uh, no! I think we should watch a drama. I vote for *Mystic River* or *Gone Baby Gone*."

"I've never seen that *Gone Baby* one," Zachary said. "I'm game."

Alexander nodded. "Only because I've never seen it either."

Sarai grinned. She passed them each their own bowl of popcorn, lightly salted with nutritional yeast. As she headed for the family room and the big-screen television, Alexander slapped her backside and she laughed. Zachary shook his head.

Hours later as the credits rolled on both movies, the trio were debating performances, the men insisting that Morgan Freeman's role in *Gone Baby Gone* was weak in comparison to Jean-Claude's role in every movie he had ever made.

"You can't compare the two!" Sarai insisted. "That's like comparing an apple with a mango and Morgan is the mango. His performance had more nuance, more definition, richer taste!"

"His performance was boring!" Zachary said, he and his brother slapping palms.

She shook her head. "I'm going to bed. I'm officially done with the both of you tonight."

"I'm right behind you, baby," Alexander said. His voice dropped to a loud whisper. "But I'm not done with you yet!" he said as he winked his eye.

She giggled as she nuzzled her nose into his neck and kissed his cheek.

Zachary interrupted the moment. "Before you go up I need to talk to you both," he said. He shifted forward in his seat, folding his hands together in front of him. Alexander pulled Sarai down onto his lap, the two staring at him curiously.

"Are you okay?" Alexander asked.

His brother forced a smile to his face, his head bobbing up and down. "I'm great. I've just made a decision that I need to share with you two."

"What's wrong?" Sarai questioned, her expression shifting into worry. "I know you and there's something wrong."

He smiled. "There's nothing wrong. I . . . well . . ." He took a deep breath and blew it out slowly. "I've decided to go back to Thailand. I'm only six weeks away from fight night and I think I should take these last six weeks back to my own gym." He tilted his head slightly, staring directly at his brother.

"You've been amazing. I have never been in better shape and I owe that to you. But you know how I need to do. It's time I stopped training with all the convenient photo ops at your gym that my sponsors love and go get down and dirty in the jungle where there are no distractions."

Sarai clutched Alexander's arm. "You're leaving?"

Her friend nodded. "I am. And I know you'll be in good hands. But it's not like I'll be gone forever. I'll be back."

"When are you going?" she asked, her soft voice quivering as she struggled not to break out into tears.

He gave her a bright smile. "Next week. I fly out next Tuesday."

The silence that suddenly filled the air was uncomfortable. Zachary's gaze shifted back and forth between them. Sarai swiped at her eyes, brushing away the mist of tears that threatened to spill over her cheeks. Alexander sat, staring down to the floor, consumed by emotion that he hadn't expected. He briefly reflected on his brother's decision and both their reactions to the news. "No," he said suddenly, lifting his eyes to stare at his twin.

"No?"

"I said no. You're not running."

Zachary shook his head. "That's not what I'm doing. I just think . . ."

Alexander interrupted him, his voice suddenly raised. "That's exactly what you're doing." He pushed

Sarai off his lap, gently shoving her to the sofa. He stood up, the gesture abrupt. "If you want to go to Thailand I can't stop you. But if that's what you want, then we're going with you."

"Excuse me?"

"Sarai and I are going with you. She's missing her father. I would like to see where you've spent half your life, and when you step into the ring to defend your title I plan to be right there by your side supporting you. Look." He moved to his brother's side, his hands extended to punctuate the point he was trying to make. "We've lost too much time already. Don't think that I don't see that things are getting harder for you, because I do. You never did well with change, and now, suddenly everything that made you comfortable is changing.

"When your wife left, Sarai was there to help you get through it. She kept things moving so it didn't feel hard. Now she's moving on and you're uncomfortable with that because you don't want anything to be different. But rather than face it, instead of embracing what the future might bring, you'd rather disappear. That's how you've always operated but not this time."

"So you plan to just pack up and leave your business for the next six weeks? What's going to happen with Champs?"

"It's going to run like the well-oiled machine that it is. I don't need to do any hand-holding at my gym. I've put together a stellar team that will keep it up and running. And with technology, I'll be updated on a regular basis. So don't you worry about my business! Be concerned about our relationship. That's more important to me and it should be important to you, too."

"Our relationship is fine. We're good, right?"

Alexander blew a heavy sigh as he shook his index finger in his brother's face. "You don't get to leave me again. You don't. You came back here and begged me to help you. You made me love you again and I refuse to miss you. I will not worry about what's happening to you or be scared that I'm not going to see my twin brother ever again. So no . . . *hell no* . . . you don't get to just pick up and leave and go live your life without me. *No!*"

Hours later the couple lay side by side, both lost in thought. Sarai was curled up against him, her bare breasts pressed tight against his broad back. Her arms were wrapped around his torso, her fingers resting against the hard lines of his abdomen. His buttocks were cradled in the warm pocket of her crotch and both marveled at how perfectly they fit against each other, like two pieces to a puzzle. Their breathing had synced, both inhaling and exhaling on the same beat, and there was no missing the easy rhythm that balanced one with the other.

Sarai pressed a damp kiss against the curve of his shoulder, the length of her hair brushing against his arm. "Why aren't you asleep?" she asked, her voice soft.

Alexander took a deep breath in, filling his lungs with the room's cool air. "I was just thinking that I probably should have asked you if you wanted to go to Thailand with Zachary. Just because I feel like I need to go doesn't necessarily mean you do."

Sarai laughed, the warmth of it filling the slight space between them. "Yes, you probably should have."

Alexander rolled his body toward her until they

were facing each other. The dim light in the room illuminated her face, the effect giving her an angelic aura. Her eyes were bright as they danced with his.

"So you don't want to go home to Thailand?"

She smiled. "I didn't say that. I miss my home and my father. I would love to go back. And I agree that we should support your brother. But it would have been nice if it had been a conversation between the two of us."

Alexander nodded. "I get it. We should have discussed it before I committed us."

Sarai trailed her finger across his cheek. "It's important to me that you see me as your partner. I want us to work together, to be equals, but ultimately I will follow you wherever you want us to go. I am . . . how they say . . . ride or die? I will be that woman for you."

He smiled, a low chuckle rumbling from somewhere deep in his chest. He could only nod his head, words to express what he was feeling caught deep in his heart. Time stood still as they eyed each other. There was an unspoken bond that existed between them, the intensity of their connection so powerful that it felt as if it had taken on a life of its own.

He wrapped his arms around her and pulled her close as he pressed his lips to her forehead and kissed her gently. His warm breath blew gently against her ear. "I love you, Sarai. I love you with everything in me. I want you to trust that and to trust me, even if I do get it wrong sometimes." He kissed her again, his lips moving to hers as he captured her mouth beneath his own.

Soon they were an entanglement of tongues, hands dancing over each other, skin heated from the intensity of their connection. When that connection was lost, Sarai pulling from him, the infraction felt voluminous. She felt tears burning hot behind her eyelids, her thick lashes stopping them from flowing over her cheeks. Her gaze was misted with joy and delight as she looked into his eyes, falling headfirst into the promises that gleamed from his intense stare.

"I love you, too, Alexander," she whispered. "I love you too. And then she kissed him again, both dropping into the wealth of emotion that embraced them.

Mama Lynn stood at her bedroom window, staring out at the yard. It had begun to snow, the first sign of a harsh winter coming down fast and furious. The gust of warm air she blew past her full lips billowed into a thick cloud of energy. She turned to stare at her husband as he called her name.

"What's bothering you, woman?" Westley questioned. He sat upright in their bed, pulling off his reading glasses as he dropped the book he was reading onto his lap. "Why are you over there looking like you lost your best friend?"

"I told you that girl was going to come between our boys. I told you. Now Zachary is leaving. We just get our family back together and now he's headed back to Thailand. You and I both know it's because of Alexander and that girl. She done gone from one to the other like she's changing her drawers. It just ain't right!"

Westley shook his head. Mama Lynn had been on a rant since Zachary had stopped by to share the news that he was leaving Boulder to return to his gym in Thailand. In Westley's mind, Sarai's role in their son's decision had never entered his thoughts. But maybe his wife was right. As he pondered the possibility, he just didn't agree. Despite the thought, he didn't bother to share his opinion with his wife.

"You can't blame Sarai for what those boys do. You can't. She loves Alexander and . . ."

"She loves Zachary too. She even said so!" Mama Lynn shouted her frustration.

Westley shouted back. "She and Zachary are friends. She and Alexander are much more than that and you know it!"

"It's a mess! That's what I know. I see how Zachary looks at her."

"Zachary is still feeling himself over his divorce. He hasn't rebounded yet and once this fight is over and he's out of training mode he can start dating again. Once he starts meeting new women and putting himself out there things will be back to normal."

"So you think it's okay for him to go?"

Westley gestured for her to come sit down beside him. She crossed the room and climbed onto the bed, leaning her thick body against his side. As she did, he wrapped his arms around her shoulders. "I think that Zachary and Alexander both have to do what makes them happy. What I also know is that our sons will work things out. They have a bond that no one will ever understand and I don't think either one of them will ever let anyone else come between them again. Not even that girl. They made that mistake once and once was all it took. That lesson has been learned."

She shook her head. "Have you spoken to Alexander? Maybe he can talk to his brother."

Westley sighed. "I'll call him tomorrow. I know Zachary was going to talk to him tonight. I'll see what he thinks and we can take it from there. Until then, you need to stop worrying."

Lynn nodded her head as she leaned against her husband's chest. Westley planted a wet kiss against the top of her head. Together they stared out at the snow falling outside, both wishing a silent prayer that God would direct all of their steps in the right direction.

Chapter Twelve

As the flight attendant prepared them for landing, a wave of anxiety blew through Alexander's gut. For a quick second he feared losing his lunch, and then just like that all was well again. Beside him, Sarai was jubilant. She looked eagerly out the plane's window as their descent brought them closer to land.

Zachary eyed them both with amusement as he fixed his reclined seat upright. There was an air of contentment that flooded his spirit, and no need to tell anyone how overjoyed he was to be back in Thailand. It was written all over his face.

As Sarai stared out to the landscape below, she was in awe of her homeland. She loved everything about the region, and over the years had met people from all walks of life who came to experience the lush jungles, amazing beaches, and world-class diving. Because Thailand was known to be an inexpensive vacation spot, tourists came in droves.

"Is my father coming to the airport?" she asked, leaning forward to look across the aisle at Zachary. "Did you talk to him?"

He nodded his head. "I think so. As long as there's

nothing going on at the gym, he'll be there to pick us up. Otherwise he'll send one of the guys and we'll see him when we get there."

She nodded as she reached for Alexander's hand and turned to stare back out the window. The two men exchanged a look, but neither had anything to say.

Alexander sensed that Sarai was concerned about coming home. Worried how her father was going to react to their relationship. He had tried to discuss it with her as they'd packed for the trip, but she'd brushed it off. Zachary had told him to be concerned.

"It's a cultural thing," his brother had said. "And he's very protective of her."

"But he let her leave and come to the United States with you. *And* he let you send her away to go to school."

"He trusted me but that didn't happen overnight. He knew I wasn't going to let anything happen to her. He doesn't know you."

Alexander had nodded. "It'll be fine. He's going to love me!"

And he wanted to believe that. He hoped that he would prove himself worthy and that Sarai's father would soon trust him as much as the patriarch seemed to trust his brother.

It felt like they'd been flying since forever, the journey taking them from Denver to Tokyo to Shanghai. Two days of travel finally had them landing in Phuket, the largest island and province in Thailand. The newly renovated airport was large, but Sarai and Zachary easily navigated them through the extended lines in immigration to the carousels at luggage pickup. The lines had been lengthy, but the airport staff had been efficient and friendly. Outside, the air was warm and humid, the tropical climate feeling like

a vacation dream come true. The sky was a brilliant
shade of blue, the surrounding waters a calming
turquoise, and there was a gentle breeze blowing lazily
about. Standing under the midmorning sun, Alexander could easily understand the island's attraction.

Sarai suddenly jumped up and down excitedly.
There was no missing the familial resemblance between
her and the older man moving in their direction. Sarai's
father, Gamon Montri, had contributed significantly
to his daughter's DNA. Despite his age, he was still a
very good-looking man, distinguished with a conservative flair. He was dressed in a collarless shirt, linen
slacks, and brown leather sandals. His dark hair was
peppered with gray, and his skin was weathered from
the sun. He wore wire-rimmed glasses, and his mouth
was turned down in a slight frown. The only hint of
excitement in his expression was the light that shimmered in his dark eyes.

Rushing to meet the man, Sarai threw her arms
around her father's neck. She hugged him tightly,
joyous tears spilling past her lashes. "Hello, father!"
she said, speaking in their native Thai.

The old man hugged her back, his own gaze misting
with tears. "Welcome home, daughter," he responded.

Alexander and Zachary both stood back as they
allowed the family their moment. Gamon kissed his
daughter's cheek before letting her go. He extended
his hand in Zachary's direction, pumping his arm up
and down.

"It's good to see you again, Gamon," Zachary said
in Thai, surprising Alexander with his proficiency with
the language.

"Welcome home, sir!"

Zachary gestured toward his twin. "This is my brother,

Alexander Barrett. Alexander, this is Sarai's father, Gamon Montri."

There was a moment of hesitation as the patriarch stood staring at him. Something in his expression put Alexander on guard and he felt himself tense. Gamon tilted his head in a slight nod as he shook Alexander's outstretched hand. His eyes were narrowed, his stare cold, and there was nothing welcoming in his stance.

"It's a pleasure to meet you, Mr. Montri," Alexander said.

The man responded in perfect English. "The pleasure is mine, sir. Welcome to Thailand." The comment was polite but not necessarily truthful.

Not seeming to notice, Zachary gave the patriarch an endearing slap on the back. "How are things going here, Gamon? Is everything still standing?"

"Yes, sir! All is good. Business is good. Everyone is working hard!"

"That's what I wanted to hear."

The ride through Phuket Town was sensory overload at its very best. As Gamon drove, Sarai and Zachary pointed out landmarks and sites, giving Alexander a mini tour of the tropical location. The journey was a plethora of sights and sounds interspersed with animated conversation between them and Gamon. It quickly became apparent to Alexander that the language barrier would sometimes be to his disadvantage. More than once he sensed them talking about him, the older man shooting him strange looks.

Reading his mind, Sarai gave him a warm smile as she gently brushed her hand against his before snatching it back into her lap. He wanted to reach out to hold her, but there was something in her demeanor that held him at bay. He sensed that she was uncomfortable with any public display of affection with her father looking on. He didn't like it, but he would respect it.

Gamon turned onto a gravel road lined with lush foliage. Coconut palms and banana trees were abundant, the thick, verdant vegetation looking like a postcard pictorial. About a mile in, the road opened onto a clearing, and Revolution, Zachary's MMA training camp, came into view. With a reputation for being a premier destination for Muay Thai, MMA, and fitness training, the facility had been featured in many a documentary and travel show, but nothing had prepared Alexander for the extraordinary facility that had been his brother's dream come true.

On the left side of the property was an extensive open-air gym. The space hosted multiple fight rings and was equipped with training bags, free weights, isolation machines, and other assorted gym equipment. The entire area was covered with a high thatched roof that allowed the breezes to flow through from the beach area that bordered the property.

On the right side of the property was a fully equipped indoor gym, rooms for dance and yoga training, and an on-site cafeteria. The back part of the property featured Zachary's private residence and thirteen additional bungalows to accommodate paying guests. Dozens of people were working out, a team of well-trained, hardworking trainers putting them through their paces.

It didn't begin to compare to the place Sarai and his brother had described. Alexander was impressed beyond measure, and he said so. "Wow!" he exclaimed. "This is really something!"

Zachary grinned. "Thanks. It's still a work in progress but I'm proud of it."

His brother nodded. "You should be."

For the next few hours, Zachary gave him an in-depth tour of the facility, introducing him to his friends and staff. When the names and faces had become a muddled mess in his head, Alexander feigned a headache, needing a reason to retire from the chatter and excitement of the athletic champ returning home.

Sarai and her father had disappeared, leaving the two men to themselves. Her departure had been swift, a quick wave of her hand before she'd disappeared out the door. He still wasn't sure what to read into the distance that had suddenly sprung up between them, but he didn't like anything about it. Not one thing. Clearly something wasn't kosher, but he wouldn't know what until he and Sarai could have a moment alone to talk.

His brother's cottage was the last stop on the tour. As they entered the comfortable space, he saw that his luggage sat in the center of the room.

"You can have the back bedroom," Zachary said. "I'd give you one of the cottages but they're all rented out."

"Where's Sarai staying?" Alexander asked.

Zachary tossed him a look. "With her father. Their home is south of us in the township of Rawai."

For a brief second the two men stood staring at each other. Zachary suddenly laughed, his head waving from side to side. "What? Did you think you two were going to be able to cozy up with each other in some love shack or something?"

"That did cross my mind."

Zachary was still shaking his head. "Welcome to Thailand. Now let me school you. What you and Sarai could do and get away with in Boulder can't be done here in Phuket. Not if she's going to save face and honor her father. She's a 'good' girl and here in Thailand 'good' girls don't fool around with or get involved with *farangs*."

"What the hell is a *farang*?"

"It's the Thai word for Europeans, or non-Thai men. It's mostly used to describe white guys. Since we're black, you and I are actually *farang dam*."

Alexander stared at his twin for a moment. "Well, damn!" he said, suddenly laughing.

Laughing with him, Zachary shrugged. "*Farang* is also the word for guava fruit. Go figure!"

He continued. "Now, the Thai women you do see being touchy-feely are usually prostitutes and you'll have to pay for the privilege. And of course there are always a few European women visiting who are always looking for a fling while they're here on holiday.

"Now, Sarai has done a fair amount of traveling so she doesn't necessarily subscribe to the traditional roles that are ingrained in the culture but she would never disrespect or dishonor her father, whether she agrees with his views or not. There is a strict moral code here. Sex before marriage is a no-no and if a 'good' girl has sex with you then she's saying she expects to be your last sexual conquest and you'll be marrying her. Usually by then she's introduced you to her family and wedding preparations are already under way."

"I do plan to marry her. I love her and she knows it," Alexander said emphatically. "That's one of the reasons I made this trip, to get her father's blessing."

"Hey, you don't need to tell me. I know how you

feel about Sarai and I know that she loves you too! I'm sure she'll sneak over to spend some quality time with you when she can. Just be mindful of what you say or do with her in public and watch the off-color jokes around Thai women. That's not acceptable either. I learned that one the hard way!"

Alexander took it all in. He looked perplexed, confusion washing over his expression. "So what do I need to do for her father to accept me? Because I'm not losing her."

"Follow her lead. When she feels it's appropriate she'll take you to her father and announce your intentions. When that happens you'll need to be ready to negotiate her bride price."

"Bride price?"

Zachary laughed. "They do that dowry thing over here, man! It's called a *sin sod*. You have to pay Pop off for having raised her well. It also shows that you can take care of her financially. And since Sarai's college educated you're going to have to pay a pretty price so don't go low-balling the old guy!"

Alexander sighed, a full grin pulling at his lips. "Can you at least drink here? Because I need one!"

Zachary pointed him toward the refrigerator. "I keep it loaded with beer for when I'm in the pool."

"You have a pool?"

His twin grinned. "Hell, yeah!"

The soaking pool was a ceramic work of art, the hand-painted tiles depicting everything that was important to Zachary. It sat off the edge of the home's patio in a private courtyard, surrounded by lush vegetation and tall trees. The water was soft and buoyant and heated to a warm hundred and two degrees.

The two brothers sat in deep conversation, both savoring bottles of Singha beer as they relaxed beneath the wet blanket that flowed around them. Dusk had turned to dark, the space lit by the bright underwater pool lights and flickering strings of miniature bulbs strung through the trees.

It had been a long day for them both, and the casual moment was much needed. Both men were enjoying their time together, reveling in the level of comfort and balance that now marked their relationship. They had promised each other that after a good night's sleep, Zachary would go back to training and Alexander would resume pushing him to work harder.

Both jumped when Sarai's sweet voice sounded unexpectedly from the sliding doors behind them. "Hi," she said as she slightly waved a hand in their direction. "I knocked but you didn't hear me."

Alexander leapt from the pool. He reached for a towel resting on a lawn chair, swiping at the moisture that dampened his skin. He practically raced to her side. "You left me," he said as he leaned to kiss her mouth. The embrace was deep and passionate as their lips moved in perfect sync.

Pulling herself from him, Sarai took a deep inhale of air; then she stepped back, putting distance between them. She stole a quick glance over her shoulder, anxiety washing over her expression.

Zachary had jumped with his brother, following close on the man's heels. "Where's your father?" he asked her as he wrapped an oversized beach towel around his waist.

She gestured toward the front of the home. "Prasong stopped to ask him something about the class schedules. I think he walked back down to the office but I know he won't be long."

Zachary nodded. "I'll go run interference," he said, giving the duo a wink of his eye. "You two do what you do but make it quick. Gamon's not going to be mad at me because you can't keep your hands off each other!"

Sarai smiled and blew him a kiss. "Thank you," she mouthed as she stepped back into Alexander's arms. She kissed him again, blowing a soft sigh over his lips.

"I missed you," he said, when they finally came up for another breath of air.

"I missed you more. And I'm so sorry. My father has gone into overprotective mode!"

"It's okay. I get it. At least I did once my brother explained it to me."

"It's just our way here." She tightened the hold she had around his waist, her hands clasped together against the small of his back.

He chuckled softly. "You could have warned a brother!"

Sarai laughed with him. "I'm sorry. I should have, but I'm so used to how it is here that I never really thought about it. But I'm sure you will be able to handle whatever is thrown at you."

"So, when are we going to tell your father that we're getting married?" Alexander questioned.

Sarai met the look he was giving her with one of her own. "Married?"

He nodded. "This isn't how I imagined proposing to you but since things are done a little differently here, I just needed to put it out there so that we don't have any misunderstandings."

Her eyes shifted back and forth as she reflected on his comment. "We've never talked about marriage," she said. "I wasn't sure that was something you wanted with me."

He chuckled softly. "I love you, Sarai. Of course I would want that with you. I don't want it with anyone else."

Sarai fell into Alexander's deep stare. His eyes were cool, his blue stare consuming. She pressed her mouth to his a second time, savoring the sweetness of his touch. Before she could respond further, there was a rustle of noise in the house, Zachary calling his brother's name.

They both took a step back from each other, hands dropping to their sides just seconds before Zachary and Gamon stepped through the door. Alexander turned, noting the look her father shot in his direction.

"What's up?" Alexander answered, shifting his eyes toward his twin.

Zachary winked. "I was just telling Gamon about your gym and the technology system you have in place to track everything. We're constantly having issues with the schedules around here. I think we might want to give it a try."

"I actually have the program on my laptop. If I can get Wi-Fi here I'd be delighted to show it to you."

Gamon gave Alexander a quick nod as he crossed his arms over his chest. He shot his daughter a look, saying something in Thai that Alexander didn't understand. Zachary laughed out loud, and Sarai blushed profusely, her face turning a deep shade of crimson. Alexander looked from one to the other. "What?"

"My father fancies himself to be somewhat of a comedian," she said, her eyes rolling skyward.

Gamon's expression was blank as he repeated what he'd said in English. "You don't look smart enough to know technology. Your head is shaped like that basketball you play games with."

Zachary laughed again, the chortle rising from deep in his midsection.

Sarai's eyes widened. "Father!"

"Do not 'father' me! This one might look like his brother, all brawn and no brains, but he is definitely *his* father's son!" There was a hint of hostility in the man's tone despite his efforts to make a joke out of the exchange.

Zachary tried to lighten the moment by laughing it off. "Brawn and no brain!"

Alexander shook his head. "I think he was talking about you too, Z!"

Zachary pounded a fist to his chest as he caught his breath. He said something in Thai, and Gamon nodded.

He shot his brother a look. "I told him not to worry. That you are very smart. That you're going to surprise him." As he eased past his brother's side, still chuckling over the amusement, his voice dropped to a low whisper. "And, boy, is he in for a surprise!"

Chapter Thirteen

Alexander was weaving and bobbing inside a fight ring as one of Revolution's best trainers schooled him on Muay Thai, or Thai boxing. The national sport of Thailand, Muay Thai is a form of close combat where the entire body is used as a weapon. It was only one of the martial arts techniques his brother employed when fighting. Zachary was also proficient in Korean hapkido, Brazilian jiu-jitsu, and karate. Alexander caught himself trying to keep pace with his twin as he improved his own proficiency in the martial arts.

Since arriving in Thailand, Zachary and Sarai had fallen easily back into their respective routines. Alexander had spent the first part of the week working with his brother's team to continue his preparation for his big match. In Boulder, Zachary had strengthened his endurance and brushed up on his boxing skills. He'd also regained the discipline he needed to keep him on top of his game. The trainers at Revolution were now fine-tuning his brother's skills, ensuring that he only brought his very best to the title championship. With much help from friends and family, the man was now in full-scale athlete mode.

Sarai was somewhat of a cause célèbre in her own right. The former Miss Thailand had quite a following of fans and admirers throughout Phuket. She was also a renowned asset to his brother's business, her opinion highly regarded by all the staff. She picked up where she'd left off, managing the facility without skipping a beat. Alexander was duly impressed.

Despite their best efforts, there was no alone time that didn't come without some challenges. Gamon watched his daughter like a hawk, and Alexander marveled at how he was able to perform his own duties and know where she was every minute. Unlike the facility at Champs, Revolution had no nooks and crannies where they could step out of sight to steal a kiss and a tickle. Revolution was wide open and totally exposed. Everyone saw what everyone else was doing, and there were few secrets that could be hidden. Despite his best efforts to relax into that, Alexander found it difficult to have Sarai so close and not be able to love on her the way he wanted. Having to temper the emotion he felt for her was proving to be more of a challenge than he had bargained for.

His opponent suddenly swept his legs from beneath him, and he landed hard on the padded floor. The landing snatched him from the reverie he'd been lost in, knocking the air from his lungs. His body hit the floor with a gut-wrenching grunt that echoed around the open-air arena. Everyone turned to stare as he rolled onto his back, sprawled flat, his legs and arms extended. He heaved air, sucking in oxygen as he struggled to catch his breath. When he finally had his breathing under control, he opened his eyes to find Sarai and his brother staring down at him. His brother was grinning with amusement. Sarai's smile widened with relief.

"That really looked like it hurt," the beautiful woman said, her eyes dancing with his.

He smiled up at her. "It didn't feel good."

Zachary laughed. "When you get it right that's how it's supposed to work for the other guy!" He extended a hand to help him to his feet.

"I think that means I've got a little more work to do." Alexander brushed the dust from his knees and chest. "And you really like doing this for a living?"

"Best thing they ever invented," Zachary answered, still grinning. "It should be a sin and a crime to make a living kicking ass and taking names!"

Alexander shook his head, still trying to dislodge the clouds from between his ears. "I think you like this a touch too much."

Sarai giggled as she pressed a small palm to his broad back. "Why don't I walk you over to the medical room and have the doctor take a look at you." Her brow was raised as she eyed him. "Just to make sure you didn't get a concussion or something."

Zachary laughed. "Yeah, why don't you two go do that? I need to talk to Gamon and I think he's checking new students into the residences."

"Make sure he collects all the paperwork and that he waits for it to be filled out. He doesn't like to wait." Sarai's bright smile radiated as she seemed to have a silent conversation with her friend.

As she and Alexander headed to the other side of the courtyard, Zachary gave them a wink of his eye and then he broke into a full gallop, running in the opposite direction.

Inside the gym facility, she led Alexander down a corridor, past the administrative offices, to the end of the building. She knocked on the door to the medical room, and when no one answered she used her key to unlock it. They stepped inside, and with a quick glance behind them, she closed and locked the entrance.

Before she could blink, Alexander swept her into his arms and captured her mouth with his own. He folded his body around hers as he kissed her, the embrace possessive and protective. His heart suddenly ached, emotion flooding his spirit. Sarai was feeling it as well as she began to shake, tears pressing hot against her thick lashes.

Their kisses were fervent and eager, and if anyone had walked in neither could have stopped. Neither would have been able to let go, the intensity of the feelings sweeping between them like a floodgate gone awry.

"God, I've missed you," Alexander finally muttered, his face pressed into her hair as he inhaled the scent of her floral shampoo.

She nodded. "I'm so sorry! I didn't think it would be like this. I just . . . I . . . I don't know what to say."

He brushed a lock of hair from her face, easing it out of her eyes. His fingers lightly swept the length of her face. "Say you're ready to tell your father."

"I am ready," she said softly. "I just don't know if he is." Sarai pulled herself from Alexander's arms and took a step back. "I'm scared he won't accept you. It would break my heart if he does not give us his blessing."

Alexander paused for a moment to think about the culture and the people he'd experienced since his arrival. Thais were very class conscious, and wealth and status were important to them. He had quickly discovered that he and his brother were an anomaly of sorts. Thais loved Americans, and they were fascinated with black Americans, not often seeing them visit the tropical paradise. What little racism he'd witnessed had been shown toward other Thais with darker skin tones, who were seen as being lower on the social ladder. Dark skin suggested that you were a laborer or perhaps a farmer who worked outside. Lighter skin tones were viewed as signs that you worked inside and were better educated. Skin whitening and lightening products were big business in Thailand.

He'd met a few Thais who'd commented openly about his skin color, but it had never been offensive, just the Thai way of political incorrectness. It would have been seen as rude elsewhere, but in Thailand it was more of a childlike attitude toward things. They made casual conversation about color, weight, and things Westerners would have been offended by. But Alexander still had to ask the question.

"Because I'm black?"

She shook her head. "Because you're *not* Thai."

Alexander took a deep inhale of air, holding the warm breath deep in his lungs. When he finally released the breath he'd been holding, it felt like a lifetime had passed between them. He shook his head. "What do you want to do, Sarai?"

She closed her eyes and took her own breath. "I just need a little more time. He's getting to know you and he likes you and I think . . ."

Alexander shook his head as he stalled her comment. He held a hand up, and frustration furrowed his brow. "This isn't going to work for me. I understand it's a cultural issue but we're adults. I love you, Sarai! Hiding how I feel about you feels foreign to me. It's not who I am. I didn't even do this mess in grade school and I dated some girls I didn't want anyone to know about! So if we have a relationship, then we're going to have a relationship no matter where we are in the world. Or we're not going to have a relationship at all."

Sarai moved against him, pressing her body back against his. Her tears finally fell, raining over the round of her cheeks. "Alex, I love you, too. I love you more than you will ever know. But he's my father and I need him to love you and me together if we're going to have any kind of future."

The silence between them grew full and thick. Alexander wrapped his arms around her shoulders and pulled her close, his hands sweeping up and down the length of her back. He pressed a gentle kiss to the top of her head. When he met her somber gaze, a wave of resolve settled over his spirit.

"If I were Thai and we were interested in each other, what would be our courting ritual? How do you all date over here?"

She smiled. "Our first date would be a group affair. I'd invite friends or maybe someone in my family to join us. We'd go to dinner, nothing overly expensive but nice. It would almost be like an interview so they could check you out. They'd ask a lot of questions and you would let them."

Alexander nodded. "So I have to have their approval to date you?"

"They need to like you, yes."

"And our dates after that? Once I've been approved? Will we still need a chaperone?"

Sarai smiled. "No. We can go out alone after that."

"And then?"

"And then I will tell my father that you are the man I want to spend the rest of my life with. I will tell him that I love you and I will get his approval."

"And then we'll be engaged?"

She laughed. "Then you'll have to go ask my father

for his permission. Here, that's called *pamanhikan*. But first you'll have to go buy me a necklace. Something really nice. It's called the *thong mun*, or engagement gold."

"Really nice like just gold nice or really nice like gold and diamonds nice?"

"Definitely gold. Diamonds are optional. You'll know it when you see it. When you come to our home you should bring a well-respected friend with you, preferably Thai, who can tell him about your good character. You should also bring pictures of your family, your house, whatever will show him what your life is like back in the States. After that you'll propose with the necklace and you'll tell my father how much you love me and why you want to be with me."

"So here you get engaged with a necklace and not a ring?"

"Yes. Then I'll give the necklace to my father and he or one of my aunts will go have it blessed by a monk. If my mother were alive she would do it. When he gives it back to me then we'll be officially engaged."

"And do we have to jump through more hoops after that or is the engagement going to be some long drawn-out affair?"

She shook her head, amused by the humor in his tone. "No. At that point we can actually live together if we want to. For the ceremony we'll just set a date with the monk and it will be official."

"Sounds like I'm going to have to go through some things."

She leaned into his chest, tightening her arms around his waist. "I promise you, I'll be worth all the effort. I will be the best wife ever!"

Alexander leaned to kiss her one last time. "Woman, you sure as hell better be!"

* * *

The soaking pool had become Alexander's favorite place to unwind. The warm waters were a soothing diversion from everything that was going on around him—and some things that weren't. For a brief moment he thought about Sarai and the courtship rituals that had suddenly become so important to her. It would probably have been too much for some men to handle. Alexander couldn't help think that with any other woman it might have been too much for him as well.

After their last conversation, she'd gone in one direction and he'd gone in the other. He was missing her, and to see her moving about the property but not be able to touch her had him feeling some kind of way. To blow off the frustration he'd been feeling, he'd gone back into the ring, testing the limits of his abilities against a trainer named Kwang. Kwang had worked him until every muscle felt like it had been shredded. Now his body hurt much more than his heart did. And the pool was the best relief.

His attention was suddenly drawn to the conversation his brother was having with two of his closest friends, an expat from Australia named Patrick, and Robert, a Thai boxer with thirty-plus years of experience. Robert was one of Revolution's head instructors, Patrick one of their best customers.

"You'd better leave that woman alone," Zachary was saying. He took a sip from the bottle of springwater he was holding. "She's just about the money. *Your* money."

Robert shook his head. "You should have said no when she asked you to fix the roof on her father's house. Now the whole family will try to bleed you dry!"

Zachary laughed with his friend. "The next time

she calls you need to tell her that all you have is dick and bubblegum and you're fresh out of bubblegum!"

Patrick swiped at his eyes, his laughter abundant. He shook his head. "Why do I always pick the wrong ones?"

Zachary laughed. "Because you keep going after the ones in the go-go clubs."

Alexander narrowed his gaze. "Go-go clubs?"

His brother nodded. "Thai titty bars. Their version of strip clubs."

"Except the girls don't strip," Patrick interjected. "They just dance."

"Badly!" Zachary added. "It's no Magic City!" he said, referring to the infamous Atlanta adult entertainment club the twins had visited for their twenty-first birthday years earlier. "But it passes the time."

"What about Miss Thailand?" Patrick suddenly questioned. "Is she dating anyone?"

"Yes, she is," Alexander interjected. He shifted forward in the warm water, turning his body in a defensive stance.

Zachary's friend shot him a look. He held up his hands. "I was just asking!"

Zachary laughed as he turned his attention toward his brother. "I hear you two are going on a date this week."

The twins exchanged glances. Alexander nodded. "I'm taking her and her cousin to dinner. On our *first* date," he said sarcastically.

"Thank goodness the girls in Bangkok are finally starting to let some of those old traditions go. I've dated a few girls there that will actually go on a first date without bringing half the family," Patrick said matter-of-factly.

"With all the beautiful women in Australia, why do you keep chasing after Thai women?" Zachary asked.

Patrick winked an eye as he swallowed the last of his beer. "I love Thai women when I'm here in Thailand! And when I'm in Morocco I love Moroccan women. Same thing goes for England and the Caribbean. I just love their women when I'm in their country!"

Robert chuckled. "Me love women, too! Love them much when my wife not home!"

Alexander shook his head as the trio broke out into raucous laughter. Hanging with the boys was a good time that took his mind off everything else. It was a roulette of beer-fueled lies about women they would never have, places they would never go, and jobs they would never work.

Twice more Patrick spoke Sarai's name, and twice Alexander was a hair shy of exposing his hand, and hers. He struggled more than once not to bust the man in his face. He was in no mood to hear any other man speak his woman's name. When Zachary put his hulking frame between them, he blew a heavy sigh, realizing that he'd probably had one beer too many. The conversation continued until his brother's alarm signaled that it was his bedtime.

The next time Alexander focused his attention on his surroundings, Patrick and Robert were gone and Zachary was pulling on his arm.

"Time for bed, A!"

"I'm sad," he said, his words slurred.

Zachary chuckled. "I know. It'll be all right."

"Sarai and I are going on a date with her cousin! You should come date us, too!"

His brother's laugh was warm and endearing. "Not this time."

"Next time. We'll invite everyone to go on a date with us. Make it a block party!"

"You're drunk!"

"Am not!"

Zachary laughed again. "Come on. It's time for both of us to hit the sack."

He pulled Alexander up, practically dragging him to one of the reclined beach chairs. Alexander sat for a moment, and when he'd regained some semblance of balance, Zachary guided him to his bed, pushing him down atop the mattress.

"Where's Sarai?" Alexander asked, trying to focus his eyes to look around the space.

"She's in your dreams, A! In your dreams."

"Then that's where I'll be," Alexander stated. And with that he was out like a light, chasing after Sarai in his sleep.

His head hurt. Alexander sat upright by the side of the pool, sucking in one deep breath after another. He hung his head in his hands, hoping to keep the throbbing that pulsed behind his brow at bay. The early morning air held just enough of a breeze to belie the rising heat that would soon consume the space, and the cool air felt like bliss against his skin.

Alexander wasn't a drinker, so the hangover he was feeling surprised him. He hadn't remembered drinking that much, and he only remembered drinking beer. The mystery was solved when Zachary suddenly stepped through the sliding glass doors, two mugs of coffee in hand.

"Good morning," his brother chimed.

Alexander winced, his twin's cheery tone too loud for the early morning hour.

"Drink this," Zachary said as he passed his twin a cup of the dark brew. "It'll have you feeling better in no time."

"What happened last night?"

"You were putting them away like water! I've never known you to drink so much."

Alexander sighed, the heavy exhale verbalizing the emotion that suddenly flooded his spirit. "Man, Sarai has me all twisted! I can't even think straight anymore."

Zachary laughed as he took the seat beside his brother. "Trust me, she's just as off sides as you are."

"Yeah? Then why is she doing this song and dance like we haven't been together for the last few months?"

"It's a cultural thing, brother. I tried to warn you."

"Did I tell you we're going on a *first* date? Is that some crazy mess or what?"

"Yeah, you told me," Zachary answered with a deep chuckle. "You had a lot to say about dating her and her cousin! And most of it wasn't about how happy you were!"

Alexander took another sip of his drink. "I like Thailand," he said, "but I am so ready to take Sarai and go back to Colorado."

"Hey, a few more weeks and you two will be married and it'll all be good."

Alexander cut his eye in his brother's direction. "What about you, Z? After the fight are you planning to stay here in Phuket or are you coming back home?"

"Phuket is my home. I love it here."

"Why? All your family's in Colorado."

"I know but it's about more than that. There's something about this place that fuels my spirit. I really like that here in Thailand, no matter where you are, even in the most modern places, their culture is still prominent. That ancient village that their ancestors built remains steadfast in everything they do. They still hold their king with the utmost respect. Tradition is important to them, and here, I sometimes feel as if I've been transported back to a time where I belong. I *really* like that, A.

"When I opened Revolution, Gamon had an astrologer calculate which day would be the most promising for success. Then the Buddhist monks were invited to come on that specific date to perform a blessing ceremony. It was amazing! Afterward we had a feast for the monks. I would have never imagined it but I stand on ceremony. I believe in the merits of ritual. I really love the divine order of things."

Zachary took a deep breath before he continued. "It's for that very reason that you've been so willing to go along with Sarai. Because the tradition of courtship that Thai families follow is important to her, it has become important to you. The hoops she's having you jump through mean something, A! Back in Boulder the only thing our family holds sacred is Mama Lynn's macaroni and cheese at Thanksgiving dinner. Hell, our own father boxed every memory of our mother away after she died, hoping we'd forget her if she was out of sight. So living here just feels right to me."

Alexander nodded as he reflected on his brother's words. A comfortable silence rose like a wall between them. Both fell into the wealth of it, embracing their ability to be together with no need for words to express what they were feeling. The inherent connection they'd been blessed with at birth had been lost for too long. Its revival had been a long time coming.

They spent another half hour in casual conversation,

the easy exchange indicative of how far they'd come together. Every ounce of vim between them was fraught with healing energy. What each had been missing for so long was suddenly abundant, both sliding back into a quiet reverie that spoke volumes about the bond they shared.

Alexander sipped the last of his coffee. The pain in his head had actually calmed to a dull ache, the relief he'd been promised slowly coming to fruition. "What's in this?" he asked, gesturing with his mug.

His brother shrugged. "I couldn't tell you. It's something Gamon blends up but it works and it doesn't taste bad. In another half hour you'll be doing handstands, you'll be feeling so good!"

Alexander nodded as a surge of renewed energy suddenly shot through him. "I don't know about a handstand but I'm ready to run."

"Then let's do it! I've got to cover ten miles before nine o'clock!"

A few days later there was no hiding his anxiety as Alexander pulled a chair out for Sarai. Her cousin, Sing Kyowa, nodded his approval as he took the chair beside her. Alexander rounded the table to the other side and sat down across from the two of them.

"So, Sarai says you own a gym, too. Like your brother's." Sing sat forward, resting his elbows on the tabletop.

Alexander nodded. "I do. It's a very successful gym like my brother's."

"I work for Bangla Muay Thai," Sing said, referring to the competition on the other side of town. "It's a better gym!"

Alexander smiled. He shifted his eyes toward Sarai.

"I hope you like this restaurant. A friend suggested it," he said, his tone smug as he emphasized the word *friend.*

Sarai had selected Baan Noy Restaurant for dinner. Located off a side road in the Chalong area of Phuket, the space was simple at best. The minimalistic décor comprised wooden tables covered with long white tablecloths, and black wicker chairs. The exterior was more warehouse than fine dining, but it was family owned and the service was exceptional. When they had arrived, Sarai had introduced him to the owners: the chef, Tai, and her husband, Fred. The couple was extremely friendly, and he had found their conversation entertaining, as they were eager to please the former beauty queen.

Sarai opened her menu, her own smile canyon wide. "It's the perfect restaurant," she said softly.

"Very nice," Sing added. "Very nice and good food, I hear."

Over prawn teriyaki and scallop appetizers, Sing peppered him with questions about his business, his parents, his education, and his basketball career. Despite his best efforts to focus on the conversation, Sing monopolizing most of it, all Alexander wanted was to give Sarai his full and undivided attention. He never realized just how much he missed her until they were together again.

But focusing was difficult because of what was going on under the table. Hidden behind the tablecloth that dropped low to the floor, Sarai had slipped off her high-heeled pump. Easing her leg toward him, she'd tapped playfully at his foot. When he'd lifted his eyes to meet the look she was giving him, she'd slipped him the slightest wink before dropping her eyes to the food on her plate.

Through their red curry duck and tiger prawn
entrée, Sing praised his uncle and explained the
branches of their family tree. Alexander had turned
back to stare at the man when Sarai tapped him again,
her manicured toes lingering for a good few minutes.
Easing his own foot from the Giorgio Brutini loafer
that he was wearing, he met the gentle caresses that
were running up and down the length of his calf.

Once or twice they locked ankles, and it wasn't
until Sarai eased her foot directly into his lap, her
toes gently caressing the protrusion between his legs,
that Alexander almost lost it, barely able to maintain
the level of stealth necessary to shield them. Across
the table, Sing was regaling him with a story about
his last amateur fight and Alexander couldn't have
cared less.

It wasn't until the cappuccino and chocolate lava
cake were served for dessert that Sing finally let Sarai
get in a word. Their conversation centered on Thailand and places she thought Alexander needed to
visit while he was there. By then Alexander was struggling to contain the raging hard-on in his pants, fighting not to explode from her flirtatious touch.

By the time the waitress brought him the check,
her bare foot was back in her heels as if nothing at all
had just happened between them. Small talk rang
through the air until he was able to stand and not
have the telltale sign of his desire be seen by her kin.

Alexander shook Sing's hand. He nodded his head
at Sarai, biting down against his bottom lip to assuage
the guilty pleasure sweeping between them. "Thank
you for dining with me tonight, Dr. Montri. I hope
that we can do it again. Soon."

Sarai smiled, her expression smug. She tossed her
cousin a dismissive look before settling her eyes easily

into his. "I would love to, Mr. Barrett. Thank you for a very nice time."

The following morning when Alexander entered the weight area, Gamon was there waiting for him. He greeted the older man warmly.

"Mr. Montri, how are you, sir?"

Gamon nodded, a quick dip of his head. "I am well, thank you. I hope that you are as well."

The edges of Alexander's mouth bent upward in a slight smile. "It's a good day, sir. I had a very nice dinner last night with Sarai and your nephew, Sing. I look forward to spending more time with your daughter. She's been very kind to me."

Again, Gamon gave him a nod, but he said nothing. Alexander continued talking.

"Perhaps you'll join us for dinner the next time, sir? My brother is very fond of you and I'd like for us to get better acquainted as well."

Gamon's stare was piercing, and Alexander felt like the old man's eyes were boring a deep hole straight through him. His silence was disconcerting, and Alexander wasn't sure what to do or say to move the conversation forward. He blew a deep gust of air past clenched teeth. Moving toward the free weights that rested on a rack in the corner, he decided to say nothing at all. Pulling twenty-five-pound weights into each hand, he turned back around to find Sarai's father still staring at him.

Gamon cleared his throat. "When you have time today I'd like to see more of your computer system, please."

"No problem, sir," Alexander responded. "Whenever you're ready."

And just like that, Gamon was gone.

Minutes later Sarai danced into the space. The look across her face made him smile, his full lips pulling into the brightest smile.

"Your father just left," he said as he met her gaze. He tossed a quick glance over his shoulder.

"I know. I saw," she said as she gestured with her eyes to the training area across the way, where Gamon stood in conversation with Zachary. The two men were huddled in conversation. The couple turned their attention back to each other.

"So did I pass last night's inquisition?" he asked.

She laughed. "Sing really liked you!"

"Sing is quite a character. Are all your family members that entertaining?"

Her laugh was like the sweetest balm. "They have their moments."

"I've never known anyone who talked as much as he talked. I don't know how I was the one being interviewed when he never let me speak!"

Sarai's smile was sunshine bright. She tossed another look in her father's direction. The man was still focused on his conversation with Zachary. Her intense stare shifted back to his and locked. "So would you like to spend the day with me tomorrow?"

Surprise pierced his expression. He eyed her with a raised brow. "Just the two of us?"

"All day," she said with a nod.

"Hell, yeah!" Alexander grinned. "You don't have to ask me twice!"

Chapter Fourteen

Sarai didn't know who was more excited for their day trip, she or Alexander. She lay across the twin bed in the second bedroom of her father's home. In the other room the old man snored loudly, his exhalation vibrating through the entire house. Sleep had been elusive, anxiety feeding on her insomnia. She hadn't had a decent night's rest since coming back to Thailand. Sleeping alone, without Alexander curled against her, was punishing. If she had her way, they would have already been back in Boulder, back to the life she envisioned the two of them having.

Her father snorted, then rolled, his own bed creaking from the breach. She knew that if she peeked in on him, he would be wrapped around the thin pillows that adorned the bed he slept in. She had often wondered if he missed her mother's presence in his bed as much as she was missing Alexander's in hers. She also found herself wondering if her mother would understand the passion that she shared with the beautiful black man. If Khim Montri would have allowed her to forgo the pretense of propriety that she was making Alexander dance in order to honor her father.

There was much Sarai found herself wondering about as she lay there missing the man who'd professed to love her more than anything else in the whole world.

Sarai was so ready to be done with the lies. She loved Alexander with every fiber of her being, and she was ready for the world to know. She didn't want to bite back the words that told him and everyone else how much love she had for him. And then she imagined her father's heartbreak if she were to break protocol and be like the women whom everyone whispered badly about.

The morning sunrise didn't come soon enough. By the time Gamon rose for the day, Sarai was up and dressed, with his morning meal ready at the table.

She greeted her father with a warm hug and kiss. "Good morning, father!"

"Good morning, Sarai. You are up early."

She nodded as she poured him a cup of rich, dark coffee. "I have a long day planned. Alexander has not seen any of Phuket yet so I thought I would take him on a trek to Phang Nga." She took a sip of her own brew, ignoring the look her father gave her.

"Won't you be needed at the gym today since Zachary and I are going to Bangkok to do business?"

Sarai shook her head. "No. Zachary has given me the day off. He asked me to give his brother a tour of Phuket. Everything will be fine."

"I'm not sure that I like the idea of you and that man spending time together. People will talk and . . ."

Sarai interrupted, her curt tone surprising them both. "People will talk no matter what I do. They will talk about me just like they talked about my mother. I don't care what any of them have to say and neither should you. I care that you trust me to do what is right for me and will make me happy. That is all I care about, father."

"I don't know that he is the right man for you, Sarai."

"What is it?" she asked, concern painting her expression. "Why do you not like Alexander? Why won't you even try to like him?"

Gamon suddenly shook his index finger at her. "You are so much like your mother. That is why people talked about her and that *farang dam*! She was impulsive and she didn't always make the best decisions."

Sarai's eyes widened at the outburst. "This is about Alexander's father?"

Gamon pursed his lips tightly together. He sat back in his seat but said nothing.

"Father? Please?" she persisted. "What did Alexander's father ever do? Was there something between him and mother?"

Gamon slammed a harsh fist against the table, the gesture startling Sarai into silence. He cut his eyes at her, his gaze narrowed and chilly. He held up his hand to silence her.

Despite Sarai's efforts to continue the conversation he would not be moved. The two finished their breakfast in silence. When she was finished, Sarai pulled on a pair of sturdy waterproof hiking boots. She packed a swimsuit, a change of dry clothes, a few bottles of water, her wallet, and a camera into her backpack.

"What time will you be home?" Gamon questioned as she headed toward the door.

"I'm sure Alexander and I will be back before you and Zachary return from Bangkok."

With one last nod of his head, Gamon wished his daughter a good day, then retreated into his bedroom, closing the door behind him.

* * *

Zachary was walking out of the door of his cottage when Sarai pulled up in front of his home. Alexander followed on his heels, skipping eagerly in her direction. His enthusiasm made his twin laugh, his thick dreadlocks waving from side to side.

"He's about to drive me crazy!" Zachary teased. "Take him somewhere. Please!"

Sarai grinned. "I'll take care of him as long as you take care of my father."

Zachary groaned. "Why does that sound like Gamon's not going to be in a good mood?"

"He's . . . how do you say? He's in his feelings?"

Alexander laughed. "I think she's definitely getting the better end of this deal, Z!"

His twin laughed with him. "I know she is!"

The early morning hour was indicative of another beautiful day. The sun was luminous and resplendent, searching for the perfect spot to settle into against the bright blue sky. Their day started with a drive through Phang Nga province, west of the Malay Peninsula. The area had once been the site of a James Bond movie, and Sarai was excited to point out the limestone rock formation jutting out of the sea that had been featured in the Roger Moore film.

Their lazy drive passed through plantations of towering rubber trees and small villages that looked like they'd never been touched by the evolution of time. When they reached the villages of Khao Lak, they stopped at the café in the Marriott hotel for a cup of coffee.

"So I still can't touch you, right?" Alexander asked, his tone teasing.

Sarai smiled. "Be good and I promise you won't be disappointed."

"I don't need to be good! You're the one pretending, remember?" His tone had morphed, raising her red flags.

She took a deep breath and held it for a split second before responding. "Are you unhappy with me, Alex?"

Alexander leaned forward, sliding his coffee mug out of his way. "I love you," he said, then repeated it a second time. "I love you and being with you makes me very happy. Not being with you is driving me mad. *That* and the lies to keep up the charade are what make me unhappy!"

"I know and I'm sorry. I thought I was doing the right thing. But now," she hesitated for a split second. "Now, I'm not so sure."

"Does that mean we can go to your father? That we can do that *pamanhikan* thing?" he asked, the word sounding like a cross between *pancake* and *hiking* as it rolled off his tongue.

Sarai laughed at his effort to pronounce the Thai word that loosely translated meant "the ceremonial merging of their two families and the official mark of their engagement." She nodded her head. "I think I need to be honest with him. I still respect the Thai ways and I don't want to disappoint my father but lying to him is probably a bigger sin."

"I agree."

"And it's not fair to you."

"I definitely agree with that." He leaned over the table to kiss her mouth, pressing his lips to hers just as their waitress paused to deliver the check.

The young Thai woman looked from him to Sarai and back again. Her eyes were wide as she tried to make sense of their situation. There was a look of disdain that appeared to cross her expression despite her efforts to not let any emotion show. Alexander grinned as he gave the woman a slight wink of his eye.

"I'm an American," he said proudly, his chest pushed forward. "And this beautiful woman is my wife. And in America, when a man gets good news from his woman he has to show her how much he loves her. It's a rule!"

The young woman gave him a slight nod and a smile, and then she scurried away.

Sarai reached across the table and rested her palm against the back of his hand. "Let's have a great day together. Let me show you the things I love most about Thailand. Then let's go home and make beautiful babies."

Alexander smiled as he kissed her one more time. "I think I'm going to like making babies with you, Dr. Montri. I think I'm going to like that a lot."

Khao Lak was surrounded by pristine beaches and warm tropical water. The views from every angle were extraordinary. Sarai and Alexander had walked the sandy shoreline hand in hand as she regaled him with stories about her childhood and growing up as an only child who had played with both her parents in that very sand.

Their mini-adventure took a somber turn as they visited the Tsunami Museum. Although Alexander recalled the news of the 2004 tragedy that had befallen the Asian coast, the massive oceanic wave ravaging the area, its full impact didn't hit him until he walked the memorial that had been built to honor some four thousand people who had lost their lives in Khao Lak.

The memorial park sat to the west of the village, by the beach. The inside of the museum featured tons of photos of the storm's aftermath. The main memorial consisted of two walls; one a bare concrete structure that was bowed and curved like a massive wave. The wall opposite was adorned with name plaques, photos, and fresh flowers paying tribute to family that were gone but never forgotten. The poignant reminders moved Sarai to tears, and Alexander wiped them from her cheek with the back of his hand.

After paying their respects, Sarai made arrangements for them with a local tour group. The jungle trek was a first for Alexander as he soon found himself sitting atop an oversized elephant that slowly waddled from side to side along the trails that ran through the thick brush, deep into the valley, allowing them to take in the stunning scenery. They connected with another guide whose enthusiasm was infectious as he led them on a bamboo raft down the river, farther into the jungle.

They were both relaxed as they sat back and the paddler maneuvered his way into the tropical rain forest. Sarai pointed out gibbons that were swinging through the trees, and as they moved downstream, there was a snake basking in the sun. The wildlife and plant life was plentiful, and in the midst of the natural surroundings, Alexander felt overwhelming joy to be in that place with the woman of his dreams.

After a thirty-minute jaunt, they floated into water that was clear and cool, bordered by an exquisite waterfall that screamed adventure. Neither could resist the opportunity to jump in for a swim, laughing and playing as if it were the most natural thing in the world for them to do.

Lunch came next, the local fare purchased from a stand on the side of the road. Sarai had assured him he had nothing to fear, and he was delightfully surprised as they dined on fried noodles with chicken, vegetables, and egg. They followed the filling meal with an assortment of fresh fruit that had been chopped into bite-size pieces and was served with a salt and chili mix to dip it in.

Once their stomachs were full, they headed to Khao Sok and the Monkey Cave that was a tourist favorite. There were a few visitors when they arrived, but it was far from crowded. A Buddhist temple sat outside the entrance to the cave, and there were stalls selling snacks to feed the monkeys. And there were a ton of monkeys! Thieving, noisy, flea-infested primates that set Alexander's nerves on edge.

"They won't bother you as long as you don't tease them," Sarai joked.

Alexander cut his eye in her direction. "Nothing to worry about," he professed. "I will leave them alone as long as they leave me alone."

She laughed as she pulled him into the cave's entrance. A faded gate opened into a large cavern with high ceilings. Inside the hollow fissure sat an oversized reclining gold Buddha that was easily sixteen yards long and just as high. There were several other large standing Buddha images, and the entire space had been decorated with religious artifacts. A monk sat meditating in front of the large statue, the man surrounded by a host of fat, lazy cats who were napping, with no cares in the world. Alexander was in awe of the place, proclaiming it a favorite after the elephant ride and well ahead of the monkey show.

By the time the two found their way back to Phuket City, they were exhausted, and invigorated, their time together reviving the emotions that had consumed them when they'd been in Boulder. Sarai pulled into Revolution's campus, guiding her car back to Zachary's front door.

She stole a quick glance down to her wristwatch. "I don't think my father and Zachary are back yet. But I don't know what time their flight was."

"How long is the trip from Bangkok?"

"Just over an hour. No time at all by plane."

"We could grab dinner," Alexander said. "I need to shower first and if you want we could go back into town to get something to eat."

Sarai shook her head. "Why don't I just arrange for the kitchen to bring something up for the four of us? I'm sure when they get back they'll both be hungry too."

He nodded, pushing open the car door. "I'll be here when you get back," he said softly, and then he leaned to kiss her cheek before pulling himself from the front seat. He ducked back down to stare at her. "You haven't changed your mind, have you? About our telling your father?"

For a brief moment Sarai thought about her father and their conversation at breakfast. She knew Alexander would worry if she told him so she chose to keep the details to herself. She reasoned that maybe Zachary could help her get some answers from her father, or his.

Her smile was easy and swift, the subtlest lift to her thin lips. "Never," she whispered softly.

He nodded, slammed the door closed, and waved after her as she pulled off in the direction of the main building.

* * *

Alexander had showered and was lounging in the warm pool when Sarai finally returned. He lay with his body beneath the water, his arms outstretched against the painted tiles, his head resting back against his neck. His eyes were closed, and he slumbered lightly, slow, easy breaths of air filling his lungs.

Missing each other had taken a toll on them both, the effect not at all what she'd anticipated. There had been moments when she'd looked into a mirror and had seen her mother's reflection in her eyes. That look that had often dimmed the light in the matriarch's smile when her heart had been someplace other than with Sarai and her father. Sarai hadn't liked what she'd seen, and she had absolutely hated what she'd seen on Alexander's face.

She wore a simple floral shift dress with casual flip-flops on her feet. Kicking off the shoes, she eased into the pool, maneuvering to his side. The warm water felt good after the lukewarm shower she'd grabbed in the women's locker room.

Alexander's eyes flew open as she straddled his body. Her dress rode up around her waist as she eased her pelvis against his lap. She wore no panties and he gasped loudly, stunned by her boldness. His arms wrapped around her, pulling her gently against him. Both hands cupped her buttocks as he held her, her knees clutching the sides of his thighs. As she slid into the embrace she nuzzled her face into his neck. Her kisses were gentle whispers of warm breath against his skin. She paused at that spot just beneath his chin, suckling the soft flesh. As she did she felt his body harden between her lean legs.

Her smile was teasing as she drew back to stare at

him. There was no denying the desire that pierced her eyes, and his. Alexander tightened his grip, the round of her bottom filling both palms. He pushed and pulled at her body, grinding the vee of her crotch against the engorged muscle that had pulled taut in his swim shorts. His breathing was raspy, and every muscle had hardened. The sensations were more than he anticipated, and he suddenly bucked, his whole body bristling with tension as he fought the urge to explode. She plunged her mouth to his, kissing him fervently. In that moment all either wanted was for him to settle the length of his cock deep into her soft folds.

When he did, Sarai rode him, both savoring the sweetest sensations of their intimate connection. He'd lifted his hips as she'd slid his shorts over his ass and then he'd kicked his trunks from around his ankles. As she'd dropped her body down hard against his, she had held her breath as he entered her easily, sliding into her sweet spot, where both knew he belonged. She had pushed and pulled against him, the slow, rhythmic motion like a choreographed dance. She plunged her body up and down against his, over and over again, soft, then harder. Their loving was swift, and when his body erupted deep into hers, his orgasm swept her right off the edge of ecstasy.

They both panted heavily, fighting to regain the regularity of their breathing. His body was still locked tightly in hers, his erection barely subsiding. Alexander stood upright, carrying her against his chest as he stepped out of the pool. As they moved in the direction of his bedroom, he tore her dress from around her, the soaked fabric falling to the floor behind them.

Once inside the privacy of his room, he dropped

her against the queen-size bed. His cock had softened slightly, falling from the wet, warm cavity that had been wrapped around him. As he fell against her, she lifted her legs and spread herself eagerly, wanting him back inside of her.

Alexander paused at the entrance to her sweet spot, his hands gently kneading her body. His caresses were heated, each pass of his hand like having a low-voltage jolt of electricity shot through her body. The intensity of the sensations was sweeping, the vibrations like nothing she'd ever experienced before. Sarai was dizzy with lust, her breath coming in fast, hard gasps. His hard dick pressed against the soft line of her thigh and it felt good to have him teasing her so unabashedly. Sarai pulled him into another deep, heated kiss. Her tongue licked his lips as she pushed her way into his mouth. Her touch was probing, her excitement spilling over in her warm breath.

Alexander ran his hands up and down her sides and back. He marveled at how smooth and flawless her skin was, the sensation against his palm like stroking silk. Then he cupped his hands around her tiny breasts and tweaked each of her nipples until they were hardened buds of dark candy against his fingertips.

Her feminine odor scented the room, and he inhaled her, his body quivering intensely. Like a bee to nectar, he slipped his hands between her legs, his fingers sliding into the sopping wetness that marked her raging desire. The gesture was rewarded with a moan of pleasure that rang like the sweetest music to his ears. Unable to contain himself any longer, Alexander slid every inch of his maleness back into her. She moaned as his mouth pressed hot against her neck, nibbling and biting at her flesh.

Everything about the two of them together was perfection. Sarai felt amazing wrapped around his hungry cock, her warm, velvet lining milking him as she clenched and tightened her muscles, every sinewy fiber pulsing with a vengeance. As he wrapped his hands around the small of her back, anchoring himself against her, he plowed his body harder and harder into hers, his organ driving into her like a piston that had lost control. He fell into a steady rhythm, bringing them both to an even higher state of excitement. She moaned with pleasure, his ministrations awakening every nerve ending in her body.

Alexander dipped his head and latched his mouth around one of her nipples. He swirled his tongue over the cone of her breast and then moved to the other, back and forth. Sarai's passion peaked as she clutched the sheets beneath them, entangling the fabric between her fingers. Her tight cunt squeezed his cock as he pumped in and out of her channel. She was hot and moist, her inner lining massaging him intensely.

His own muscles tingled, his cock desperate to shoot. He pumped faster and faster, in and out. They both moaned and grunted as their climax neared, and then he suddenly let go, riding the waves of pleasure that coursed through him like a volcano. He groaned, the deep vibrato rising from someplace low in his center. As he came for the second time, shivers of sheer pleasure pulsed from Sarai's feminine core and she screamed his name, clutching at him hungrily. Her body went rigid, and she cried out, her soft voice piercing.

The couple thrashed about until their excitement ebbed. Spent, the two lay side by side, dropping readily into their love for each other. The whole experience felt surreal. As he continued to caress her, they both fell into a wonderful sense of peace and content-ment, neither concerned that it might not last.

Chapter Fifteen

Alexander was startled out of a deep sleep. Beside him Sarai was curled in a fetal position, her back and buttocks pressed against his side. Turning slightly, he eyed the alarm clock on the nightstand. It had been a good two hours since they'd fallen into his bed, loving each other as if they needed to make up for lost time. He cupped his palm between his legs, lightly stroking the tender appendage that pulsed from the sweet memory.

Something suddenly drew his attention, and he lifted his torso slightly. He listened intently, noise coming from outside his bedroom door, and then it hit him. Zachary and Gamon had returned. A wave of anxiety pinched him hard in his side.

Leaning his face against hers, he pressed his index finger to her lips as he whispered softly into her ear. "Shhhh! Sarai, wake up, baby! Your father is here."

Sarai's eyes shot open, flickering back and forth. Alexander could actually feel her heart start to race, her naked body shaking as if she were cold. The two exchanged a look as Alexander drew his finger to his own lips, blowing out the softest breath. "Shhhh!"

Outside the door they heard his brother calling his name, both tensing, knowing that it wasn't locked. Alexander threw back the cotton sheet that had covered his long legs. Rising from the bed, he grabbed a pair of shorts and stepped quickly into them. Sarai had sat upright, drawing the bedclothes up to her chin. Her eyes were wide and glossy, fear painting her expression.

"It's going to be okay," he whispered, hoping to assure her.

She nodded, but her expression wasn't relieved, Sarai still looking as if her whole world were about to fall apart. The look suddenly held his heart in a vise grip. He turned and exited the room.

Just as he stepped into the hall, Zachary rushed him. Concern washed over his brother's face, his eyes widened. He carried Sarai's gym bag, slamming it into Alexander's chest. He hissed between clenched teeth. "Gamon's in the kitchen!"

With a nod Alexander tossed the bag into the room behind him and quickly closed the door. Both he and Zachary could hear the patter of Sarai's feet as she jumped from the bed and crossed the room.

The brothers moved together into the living space, Alexander following on Zachary's heels. His twin feigned a casual conversation, trying to make light of the moment. Alexander asked about Zachary's day.

"How did everything go?" he questioned. "Did you two have a good flight?"

Amusement shimmered in Zachary's gray eyes. "It was a good day but I'm sure it wasn't nearly as good as your day," he said mockingly.

Gamon had moved from the kitchen to the patio, taking a seat at the glass-topped table beside the pool.

As both men stepped outside to join him, Alexander's eyes immediately went to his swim trunks floating on top of the water and the floral dress abandoned on the concrete walkway.

Zachary noticed both items as well, shooting him a look. His head waved, amusement dancing in his eyes.

"Mr. Montri, hello," Alexander chimed, ignoring the look his brother was giving him. He stepped directly in front of the man, hoping to block his view.

Gamon nodded his head in greeting. He refocused his attention on the plate of food he'd been enjoying. Zachary had reached down to snatch the floral fabric from where it rested. He tossed the garment into a basket of towels that rested in the corner and made a joke about finding a new cleaning crew.

Alexander tried to make conversation. "Sarai arranged for the food," Alexander said. "She thought you two would be hungry when you got back."

"And where is my daughter?" Gamon suddenly asked. His eyes locked with Alexander's as he bit into a forkful of baked fish.

"You didn't see her down in the office?" Zachary interjected. "I saw her car parked down there."

The older man shook his head. "I didn't go to the office."

Alexander nodded. "When she dropped me off she said she was headed to the cafeteria. Then I fell asleep," he said, the partial truth not a full lie.

Gamon lowered his stare back to his plate.

Alexander turned abruptly. "I think I'll go get something to eat, too," he said.

"Sounds like a good idea," Zachary said as he followed on his twin's heels.

When the two men were in the other room, Zachary

whispered, "You two are so busted!" He laughed heartily. "Busted!"

"Shut up!" Alexander whispered back. "Why didn't you just take him home?"

"He didn't want to go home!"

Shaking his head, Alexander looked down the hallway toward the closed bedroom door. He suddenly imagined Gamon finding his only girl child naked in his bed, the subsequent fallout a drama-filled, made-for-TV special. Despite wanting them to be open with her father about their relationship, he didn't want the news to be a Jerry Springer moment.

Both men were suddenly surprised to hear Sarai's voice, the young woman in conversation with her father. They were speaking Thai, and both seemed to be in a good mood. Zachary looked at him, his own expression even more curious. The two grabbed their plates and headed back outside.

Sarai was standing by her father's side, one hand on her hip. Their conversation was animated but there were smiles on both their faces. Sarai had changed back into the blouse and khaki pants that she'd had on earlier in the day. She'd pulled her thick tresses up into a casual bun. No one would have guessed that she'd been buck naked in his bed just minutes earlier.

She greeted the two of them with a wide smile across her face. "Hi, guys!"

Alexander grinned back.

"Where'd you come from?" Zachary questioned teasingly.

She pointed toward the gate that led to the rear of the property. "One of the new students had an issue with her door over at the cottages. We were just trying to get that resolved."

"It could have waited until tomorrow. I would have taken care of it," Gamon interjected.

She drew her hand across her father's narrow shoulders. "I know, Father. I just wanted to make sure she felt safe," Sarai said, fueling her own little white fib with an element of truth.

"Thanks for looking out," Zachary said. He gestured with his plate. "The food is really good too!"

"Just returning the favor," she said smugly. She moved to an empty chair and took a seat.

The rest of their conversation was easy. Alexander's enthusiasm was contagious as he shared the day's experience. Zachary was excited as well to fill them in on his decision to add additional housing to the property. The architect that he'd used before was based in Bangkok, and their meeting earlier that afternoon had gone better than he'd anticipated.

"Do you have the space to build?" Alexander asked.

His brother nodded. "I own almost five acres of land that borders this back lot. We're growing so fast and we have so many people trying to come and train with us that I really need to increase the housing."

Even Gamon had more to say, commenting periodically. He spoke more in that next hour than Alexander had ever heard him speak his entire time in Thailand. His conversation centered on the Bangkok site where the UFC battle would take place and the training facilities close by that were excited for an opportunity to have Zachary grace them with his presence, sure to boost their reputation.

"So did you select a gym?" Alexander asked.

His brother nodded. "I'll go back to Master Todd's," he said. "The owner is a friend of mine."

Gamon shook his head, not agreeing with the man's decision. There was a brief exchange between them that was short and curt, but Zachary seemed to have made up his mind, and Gamon let it go.

"What am I missing?" Alexander asked, looking from one to the other.

Zachary shrugged. "Gamon doesn't like Master Todd. The last time I trained there the two exchanged words about the people Todd allows in his gym. Gamon is worried that he associates with an unsavory element."

"Should you be worried?" Alexander questioned.

Zachary shrugged. "I'll be renting the entire gym this time. No one will get in that we don't let in."

When father and daughter rose to leave, Gamon pointed toward the pool. "Which one of you lost something?" he asked, pointing toward the floating boxers. His gaze skated between the two brothers, finally resting on Alexander's face. The energy that danced in the man's eyes was taunting, taking on a life of its own.

Alexander blushed, color rushing to tint his cheeks a deep shade of vibrant red.

Sarai interjected, saying something in Thai and Gamon responding in kind. The exchange made Zachary bust out laughing.

Alexander eyed them all anxiously. "What?" Alexander asked, looking from one to the other.

Gamon gave him a look. "You blush like a girl! Makes you look guilty!" he repeated in English. "Instead of worrying about your pants, they need to be asking about the woman in your bedroom and that dress over there that she probably needs!"

As Zachary slapped him against his back, Alexander locked eyes with Sarai, her small hand clasped over her mouth to stifle her gasp. Another wave of embarrassment flooded his face, and there was nothing at all that he could say.

* * *

The clock chimed midnight, and the two brothers were still laughing together. Alexander had called to check on Sarai after she and her father had gone home. She too had been amused by her father's assumptions. Alexander knew that one day he'd look back and find the whole situation as hilariously funny as Zachary and Sarai did, but it wasn't happening that day.

"So, now Gamon thinks I'm a womanizer. He's never going to accept me being in a relationship with his daughter!"

"Don't be such a drama queen. It's not that bad," Zachary laughed.

Alexander gave his brother an evil eye. He pouted profusely, finding nothing at all humorous in his situation.

"Don't look at me like that! I didn't have anything to do with your mess!"

Alexander sighed. "So what do you suggest that I do now? How do I make this right?"

Zachary responded almost immediately. "Just get a good night's rest. I'll take care of everything."

The next morning Zachary had absolutely nothing to say about his brother's personal problems. He had thrown himself back into training, winning his upcoming fight the only thing on his mind.

Gamon had gone back to ignoring him, having nothing at all to say to him. Despite his best efforts, nothing Alexander did or said seemed to move the man. It went from bad to worse when he discovered that Sarai had disappeared to places unknown, no one telling him anything. And she had disappeared, leaving Thailand without a word of good-bye.

He'd been blowing up her cell phone, trying to reach her. His calls continually went to voice mail, and there was no return call. Nothing. Radio silence. He didn't know whether to be worried or angry. His emotions wafted from one to the other, most especially when Zachary and her father didn't seem to have an ounce of concern at all.

Alexander was throwing punches at a sand-filled sack, his frustrations vibrating with each pounding smack. He could see his brother on the other side of the property, sparring inside a fight ring with one of his trainers. Gamon stood at the cage entrance watching. The open-air space overflowed with spectators.

UFC fight executives, corporate sponsor representatives, and sports writers from all around the world had besieged the property, everyone trying to get a small piece of his brother's time. Alexander had taken to running interference whenever it was necessary to give his twin a little peace of mind. When one of the young staff members called his name, gesturing for his attention, he figured it was only to have him point a potential problem away from Zachary toward another direction.

"You have . . . phone . . . call," the young man said, his English stammering.

Confusion washed over Alexander's face.

The kid pointed toward the main building. "You . . . have . . . phone . . . call," he repeated, enunciating each word slowly.

Alexander nodded, pulling at the wraps that covered his hands. As he jogged across the courtyard, he couldn't begin to know who was trying to reach him that wouldn't just call him on his cell phone. The man at the front desk pointed him to an old-fashioned rotary phone that rested on a wooden desk. He pulled the receiver to his ear.

"Hello?"

"Alex?"

Alexander tossed a look over his shoulder before he spoke. The desk clerk was lost in conversation with another staff member. "Sarai, is that you?"

"Alexander, hello! How are you?"

"Baby, I'm good! Where are you?"

"I'm in Hong Kong."

"Hong Kong? What are you doing there?"

"I had a photo shoot for the Miss Universe organization. I'd completely forgotten about it. I didn't have time to tell you before I had to leave but I had asked my father to tell you that we would speak when I returned."

"I didn't get that message, baby! I've been pulling my hair out trying to figure out what happened to you."

"I'm so sorry! I actually forgot my phone. I'm sure it's still sitting on my father's kitchen table. I didn't realize I'd left it until I got to the airport and I went to text you."

Sarai didn't bother to add that she'd been distracted by her father and his rants about Alexander's character. They had argued most of the night and she still didn't understand why Gamon was against her relationship with Alexander or what had occurred in the past that had him hating Alexander's father.

"When will you be back?"

"We finish up tomorrow. I'll fly out right after. I get in late so I probably won't see you until Friday morning."

Alexander tossed another look over his shoulder.

The two men were still lost in their own conversation, paying him no mind. "I miss you, Sarai."

"I miss you too and I wanted to hear your voice."

"You really need to stop leaving me the way you do." There was a hint of attitude in his tone, the wealth of it edged in humor.

"I didn't leave you! And I promise I'm coming back soon."

Alexander felt himself grinning foolishly. "I love you, Sarai," he said, his voice dropping two octaves.

He sensed her smiling on the other end.

"I love you, too, Alexander!"

Sarai passed the cell phone she'd borrowed back to its owner. The former Miss Indonesia, Leah Surya, gave her a bright smile as she dropped the device back into her purse.

"Thank you so much," Sarai said. "I can't believe I forgot my phone!"

"You're very welcome! I'm so excited for you. Your new beau sounds like quite the catch."

"He's incredible!"

"And he's cute," Miss Jamaica, Jeannette Ferrell, interjected. "I've been following his career since he was playing college basketball."

Sarai smiled at her friend. "Down, girl!"

Miss Jamaica laughed. "Is his twin brother married?"

"How did you know he had a twin brother?" Sarai asked.

"I told you I've been following him. And his brother!" Miss Jamaica pulled up her Facebook page on her iPhone. She slid her finger across the screen, pulling up the page for Champs and then for Revolution, the two gyms both recently updated with images of the brothers together.

Miss Indonesia grinned as she leaned to stare at the iPhone screen. "They are cute! I've never dated black men before. What's that like?"

Sarai shook her head. It had been a few months since she'd last seen the two women who had made her pageant years a fun experience. The bond between the three had been about their mutual interests in those things unrelated to their pageant lives. All three had a passion for health and exercise and all three had been determined to build futures that revolved around their own needs and wants and not the expectations of their families.

"It's just like they say," Miss Jamaica interjected. "When you go black you never go back!" she said with a deep chuckle. "The darker the berry, the sweeter the juice!"

Sarai laughed with her. "Everything about my Alexander is perfect!" she said. "That's all I need to say about that!"

Her friend rolled her eyes skyward. She leaned forward to whisper, the gesture conspiratorial. "Is it true that they're very large?" Miss Indonesia asked, gesturing crudely with her hands. The woman tossed a quick look over her shoulder before leaning even closer.

Sarai blushed profusely, her face turning a deep shade of red. She opened her mouth to speak, then closed it, sucking air like a guppy.

Miss Jamaica laughed as she answered the question. "Yes," she said. "They are *very* large. Black men are very well endowed. What they say is true. They are blessed beyond measure!"

Sarai shook her head. "Now you know that is not

right. Not all black men are large. Just like not all
Asian or white men are small. We shouldn't be stereo-
typing them! That's not right."

"So you are saying that your man is not so big?"
Miss Jamaica teased.

Sarai laughed. "I didn't say that at all. We are not
talking about my man like that!"

Miss Indonesia waved a dismissive hand, then
grinned brightly. "I must date black! I must find me a
beautiful black man for a boyfriend."

Sarai laughed again. "But you have a boyfriend!"

"I do. He's rich and he's very good to me, but
he's"—she leaned forward again, whispering across
the table—"small!" She winked her eye and held her
thumb and forefinger about an inch apart. "Small
doesn't work so good!"

The laughter that rang around the table felt good
to Sarai. The opportunity to work with her old friends
and be able to spend some quality time with them
had come at the perfect time. Sneaking out of
Alexander's window to keep her father from catching
her in his bed had been a moment of revelation for
her. Alexander deserved better.

Alexander deserved her being honest with her
family and friends. He had proven himself more than
worthy, and if she intended to be a good wife, she
needed to honor him as her husband as much as she
honored her father. And she needed to have started
weeks ago. Even though he'd been a good sport with
the teasing, she felt bad that she had put him in the
position to not be honest, and when she returned to
Phuket she intended to make things right.

Alexander had her heart like no one else. She loved
him. She'd been raised that women showed their

love, words not necessarily needed. But in that moment Sarai was determined to not only demonstrate her feelings through her actions but to shout them out for everyone to hear, every chance she got.

Alexander was ready to settle down for the night when Zachary bogarted his way into his room. "What are you doing? Why aren't you dressed?"

"What? I'm going to bed. Why would I be dressed?"

His brother shook his head. "No. Get dressed. We're out of here in thirty minutes."

"Where are we going?"

"Your bachelor party, bro!"

Alexander sat upright in his bed. He stared at his twin, his eyes blinking rapidly. "Excuse me?"

Zachary laughed. "I need to blow off some steam so we're going out. Since you'll be off the market in a few days it's a good time to give you one last blowout with the guys! So, it's your bachelor party! Just don't tell Sarai because she will kill us both."

"Why?"

"We're taking you to a go-go club!"

Thirty minutes later Zachary and Alexander piled into a small van driven by Zachary's friend Patrick. His other friend Robert rode shotgun. Sarai's cousin Sing, another cousin named Pom, and a bantam-weight UFC fighter named Fabricio Aldo, who trained under his brother's tutelage, rounded out the group. They were all raucous, slightly inebriated, and excited to be headed straight for trouble.

"Your brother says you need a woman!" Patrick exclaimed. "We are going to find you many beautiful women. You only have to choose whichever one you want!"

Alexander cut an eye at Zachary, who was laughing loudly.

"Just be mindful," Fabricio said. "Thailand has beautiful women. But some of them come with surprises!"

Alexander's head snapped in the man's direction. The other men howled. Fabricio nodded his head as he continued.

"The last time I go to the bars with your brother and his friends, they leave me. I find my way to this club and the women, they pull me inside. I go because they are all beautiful women." He gestured with his hands. "Big beautiful breasts, small waists, nice curves. They dance and I am very excited. I meet two who want to show me good time!"

"For a price!" Zachary interjected. "They weren't free! Don't forget that part."

Fabricio nodded. "Cost me much money! One thousand baht!" he said, referring to the Thai currency.

"Each?" Alexander asked.

The man shook his head. "No, one thousand baht for both!"

Zachary was still laughing, knowing that Alexander was calculating the exchange rate in his head. When his brother blinked, he already knew what his twin was thinking. Trying to fathom how two prostitutes who had cost the man less than thirty dollars for the night had him feeling that was expensive. The two traded glances as the other man continued.

"I am having good time. We are dancing and kissing and touching and then they start coming out of their clothes."

The others in the car bust out laughing, all having

heard the story before. Fabricio was shaking his head as he came to the punch line. "And my beautiful women were beautiful *kathoey!*"

Alexander looked to his brother for translation. "What's *kathoey?*"

Zachary was clutching his chest, cackling heartily. "Ladyboys!" his twin exclaimed as he caught his breath. "Women with boy parts!"

"Chicks with dicks!" Robert added for emphasis.

Alexander nodded his understanding. Thailand was infamous for its transgender women and effeminate men. They were actually considered a third gender and generally accepted by the community. Most worked in traditional female occupations and were a large facet of the sex trade that was so prevalent in the country. Many were extremely attractive, having undergone medical procedures to make themselves more feminine. Breast implants, hormone treatments, silicone injections, and Adam's apple reductions were a Thai staple for those wanting to transition. He easily understood how some men might be misled.

Sarai had schooled him the day she'd taken him around Phuket and an attractive woman had waved him over. The stranger had grabbed his arm, calling him "chocolate man" excitedly. Sarai had stepped in, putting the woman in her place and telling her to back down. The conversation had been in Thai, but there had been no misunderstanding what was being communicated. The other woman had dismissed them both with an eye roll and had turned her attentions to a young boy with blond hair and a pimply complexion. When Sarai told him his admirer had actually been male, he'd been completely taken aback.

He grinned. "Well, that's not going to be a problem for me tonight. I'm not looking for any kind of female companionship."

Robert laughed. "Men are always looking for female companionship. I have a wife and I am still looking!"

Their banter continued through Phuket Town. It was rowdy, raunchy, and ridiculously out of character for the twins. But they were enjoying the camaraderie, the bawdy jokes, and the free drinks as friends and strangers alike wanted to toast the two black athletes.

Sometime during the late-night hour, they found themselves on the west end of town in Patong. Laughter was overflowing as they maneuvered through the streets toward Suzy Wong's A Go Go. The newly renovated space was a longtime favorite of expats, and they boasted having the sexiest girls to be found in Phuket. The outside facade was an amalgamation of red paint, Chinese decorations, and one massive door. Hawkers, both male and female, stood outside, promising guests a good time to try and lure them inside.

Once inside, the Asian theme was continued with displays of masks and swords and waitresses in pretty silk dresses. Then there were the dancers. Center stage six rail-thin women dressed in skimpy blue and white cheerleading outfits were bouncing and gyrating in a poorly choreographed dance routine. Smiles were wide and temptation was abundant. The men split up, retreating to different areas of the club. Patrick, Robert, and Pom took front-row seats on the stools that surrounded the dance floor. Fabricio eased his way over to the spanking corner for some ass-smacking fun. He was soon going blow for blow with an older Thai woman who'd pocketed some of his money.

The twins retreated to one of the cushioned sofas in a corner, Sing following behind them. They were quickly surrounded by dancers hoping to lure one or the other, maybe even both, to a back room for some private entertainment. Zachary ordered beer for the three of them, then sunk back against the cushions to eye the entertainment.

The music was a playlist of seventies rock and roll, techno-funk, and dance pop. The next dance set featured three girls in the barest black lingerie, black high-heeled boots, and cowboy hats. There was a lot of girl-on-girl action, and the crowd responded enthusiastically. By the fourth dance routine, Zachary's three friends had disappeared to the back rooms, the women dragging them there each looking like they'd hit the jackpot.

Zachary shook his head as he sipped on his beverage, Sing talking nonstop about absolutely nothing. Despite his air of indifference, there was one young woman who was anxiously trying to catch Alexander's attention. After her second attempt, dropping her lean frame into the seat beside him, her hand trailing suggestively along his thigh, he'd insisted on trading seats with his brother, moving to sit between him and Sing.

Zachary laughed at his discomfort. "She won't bite. Not if you don't want her to!" he teased.

Alexander shook his head. "You are not going to have Sarai kicking my ass over some dumb mess like this. She will never have any doubts about me being faithful."

"No one says you have to do anything. Just enjoy the attention. It's good for you!"

"I'm not that drunk. And neither are you."

His brother grinned. "Yeah, I'm holding back. I can't afford to get myself into trouble and there's nothing but trouble up in here," he said as the same girl sat down to rub on his leg.

The last dance routine of the night featured the few dancers not entertaining customers in the back. They wore white bikinis and Catwoman masks. Their sultry gyrations were a half beat off from the music, but no one noticed. Fabricio and Pom had joined them on the couches, but Robert had yet to return.

"He must be like the Energizer Bunny!" Alexander joked.

Zachary grinned, waving his head. "That fool popped a little blue pill before the first lap dance. He'll probably be *up* for another two hours!"

The men laughed. Sing stretched his arms outward and yawned. Alexander gave the man a nod, pushing his last bottle of beer across the table. "I'm done," he said.

Zachary shifted his leg away from the young woman who was still rubbing on him. Reaching into his pocket, he counted off five bills, each imprinted with the image of Thailand's beloved king. Each note was the equivalent of one thousand baht. He pressed the money into the girl's hand and leaned to kiss her cheek. Then he waved her off, all of them chuckling as she skipped across the room. Excitement flooded her spirit. He tossed back the last sip of his own drink. "Yeah," he said. "We need to get some rest."

"You keep tipping like that and you're not going to be able to get rid of these girls," Fabricio said as two more came rushing across the room in their direction.

Pom stood up, moving between them and Zachary.

There was an exchange in Thai before both turned, stomping off in anger.

"Especially when they haven't worked for it," Robert said, suddenly joining them. The man was grinning from ear to ear.

Zachary shook his head. "Don't come to my place when your wife puts you out," he said, directing his comment at his friend.

Robert laughed. "My wife knows her place," he said. "Besides, if she did what some of these other girls will do I wouldn't have to pay for it."

Alexander shook his head. "Maybe if you stopped paying for it your wife would do it," he said.

Robert shrugged. "Marry a nice Thai girl and come see me in a year. Thai girls don't keep things interesting in the bedroom once they get married. Just ask all the husbands in here buying what they want."

"It might be more about the men they married than it is about them. You might want to think about that," Alexander said as he sat forward in his seat, narrowing his gaze on the man.

Robert shrugged. "I'm still holding it down!" he exclaimed.

"You're holding it down as long as you have your Viagra," Fabricio interjected, all of them laughing.

Zachary tossed his twin a look, a wide grin spreading across his face as he read his brother's mind.

Alexander laughed with the crowd. He didn't need to say that he wouldn't be having that problem in his marriage in one year or ten. He wouldn't be having that problem ever!

Chapter Sixteen

Sarai had only been back a few minutes before everyone wanted to tell her about the boys' night out. She smiled and laughed as the tall tales put Zachary and Alexander at the scene of some very shady activity. It was only what her cousin Sing had to say that was of any interest to her. As he recapped their evening for her and her father, it made her heart jump with sheer joy to know that Alexander hadn't fallen prey to any of the vultures that had been hunting him.

Gamon watched his daughter as intently as she eyed him, both eager to know how the other would react to Sing's news.

"Alexander is a good man," she said softly after Sing had moved on to gossip elsewhere.

Gamon's gaze shifted to the weight area, where Alexander was spotting Zachary through his weight routine. His stance widened as he crossed his arms over his chest.

Sarai continued. "He will be a good husband."

The man turned back to his daughter. "Who says

he is looking for a wife? American athletes have many women, and children with all of them."

"Not Alexander. He will have one wife and she will mother all of his children. I know this."

"Maybe yes. Maybe no. I don't doubt that he will find a nice American girl to spend his life with since that is where his home is."

Sarai paused, taking a deep breath before responding. "He has found a good Thai girl and they will make their home in America and also here in Thailand."

Gamon was tapping his foot against the grassy knoll. He dropped his arms down to his sides, his hands clenched in tight fists. He and his daughter were still staring each other down.

Sarai took another deep breath. "I love Alexander, Father. And he loves me. We plan to marry and I really want you to accept him."

Her father's gaze moved back to stare at the black man, he and his brother laughing together. Sarai continued to plead his case.

"Alexander will be a good husband. He is very protective and I trust that he will take care of me. You will not be disappointed, Father."

It felt like an eternity before Gamon finally responded. "Will he come for my permission?"

She nodded. "Yes. He has great respect for me and our traditions, Father."

Saying nothing else, Gamon turned and headed toward where Alexander and Zachary stood in conversation. Sarai stood watching as her father interjected himself into their discussion. She could tell, without being told, that whatever he was saying centered around Zachary and his training regime, nothing feeling out of place or abnormal. It would be another hour before she could speak to Alexander, the man excited to welcome her home.

He smiled brightly, wanting to pull her into his arms, but Gamon's staring at the two of them kept him from doing so. Sarai brushed her hand against his arm. He'd been working out, and sweat poured down his body like water running from a faucet. He swiped the rise of perspiration from his brow.

"Did you have a good flight?" Alexander questioned.

"I did. It was a great trip. The business went fast and I was able to spend time with some old friends."

"Well, I really missed you," he said, his voice dropping. "I'm glad you're back."

She smiled, the sweet bend to her mouth causing a wave of heat to course down his spine.

Alexander fought the urge to shudder as he tossed Gamon a look. The man was still eyeing him with a narrowed gaze. "Why is your father mean-mugging me? What did I do?"

Sarai laughed. "Mean-mugging? Is that like the evil eye?"

"That's exactly what that's like."

She was still giggling. "You didn't do anything. He just knows that I love you."

Alexander's eyes were large saucers. "You told him about us?"

"I did."

He took a step toward her, closing the divide between them. "What did he say?"

Sarai pressed her palm to his chest. "He asked me if you were coming to get his permission."

"And you told him yes, right?"

Sarai shrugged, the gesture meant to tease him.

Alexander laughed heartily. "You better have! Don't play with me, Sarai!"

As Gamon turned abruptly, suddenly headed in the opposite direction to go run some errand, Alexander grabbed her hand, pulling her along with him to go speak with his brother.

Zachary's gaze raced from one to the other as he paused, resting the free weights he was working with back to the ground. "What's up with you two?" he asked. "Why are you two grinning like you just won a lottery?"

Alexander squeezed Sarai's fingers. "I need your help. I need to do that pumpkin thing to get Gamon's approval to marry his daughter."

"*Pamanhikan.*" Sarai giggled as she corrected his pronunciation.

Alexander tossed her a nod. "Yeah, that thing!"

Zachary laughed. "A, you're a day late and a dollar short, my brother! I already have you covered."

Alexander looked confused, and Sarai laughed, the lilt of it warming his spirit.

His brother grinned. "It'll all make sense tomorrow. Then you two will be stuck with each other for good."

The following day the whole vibe around the athletic facility shifted into high overload. Everyone was on edge. Energy levels were super intense, and the excitement was one firecracker away from exploding. Gamon had declared a moratorium on everyone else's training, the entire camp focused on Zachary. They were just days from him defending his title, and all hands were on deck to help.

The two brothers had started their morning with

their usual run, but the alone time both relished had been bombarded by a cavalcade of fans, sports enthusiasts, and reporters running with them. They looked like they had a marathon following on their heels, trying to keep up.

"This is crazy!" Alexander said as they rounded a narrow passage that dropped them at the bridge that connected the island to the mainland.

From there they followed the route to Haad Sai Kaew Beach, an endless stretch of sand and sun. Miles of solitary beachfront property lay before them, the area completely deserted. The water that kissed the sand's edge was as blue as Alexander's eyes. And above their heads, the new day's sun colored the sky in striations of yellow, orange, and gold.

Zachary didn't respond to his brother's comment until they were kicking up sand, the spray of ocean water hitting them in the face. "We go to Bangkok this week and it's going to get even crazier. But things will settle down after the fight."

Alexander nodded. His calves had begun to burn as both men fought their way through the damp sand. He had broken out into a slight sweat and was panting softly.

"Did you pack a suit?" his brother suddenly asked, his own body temperature seeming as if it had barely risen. "Or do you need to borrow one of mine?"

"A suit?"

"Yeah, a suit, white dress shirt, nice necktie, leather shoes?"

Alexander shot Zachary a look, confusion wafting from his stare. "Yeah, why?"

"You'll need to dress up tonight when we go to the Montri home. I don't know if Gamon's sisters will be there to represent Sarai's mother or not, but you'll need to make a good impression. With your luck, the whole family will turn out."

"I thought it was just supposed to be a conversation between me and Gamon?"

"It will be but it's also about the ritual and I will be there as your sponsor."

Alexander nodded. His lungs were beginning to burn, and it was becoming more of a challenge to talk and breathe. Behind them runners had begun to drop like flies, and Alexander realized there was a method to his brother's madness. They reached an incline that began the path back to the gym. Every step was taxing, but side by side the two brothers were easily outrunning the rest of the pack.

"Damn! I still have to go buy a necklace! That thong moon gold gift thing!" Alexander suddenly exclaimed, a wave of panic crossing his face.

Zachary glanced down to his wristwatch. "It's already being handled. I have a jeweler friend who's going to stop by the house when we get back. He'll bring a nice selection of pieces for you to look at and choose from. And it's called *thong mun*. It's the least I can do to help you get this show on the road."

Alexander laughed. "Did you write down what I'm supposed to say, too?"

His twin laughed with him. "You're on your own there. I can't do everything for you!"

They dropped into a comfortable silence, the early day's sun beginning to bear down on them. Both slipped into their own thoughts as they pushed each other to run faster and work harder, the last of their run taking them back through the streets of Phuket Town. As they turned onto the road that led them back to Revolution, Alexander called his brother's name.

"Yeah, A?"

"Thanks. For everything! I owe you!"

Zachary chuckled. "My brother, you just don't know how much!"

By the time they crossed the courtyard at Revolution, only two or three runners were still tagging along behind them. The others had run out of steam miles back. As they came to an abrupt halt in front of the cottage, Alexander was surprised to see Sarai's car parked in the roadway. He shot his brother a look, and Zachary grinned. He walked in slow circles, his hands gripping the sides of his hips as he sucked in air to catch his breath.

Zachary moved into the house first, then stepped aside. As Alexander entered after him, he was greeted with a loud scream, Mama Lynn shouting her excitement.

"Surprise! Surprise!" The old woman rushed them both, hugging and kissing one and then the other.

Alexander grinned as their father stepped forward to greet them. Sarai stood quietly in the back of the room, her hands clasped together as she watched the family reunion.

"When did you two arrive?" Alexander asked, looking from one to the other.

Westley shook his hand. "We just got here a few minutes ago. Sarai picked us up at the airport."

"Lord, that's a long flight!" Mama Lynn exclaimed.

Alexander wrapped his arms around the matriarch and hugged her close. He kissed her cheek. "Zachary didn't tell me you two were coming in for his fight."

Westley laughed. "He didn't tell us that either. We thought we were coming for your wedding!"

Mama Lynn nodded. "I didn't know what to bring!

Your brother didn't give us a whole lot of details. Couldn't even pack my wigs the way I would have liked!" Her hair was pulled back into a ponytail, the strands wrapped around a nylon donut roll to give her an oversized bun at the top of her head. She brushed her fingers across her hairline and earlobe, flattening any wayward strands.

"You look beautiful, Mama!" Westley said, moving to give his wife a warm hug. He turned toward Alexander. "Now, son, why don't you tell us what's going on with you and Sarai."

Taking a deep breath, Alexander shared everything that had happened since their arrival in Thailand. With Sarai's help he explained the Thai formalities facing them and what needed to happen for the two of them to marry.

As they talked, amusement danced across his father's face, the patriarch shaking his head from side to side. "You can always fly back to Colorado and just go down to town hall," Westley said. "It worked for us!"

"I think it's just so exciting!" Mama Lynn exclaimed. "You don't want to go to town hall!"

Zachary shrugged as he tossed his twin a bottle of spring water, chugging back his own. The two brothers exchanged a look, their silent conversation speaking volumes.

Alexander nodded his head, his eyes glazing over as he struggled to contain the emotion sweeping through him.

Zachary slapped him against the back. "I told you I had you. You can't *officially* propose without the parents *officially* meeting."

Twisting the water bottle between his hands,

Alexander moved to Sarai's side. He wrapped his arms around her shoulders. Her eyes were wide, and she blushed at the sudden attention that shifted in her direction. She pressed her hand to his chest, his heart beating rapidly beneath her palm. He kissed her forehead gently, his lips lightly brushing her flesh. And then he kissed her mouth as if he were kissing her for the very first time.

Mama Lynn swiped a tear from her eyes. "I swear! You all are *trying* to make me cry!"

Zachary had arranged for a car service to pick the family up at his home. When the stretch Lincoln limousine pulled onto the property, the commotion among the spectators was palpable. The reporter from the *Phuket Gazette* and a cameraman with Phuket TV both rushed forward, stopped short by Pom and a team of employees who'd been put into place to give the family some privacy. Both were excited when Zachary waved them over, he and Alexander posing for pictures.

Side by side, the two men were extraordinarily handsome, both meticulously dressed. Alexander wore Prada, a navy blue design with a starched white dress shirt and paisley tie. He sported a fresh haircut and shave, his edges pristinely lined courtesy of his father. Zachary's suit was a custom fashion-forward design in gray cotton pinstripe with a pale gray shirt and silver tie. His dreadlocks had been freshly twisted and oiled, and hung loose past his shoulders. Both men could have easily graced the cover of any high-fashion magazine.

"What is the occasion?" the reporter asked as he snapped a series of photographs.

Zachary introduced his twin. "This is my brother, American basketball star Alexander Barrett. He has fallen in love with a beautiful Thai girl and we are headed to visit her family so that he can formally ask for her hand in marriage."

Despite knowing more of the language than when he first arrived, all that Alexander understood of his brother's comment was his name, the words for *beautiful Thai girl*, and *pamanhikan*. He also understood when they extended their congratulations, and he nodded, smiling for a few more photos.

Inside the limousine Zachary grinned. "Thais are big on appearances. When that hits tonight's news and tomorrow morning's newspaper, Sarai is going to be the envy of every girl in the country!"

"Of course she is!" Mama Lynn exclaimed. "She's marrying my baby! Both you boys are quite the catch for any girl. And Zachary, when you find the right girl she's going to be the envy of every girl in the country, too!"

Alexander shook his head. "God, help us!" he muttered under his breath, suddenly worried that he might commit a social faux pas and insult the entire nation. Anxiety was suddenly kicking in with a vengeance, and the family laughed, trying to ease his nerves with jokes and anecdotes.

Minutes later the driver stopped in front of the Montri home. A small crowd of curious neighbors had all come out to see what was going on. Zachary gestured for Alexander to take the lead, so he took one breath and then another before stepping out of the luxury vehicle. Reaching back, he extended his

hand toward his stepmother to help her out. His
father and brother followed.

At the home's entrance, Sarai opened the door to
welcome them. Beautiful bouquets of plumeria decorated the space, the soft floral aroma scenting the
air. But their beauty didn't compare to hers. She was
dressed simply, a silk dress in a soft peach tone adorning
her body. She'd twisted her hair into a side ponytail,
and simple gold earrings complemented the look.
Her smile was bright, and Alexander was instantly at
ease the moment he saw her.

"Welcome to our home," she said as she stepped
aside, gesturing for them to enter.

Sarai guided them into the living space, where
Gamon sat flanked by three older women. Nervous
energy suddenly filled the home as Sarai made the
introductions.

"Father, Aunties, allow me to introduce you to
Alexander Barrett and his parents, Mrs. Lynn Barrett
and her husband, Mr. Westley Barrett."

"Mr. and Mrs. Barrett, this is my father, Gamon
Montri, and my aunts," she said, calling each of their
names. "Auntie Lawan and Auntie Manee are not
related to us by blood, but they helped my father
raise me after my mother's death. Auntie Rune is my
father's youngest sister. The baby of the family. His
oldest sister lives in England with her husband and
can't be here."

The tension that suddenly filled the space was palpable. Sarai's aunts welcomed them in Thai, smiles
and nods abundant, and then the whispering began
as recognition swept through the room. Gamon
slowly came to his feet, his eyes locked on Westley
Barrett. Sarai and Alexander both shifted their gazes

back and forth between the two men, acutely aware
that something wasn't quite right. Mama Lynn looked
confused, her own gaze shifting to Zachary for some
answers.

Westley extended his hand to shake Gamon's but
the other man never extended his arm to return the
gesture. After Gamon left him hanging he pressed his
hands together as if in prayer, holding them at chest
level. *"Wai!"* he exclaimed, the Thai greeting sounding like the English word *why*. The aunties giggled,
their heads bobbing gleefully as they greeted him
back.

It surprised Alexander, a smile pulling full across
his face as Zachary winked an eye at him.

Westley continued. "It's good to see you again,
Gamon. My wife and I would like to thank you for
your hospitality." He reached for a box that Zachary
carried, extending it toward the other man with both
hands. "Please, accept this as a token of our appreciation," he said.

Gamon's stare shifted toward Mama Lynn, who was
grinning brightly. "Thank you," he said, resting the
gift on the table by his side. He turned abruptly and
dropped back into his seat.

There was an awkward silence as Sarai gestured for
them all to sit. She reached for Alexander's hand,
drawing him to her. Side by side, they were a stunning
couple, and there was no missing the emotion they
shared; love like a warm blanket wrapped around their
shoulders. Zachary moved to his brother's other side,
and the two gave him a nod, gesturing with their eyes.

Alexander took a deep breath, and then he spoke.
"Mr. Montri, Aunties, my family and I are here because
I would like to ask for your permission, sir, to marry

your daughter. I love Sarai and I would like to be a good husband to her. I have a home and a very successful business back in the United States and I want to share everything that I have with her."

Gamon pondered his question for a brief moment. "And why do you want to marry my daughter and not someone else's daughter?"

Alexander took a step toward her family, gesturing with his hands. His words were suddenly poetic. "Sarai brings me immense joy. She makes me smile. I am a better man because of her. She has my heart and I breathe because she is my air. I don't hunger for anything because she is my nourishment. Your daughter is my lifeline and I would only be a semblance of myself if you were to deny us a future together."

As Alexander spoke, his brother translated for the old women. There was a rumble of mutterings as they whispered together, faces glowing with wide, toothy smiles.

Zachary stepped forward, his hands clasped together in front of him. "Gamon, I come on my brother's behalf. I speak to you as one friend to another. You know me and you know I am an honorable man. When I tell you that Sarai will want for nothing, you can trust that with your life. My brother loves her with his whole heart and he will cherish her forever. You have my word that he will be a blessing to you and your whole family."

Alexander reached into the inside pocket of his suit jacket and pulled out a velvet box. He stepped in front of Gamon and lifted the top. Gamon eyed its contents intently before lifting his gaze to meet Alexander's. The women beside them were fanning themselves, unable to contain their excitement. The patriarch gave Alexander a nod but said nothing.

Moving back to Sarai's side Alexander reopened the box for her to see what was inside. The stunning piece of jewelry that lay before her was an intricate design of gold and diamonds. It was a dropped collar, the gold looking like delicate lace entwined in a bed of teardrop diamonds. He had known it was the perfect piece the moment the jeweler had shown it to him. It had taken Alexander's breath away. He prayed that it would do the same to Sarai.

Her eyes widened, tears suddenly misting her gaze.

"Will you accept my proposal, Sarai?" he asked.

Sarai nodded, her smile widening. "I'd be honored." Taking the gift from Alexander's hands, she moved to where her father sat and dropped down onto her knees. With a bowed head she extended the box toward him. "Will you give us your blessing, Father?"

Gamon hesitated for a brief moment, once again looking in Westley's direction. He suddenly gestured for the man to follow him and the two disappeared from the room. Their departure was abrupt and unexpected. The aunties resumed their whispering, concern shadowing their expressions.

"What's going on?" Alexander asked, looking to his brother.

Zachary shrugged. "You got me!"

"Do you know?" Alexander asked Sarai, who was chewing nervously on her bottom lip.

She met the look he was giving her and shook her head. Despite her optimism, something about the turn of events didn't feel encouraging.

"This is ridiculous," Alexander muttered under his breath. "We're eloping," he whispered between clenched teeth. "I've had just about enough of this craziness!"

She reached for his hand and squeezed it, knowing in her heart of hearts that if her father didn't give them his blessing, marrying Alexander might not be an option for her. Ever.

He seemed to read her mind, the frustration and fear across her face. "You do want to marry me, don't you?" he asked.

Tears misted Sarai's gaze. "Of course I do," she whispered between her own clamped teeth. "I want that more than anything in this world but I also want my father to support us the way I know your father supports us." She brushed a tear from her cheek. "I need him to give us his blessing!"

"It's going to be okay," he said and then he exited the room, moving to the patio outside to join the two patriarchs, his brother close on his heels.

Gamon and Westley stood toe to toe, the two men in heated discussion. The twins were both surprised to hear their father speaking fluent Thai. Heads were waving, hands were shaking, and clearly, whatever it was between them had finally come to a head. The brothers stood watching, heads snapping left and right as if they were watching a tennis match.

"What's he saying?" Alexander asked as Zachary stood listening.

"Apparently Dad and Sarai's mother had a serious fling," Zachary whispered. "Really serious! Everyone thought Dad was going to marry her but when he left she stayed behind."

Alexander rolled his eyes as he eyed both men,

desperate to understand why their past drama was interrupting his marriage proposal.

Zachary suddenly gasped. "Sister?" The look he tossed his brother was gut-wrenching. He switched from English to Thai, inserting himself into their conversation.

Alexander suddenly looked anxious. The moment was surreal. He felt like his life was flashing before him. He tried to make the pieces fit. What he knew and what he didn't. His father had said his relationship with Sarai's mother was before their mother. So it wasn't possible. Or was it? Westley had secrets, things his sons didn't know. But he wouldn't have said nothing about Sarai possibly being his half-sister. Even if he wasn't sure, he wouldn't have allowed the two of them to fall in love to only have their hearts broken. Alexander desperately needed it all to make sense. "What sister?" he snapped. Loudly. "Please, God, do not tell me Sarai is our sister!"

Both Gamon and Westley turned to stare at him, their conversation coming to an abrupt halt. The moment was awkward and then Gamon started to laugh. When he did, Westley followed, and seconds later Alexander was staring at the three of them chuckling like they'd just heard the last punchline at a comedy show.

He shook his head. "Would someone please tell me what's going on?"

Gamon pointed a finger in Westley's direction. "Your father, he broke my sister's heart."

Westley swiped a large hand across his eyes. "All your family cared about was my money," he said, "and I didn't have any money!"

Gamon went off on another tangent, chastising

the American's bad behavior. When he was done, Westley apologized, genuinely regretting everything that had happened. Contrition furrowed his brow as he tried to explain himself and plead his son's case.

"Look," he said, "I can't change what happened. If I could, I would. But your sister married a great guy. He made her happy. Now, that's all in the past. We need to focus on the future. Our children's future. My son is a good man. He is a better man than I ever imagined being. And he loves your daughter. He would do anything for her. He wants to make her happy and you should let him because your daughter loves him back. Besides, you and I both know Sarai's mother would have loved him, too. She would have wanted this for your daughter."

Gamon stood in reflection for a good minute, staring out to the fields that bordered his property. He turned toward Alexander and extended his arm and they shook hands. "My daughter is waiting," he said as he turned, heading back into the home. As he passed by Westley he tossed him one last look. "My sister married a man with a face like a frog. She wasn't that happy."

As Gamon disappeared inside Alexander crossed his arms over his chest, his hands clasped tightly beneath his armpits. He felt himself tearing up and he was successfully fighting the sensation right up to the moment his brother touched him, slapping him warmly against his back. He closed his eyes and shook his head, the tears burning hot behind his lashes.

His father called his name and when he opened his eyes, Westley wrapped him in a warm bear hug. "I'm proud of you, son," he said. "I'm proud of both you boys."

Zachary shook his head. "I am so confused!" he exclaimed. "I thought you had a thing with Sarai's mother?"

Westley laughed, his voice dropping to a loud whisper. "I did, but let it go for now or your brother and that girl will never get married!"

Back inside Gamon had returned to his seat by the aunties, the old women admonishing him for disrupting the moment. When Alexander moved back to Sarai's side she was shaking, her eyes tinted red from crying. He wrapped his arms around her and hugged her close. She was still clutching that velvet box tightly. He leaned to whisper in her ear.

"Please ask your father again for his blessing," he said softly.

With a nod of her head Sarai moved back in front of her father, bowing down a second time. She lifted the box and extended it toward him.

"Father, will you give Alexander and me your blessing to be married?"

Gamon's gaze danced across his only child's face as she eyed him eagerly, anticipation thick and full between them. In that moment he wanted only the very best for her. He loved her and despite all of his other issues he wanted her happy.

Reaching out he took the velvet box from her. His smile lifted slowly as he nodded his approval, and when he did, her aunts cheered with excitement. Mama Lynn clapped her hands together, her own joy overflowing. Alexander blew a sigh of relief as Gamon stood, reaching to shake his hand one more time.

The aunts gestured for Mama Lynn to join them in

the kitchen. They had prepared a feast of food for the entire family to celebrate the occasion. The atmosphere was suddenly relaxed as discussion immediately started about the wedding and everything that needed to be done to prepare.

"I will speak to the monks and we need to consult the astrologer for the best day," Gamon said.

The women were suddenly talking guest lists and colors. Alexander and Zachary filled plates with food and settled down into a corner as Gamon and Westley became better acquainted, the two men discussing the upcoming fight.

"And you are sure about this, A?" Zachary asked. "Because this marriage needs to be forever."

On the other side of the room, Sarai met the look Alexander was giving her. Joy shimmered across her face as her female relatives fawned over her. She smiled, and in that moment, everything felt right in Alexander's small world.

He turned back to his brother. "I am, Z! It's the only thing I've been sure about in a long time."

Chapter Seventeen

Bangkok was a host of contradictions. The sprawling metropolis was hot, polluted, and chaotic with the worst traffic nightmares, yet it thrilled with vibrancy and energy, playing to tourism with its bright lights and attractions.

The views from hotel windows magnified the natural landscape that shaped the city's layout. Canals that branched out from the Chao Phraya River snaked through the heart of the city, complemented by floating markets that highlighted the daily life and cultural custom of the people who lived there.

The Barrett family was staying in connecting suites at the Mandarin Oriental Bangkok. The luxury five-star hotel was renowned for its timeless style, and Zachary was excited to be able to gift the accommodations to his parents. But after checking them all in, he'd said good-bye, kissing and hugging them warmly.

"You aren't staying?" Mama Lynn asked.

Zachary shook his head. "I'm sleeping down at the gym. I can't get too comfortable," he said.

Alexander had nodded his understanding, but he also addressed his concerns. "You need to slow your training down. You can't go at the same pace you've been working. Your training sessions have been super intense and your body needs to heal as much as possible before fight night. Maybe some pampering might be good for you?"

"I know but I really need to stay in the zone. I'll get plenty of pampering once I win this belt."

"How can I help?"

"Help your woman with the wedding plans. She's got a ton of things to get done before next week."

Alexander laughed. "And tell me again why we're having the ceremony so soon?"

Zachary laughed with his brother. "Because the astrologer said next week is the best time to ensure a long-lasting union, our parents will still be here, and the monks have agreed."

"Well, there must be something I can do for you?"

Zachary nodded. "Gamon and I have got everything covered from here but the night of the fight I would really like for you to be with me then. By my side."

"I wouldn't be anyplace else. I'll have your back, like you've had mine."

The two men pumped fists, then pulled each other into a warm hug. When their family walked into the room, they were still holding tight to each other.

"How's Thailand?" Dan asked, his deep voice echoing over the phone line.

Alexander grinned into the receiver. "Thailand has been an experience. Right now I'm in Bangkok!"

"You and your brother have been all over the sports news! It's been good publicity for the gym."

"How is my business holding up without me?"

"Business is great! You're actually going to turn a profit your first quarter!"

"Nice!"

"And we're hosting a live fight-night event to watch your brother defend his title. In fact, I just confirmed the HBO order to ensure it's going to show on all the big-screen TVs around here."

"That's a great idea! If I can I'll try to get a minute of camera time and plug the gym."

"So when are you coming home? We have a lot going on in terms of marketing and promotion and since you're the face of Champs it would be really good if you were actually here."

"The fight is on Saturday night and then the wedding is next week—Thursday. I'll be home sometime right after that."

There was a brief moment of silence as his friend, Dan, pondered his comment.

"What wedding?"

Alexander laughed. "Sarai and I are getting married!"

"You're kidding me, right?"

"I'm dead serious, my friend! I asked the girl to marry me and she said yes! We're having the official ceremony here in Phuket and then we'll have another reception or something when we get back to Colorado."

"So you're definitely coming back to Boulder?"

"Boulder is home, boy!"

Their conversation continued for a good few minutes as Alexander updated his friend on everything that had happened since his coming to Thailand. With plans in place for his return and him feeling comfortable that everything was going well with his business ventures, he ended the call on a happy note.

Moving to the massive windows that looked out on

the city, he took a deep breath and then another. In the distance, lights flickered like a holiday event gone wild. His parents had gone to dinner, Westley promising Mama Lynn a romantic evening. Alexander had slipped his credit card into his father's hand and had insisted the couple go have fun without being concerned about their spending. His father's penny-pinching could sometimes be a source of consternation, and he hadn't wanted the man's prudence to keep Mama Lynn from doing something she wanted to experience. He felt like it was the least he could do after everything they'd done for him.

Moving back across the room, Alexander reached for his cell phone. He hadn't heard anything from Sarai since they'd parted ways at the airport. There had been a host of details that needed to be settled with the UFC and the training facility that was hosting Zachary and his team. Sarai had dived headfirst into her managerial role, both Zachary and Gamon deferring to her judgment while they focused entirely on what Zachary needed to be prepared.

He dialed her number but got her voice mail. Just as he was wondering where she might be, there was a knock on his door. The light rap was unexpected, and for a brief second it startled him.

"Who is it?"

A thickly accented Thai voice echoed on the other side. "Room service! I'm here to turn back your bed, sir!"

Moving to the entrance, Alexander pulled the door open and was overjoyed to find Sarai standing on the other side.

"Do you just let any woman come in and turn your bed down?" she said teasingly.

Alexander laughed. "I try to save things like that

for my woman but she's been off doing her own thing and I haven't heard from her!"

Sarai wrapped her arms around his neck and hugged him. "Your woman has been working too hard!" she said as she moved into the room and he closed the door behind them.

"How's it going?" he asked as she moved to the sofa that sat room center and took a seat.

"Zachary is all settled in. I confirmed everything with the caterer who is handling his dietary needs, and my father seems to have a handle on everything else. The UFC is really happy with him. His sponsors are even happier and when he wins it's going to be a real boost for his career. I'm glad that you've been here to help him. He really needed you."

"I really needed him. I just didn't know it," he said as he sat down beside her.

Sarai smiled, reveling in the emotion he exuded as he thought about his twin and everything that had happened with the two of them. Both men had found balance and comfort with each other, and the wealth of what they'd been feeling had been a blessing for the rest of them.

She leaned into Alexander's side. "Have you eaten anything?"

He shook his head. "I haven't been hungry. There's just been so much going on."

"I haven't eaten either. Would you like to go out and get something?"

Alexander thought for a quick minute. "Why don't we order up room service and just stay in? We haven't really had any time together since we got engaged." He smiled.

"I would really like that," she answered as he stood up to find the hotel menu.

Minutes later as they waited for their traditional
Thai meal of deep-fried chicken and crabmeat spring
rolls, prawns with pineapple curry, and jasmine rice
to be delivered, their conversation turned to their
pending wedding.

"So what do I need to do?" Alexander asked. "Because I'm sure there's a hoop or two I need to jump
through. Getting married has to be as hard as getting
engaged was."

Sarai laughed. "It won't be nearly as difficult, I
promise."

He nodded. "Let me ask you something," he said
as he sat back down.

"Anything."

"If I asked you to forgo a Thai ceremony and just
go back to Colorado with me and get married at the
courthouse, would you?"

Sarai studied his face for a brief moment. He was
eyeing her intently, his expression too serious for
comfort. She nodded her head slowly. "If that's what
you wanted. Yes, I would. I just want to be your wife,"
she said, her voice dropping to a low whisper.

Alexander smiled as he raised her hands to his lips,
kissing her palm gently. "I love you, Sarai. I hope that
you know that."

"I do and I love you. I want to make you happy,
Alex."

"You do, baby. You make me very happy. And I
want you to have the wedding of your dreams."

Her smile was canyon wide as she dipped her head,
gratitude billowing across her face.

"So, how long do I have you for? Is Gamon going
to be looking for you?"

She giggled. "No. My father knows I'm here with
you. We're engaged now, remember?"

"It's like that? Girl, we should have gotten engaged weeks ago!"

Their conversation continued until well after their late-night meal was delivered and consumed. After savoring the last bite, their stomachs full, they moved from the dining table back to the sofa. Holding hands, the two settled back in their seats, falling into the silence that painted the room. For some reason, Sarai found herself unable to focus. She had no words for the thoughts that were going through her mind, but in that moment her head was clouded, a range of emotion suddenly consuming her.

Their hands were still joined, Alexander's fingers interlaced between her own. He'd developed slight calluses across his fingers from working out so hard, but his touch was soft, almost feathery against her skin. She lifted her eyes to stare at him. Lost in his own musings, his blues eyes stared at the views outside the windows. Sarai leaned her head against his shoulder, a soft sigh of contentment blowing past her lips.

Alexander felt his heart leap into his throat. His nostrils were suddenly filled with the scent of the peppermint oil and lavender soap that Sarai had bathed in. The nearness of her had his senses on alert, and his skin tingled from the sensation of her soft hair brushing against his arm. They sat for a few more minutes; then Sarai disengaged her hand from his. The gesture was slow and deft as she began to caress his palm and wrist tenderly with her fingertips.

Alexander's pulse was suddenly racing. The impulses emanating from every pore were hard core, an irresistible urge to take her right then and there compelling. The intensity surprised him, desire going from zero to ten in a split second. There was no hiding the wanting that had risen full and hard in his southern quadrant. Her hand suddenly strayed into his lap, and she began to caress the fabric of his slacks over his thigh. Her touch was teasing, purposely avoiding the protrusion that shifted between his legs. Closing his eyes, he let himself fall into the delicious sensations.

Alexander shifted his body and extended his legs outward. He wrapped his arms around her shoulders, his own hands slowly caressing her arms and back. His eyes were suddenly drawn back to his lap as her hand continued to move upward. She trailed her nails slowly, the teasing beginning to take on a life of its own as she stroked him over his clothes. Their gazes connected for a brief moment, the look she gave him causing his breath to catch deep in his throat. He gasped, suddenly unable to form a coherent thought.

Alexander bit down against his bottom lip as Sarai pulled at his zipper to release him. He lifted his hips to help pull his slacks and briefs past his hips. His whole body quivered when she suddenly brushed her cheek against his cock, her warm breath teasing the head of his organ with each pass. He tried to say her name, but nothing passed his lips but a loud moan.

Sarai held him in the palm of her hand, her fingers drawing up and down against the dark skin. She lowered her face against him, nuzzling him with her cheek and chin. Her touch elicited a heavy sigh of pleasure from Alexander. He trembled, reclining his body even more. The anticipation was overwhelming, and the throbbing between his legs had his whole body pulsing with heat.

"Just like that," he whispered as he wrapped her fingers around his shaft and guided her ministrations.

Sarai stroked him slowly, each pass long and firm

as she watched his face. Pleasure flushed his cheeks, and he bit down against his bottom lip, his eyes half closed as he panted softly.

Alexander suddenly felt himself being sucked down into a vortex of pure, unadulterated desire, and he slid like melting butter into the sensations. Sarai's mouth was heated and wet, and she blew him with warm breath, sucking him in and out. He grabbed the sides of her face with both hands, making love to her mouth as he pushed and pulled his hips in sync with the massaging action of her lips. She dropped to her knees to better position her head over his crotch, and every muscle in his body felt like rubber as he watched.

Watching her pleasure him, her head bobbing up and down, sent him over the edge. He murmured her name over and over again as if in prayer, the soulful mantra resounding through the room. His orgasm was intense. He spewed his seed on a down stroke, and Sarai never missed a beat, continuing to knead and suck and caress him with her lips until she'd milked him dry. Her mouth never left his flaccid member as her tongue continued to flick back and forth against his flesh. And then he fell into a deep slumber, her name still vibrating out of his mouth.

When Alexander opened his eyes again, the lights in the room had been dimmed. It was eerily quiet as he lay across the sofa, his gaze adjusting to the barest hint of light through the space. Someone had draped a blanket over his body, and it was pulled up to his shoulders. As he threw his legs onto the floor, he realized he was naked from the waist down. Looking around, he found his pants, briefs, and socks folded into a neat pile on the coffee table. His shoes rested beside the couch. He palmed his manhood and realized he needed to use the restroom, a full bladder anxious for his attention.

Rising, he headed toward the bathroom. As he moved in that direction, he pulled his T-shirt up and over his head and tossed it to the floor. Minutes later, with relief found and his hands washed and dried, he moved into the suite's bedroom. He was pleasantly surprised to find Sarai sound asleep in his bed. She lay in the center of the mattress, her body curled tightly around her pillow. Her hair lay loose around her head, the luscious locks a mass of thick waves.

She was naked, the sheets tangled around her feet and falling down to the floor. Alexander stood watching her for a good few minutes. She was the most beautiful creature he'd ever beheld. She looked angelic and fragile, and he thought about how much he loved her. Knowing that she loved him had his heart beating a drum line in his chest, the pulsing sensation surging through every inch of his body. He suddenly wanted her again, trying to imagine if there would ever come a day when his desire would pale and he wouldn't want more of her.

He eased himself onto the bed, lifting one knee and then the other as he crawled up against her. He laid his body down beside hers, settling into the heat that billowed off her skin. Her lips were parted, her breath an easy exhale of air. It was like she was begging to be kissed. He lowered his face to hers to oblige. He touched her upper lip with the tip of his tongue, the gesture gentle and teasing. Then he slowly sucked her bottom lip into his mouth.

Sarai woke with a slight start, a gasp of surprise and pleasure blowing into his mouth. She purred, the soft

sound like a caressing breath against his ears. Sarai
ran the tip of her own tongue over Alexander's full
lips. Delight rose up in his throat as he moaned his
pleasure against her tongue.

As he kissed her, his hands walked a heated trail
over her body. His easy caresses were intoxicating,
and she soon found herself drunk with wanting. The
kiss was loving and intimate. She wanted to find the
words to describe the wealth of sensations his touch
was bringing forth, but the erotic sensations made
thinking difficult. It was a tender moment, teasing
and playful as they gently savored each other's taste.

Their kisses grew deeper, longer, and more insis-
tent. Both found themselves lost in the tide of their
growing passion. The dance that unfolded against the
bedclothes was a graceful give and take, bare skin kissing bare skin. Their naked bodies were heated, damp
with perspiration, sweat puddling in intimate places.
Their mouths never parted as he fondled her breasts
and palmed her buttocks, his body melting like
butter against hers. They were both panting like
they'd run a race. He licked her throat, her breasts,
suckling her hardened nipples as his hands kneaded
her thighs and caressed her abdomen. He parted her
legs, his fingers tapping gently at the damp fold. He
teased her clit with his thumb, gently rolling the engorged nub between his fingers. Her legs fell open,
parting widely as she urged him to settle in.

As he pushed his body into hers, he pressed his
mouth back to her parted lips, his tongue plunging
as deeply into her eager cavity as his cock plunged
into the folds of her inner lining. Sarai stifled a low
sob, the intensity of his kiss keeping her from crying
out. He pushed and pulled himself into and out of
her, his loving intense, demanding, urgent.

They were an entanglement of arms and legs as they gyrated from one corner of the bed to the other. Beneath the soft lights that reflected into the room, both marveled at the beautiful contrast between her pale skin and his darker complexion. They were an exquisite blending, the sheer magnitude of how beautiful they were together overwhelming them both.

They made love over and over again. Time seemed to stand still, everything falling into place to do their bidding. When the first sign of light shimmered through the windows, the morning sun beginning to rise against the Bangkok skyline, Alexander was still wrapped around her body. As Sarai lay curled in the armor of his arms, sleep slowly beginning to take hold, he kissed her one last time, then finally closed his eyes.

Chapter Eighteen

Breakfast was about to be over and lunch was about to start when Sarai and Alexander found their way to the Verandah Restaurant. His parents were just finishing their meal, the two plotting out their day. With only a few hours before they would all have to be ready for Zachary's fight, neither wanted to stray too far from the hotel.

Sitting outside with a wonderful view of the river, in the fresh air, was exactly what Sarai and Alexander needed to shake the sluggishness that was hanging heavily over them. Alexander imagined a cup of hot coffee would also help.

As they approached the table, Mama Lynn laughed warmly.

"Good morning, sleepyheads!"

Westley tossed them both a raised brow. "Looks like you two done started the honeymoon already," he teased.

A blush colored both their cheeks, Alexander waving his head from side to side. "Good morning," he said as he leaned to kiss his stepmother's cheek. He pulled out a seat for Sarai, and they both sat down.

"Did you two sleep well?" the matriarch asked.

Sarai nodded, cutting an eye at Alexander.

"I'm glad someone did," Westley said. "I was too wound up to sleep. Have you talked to your brother this morning?"

Sarai nodded again. "I spoke to my father a few minutes ago. Zachary was watching cartoons and eating Cheerios! He said to tell you that he wants all of us to come to the arena at six o'clock. Alexander, he wants you and your father to walk the gantlet with him and there are reserved seats for us all."

Alexander laughed. "The breakfast of champions!" he said, the meal one of their favorites when they were boys.

Westley nodded, turning toward his wife. "We might as well stay in and relax. Maybe rest by the pool. We only have a few hours before we have to be ready."

"I was hoping to do a little shopping," Mama Lynn said, clearly not agreeing with his game plan.

Sarai shifted forward in her seat. "I would love to go shopping with you," she said. "And we won't need to go far. They have plenty of shops within walking distance."

The older woman clapped her hands together excitedly. "Maybe I can even find me a wig store!"

Alexander laughed. "Sounds like I'm sitting by the pool with you, Pop!"

His father nodded. "Looks like you need it, too."

A waitress came to take their orders. Alexander selected an omelet with fresh herbs, tomato, mushrooms, Gruyère cheese, ham, and asparagus, and a glass of papaya juice to go along with his pot of coffee. Sarai order roasted snow fish with sautéed spinach and mushrooms. Once the food arrived, the two ate eagerly, suddenly realizing they were starved. Once they'd eaten, the two women blew the men kisses and headed to the shops.

"She's a sweet girl," Westley said, his gaze following behind the two women. "Real sweet. And I like her father even if he is a pain in my ass. Although I still don't think he's sure about you yet."

Alexander rested his juice glass on the table, turning toward his father. "Did he say something else to you that I should know about?"

"Just that he was happy that you had the financial resources to take care of his baby girl."

His son shrugged. "It's all good."

"They've got some funny ways over here, son. That's one reason things didn't work out with me and her mother. It always felt like it was more about my money and what I could do for her family than it was about me and what we were feeling for each other."

"So is that why you left and never came back?"

The older man cut an eye in his child's direction. "I just shared that with you because I want you to be sure about marrying this girl. So, that's all I'm saying. It's not too late if you want to change your mind."

Alexander rolled his eyes skyward. "So are you going to tell me about you and Gamon's sister? And how Sarai's mother fit into the mix? It seems like you had some kind of love triangle going on while you were here."

Westley leaned back in his seat, his mind seeming to drift into the past. He sighed as his gaze shifted back toward his son. "I was young and dumb. I was stationed at the US Embassy in Bangkok and I was only a few short months away from being transferred back to the States. I had met Gamon's older sister, Tai, first. She was a nice girl but she wasn't as innocent as her brother seems to think she was. She wanted a husband, she wanted out of Thailand, and she was willing to do anything and everything to make that happen. Of course, Gamon couldn't see it. He was as protective of his sister as he is with his daughter. But Tai, well let's just say she knew some tricks that kept a few of us coming back for more, if you know what I mean. But I would never tell her brother that."

Westley took a breath as he continued. "Then I met Sarai's mother. Khim was everything Tai wasn't. Khim managed to steal my heart and I almost gave up everything to stay here with her."

"So you loved her?"

His father gave him a look as he nodded his head. "I did. I loved Khim very much. Back then I didn't know that it was possible to love someone as much as I loved that woman."

"So what happened?"

"You've seen enough to know that their culture is very different from ours. You marry a girl here and it's expected that you'll support her whole damn family. I just couldn't handle all of the demands. Every time I turned around Khim's family wanted money. Someone always had their hand out and Khim didn't seem to understand why I had to say no. Back then, by their standards I was rich! So one day I gave her an ultimatum. Me or them. I was ready to take her back to the States and I really thought she loved me enough to leave. I honestly believed that we didn't need anyone else as long as we had each other. I thought we were all the family we would ever need."

Westley lost himself in the memories for a moment, as he was taken back to a time he'd long laid to rest. He sighed, the weight of it like a heavy brick being launched into a glass window as he continued. "Khim couldn't leave and I couldn't stay. We kept in touch, wrote letters to each other for a few years, and then she met and married Gamon. A few years later, I met your mother and fell in love with her and we both moved on with our lives. End of story."

Alexander nodded. "Sarai doesn't think her mother ever stopped loving you. She thinks she regretted how your relationship ended."

Westley shrugged. "Neither one of us had time for regrets. Gamon loved her. And he took good care of her. She loved him back and they worked very hard to make each other happy."

"How do you know that?"

"Because when I found out about her and Gamon, I came back to try and change her mind. I begged her to leave him and be with me. But she turned me down."

"Gamon doesn't know this, does he?"

Westley shook his head. "He may have suspected. He knew that Khim and I were acquainted. But there was no reason for him to know anything else. Khim chose him. Not me. It was enough that he thought I did his sister wrong."

Alexander shifted his eyes to the river boats that bobbed out on the water. When he turned back to his father, the old man was staring at him. He met the look evenly with one of his own. "I'm not going to change my mind. I love Sarai. I love her with every ounce of breath I have in me and I'm not going to lose her."

Westley nodded. Another moment passed before either spoke; then his father broke the silence. "I'm glad you and your brother are doing well together. Family is very important. Don't you ever forget that."

The two men stood up, and Alexander gave his

father a fist bump. "Let's go check out the pool, Pop,"
he said with the wink of an eye.

Westley chuckled. "A bikini or two sure wouldn't
hurt right about now!"

A crowd was already beginning to line up at Ra-
jadamnern Boxing Arena. When Alexander and his
parents arrived, Sarai was already there. Gamon had
called for her hours earlier, needing her to run interference with the media and sponsors trying to pull at
Zachary's attention.

Gamon greeted his future son-in-law warmly, then
pointed him toward the dressing room. His brother's
team were all standing anxiously out in the hallway,
awaiting permission to go inside. But permission wasn't
being given. "He only say you," Gamon pronounced.

"Go make sure he's okay," Westley admonished,
concern furrowing his brow.

Alexander cast his eyes around, everyone staring
back at him. With a quick nod, he sauntered the
length of the hallway and entered the closed room.

Moving into the space, he found his brother and
Sarai huddled together in a corner of the room. She
was holding both of his hands, their heads bowed
together, foreheads brushing against each other. A
wave of jealous emotion hit Alexander broadside, and
he felt himself bristle with indignation. His entire
body was suddenly a constricted knot. He clenched
his fists, and his jaw tightened.

He was just about to speak when Zachary suddenly
looked his way. A wide grin blossomed full across his
twin's face, and relief seemed to flood the other
man's entire demeanor. Beside him, exhilaration

gleamed from Sarai's eyes. She was excited to see him as well. There was something in that moment that flooded Alexander with emotion he'd not been expecting, and he bit down hard against his bottom lip to regain a sense of control.

"Hey, it's about time!" Zachary exclaimed. "You had me scared for a minute."

Alexander nodded. "I didn't mean to be late. Blame your mother. It took her forever to get ready. Something about the Asian hair she bought from an Asian." He chuckled, trying to lighten the moment.

Zachary gestured for him to join their little circle. "Come pray with me," he said.

As Alexander stepped between them, Sarai trailed her hand against his back. Concern pierced her expression as she noted the tension that had tightened the muscles across his back. She met his stare, her gaze questioning. "Are you okay?" she asked.

Alexander nodded, feeling slightly foolish. He said nothing, only leaning to press a damp kiss to her cheek.

Zachary grabbed his brother's hand, and Sarai grabbed the other as the trio bowed their heads together. The blessing was short and sweet, his twin asking God to guide his punches, followed by Sarai echoing the sentiment in a Thai prayer for luck.

"Sarai, can you give me and Alex a minute, please?" Zachary asked. "Tell everyone we won't be much longer."

"Of course," she said. She leaned to kiss Zachary's cheek, then pressed her lips to Alexander's lips. She gave him one last look as she brushed her hand down the side of his face in a sweet caress.

The brothers watched as she exited the room,

closing the door behind her. Zachary reached for the rolls of tape and passed them to his twin. "I didn't want anyone else to wrap my hands. Do you mind?"

Alexander shook his head. The two men stood toe-to-toe as he began to wrap the protective layer of material around his twin's palms.

"You got jealous there for a minute, didn't you? I saw it on your face."

The brothers locked eyes. Alexander hesitated for a brief second before responding. "Yeah," he said. "I did. You two looked very cozy there for a minute. And, I'll be honest, it surprised me."

Zachary blew a deep sigh. "We've come too far to fall apart now, A!"

"I agree. I guess I still have some work to do."

"Your girl's always been good luck for me. She made me pray my very first fight and she's prayed with me each time since."

"She loves you."

"She's *in* love with you. And damn, bro, I love you both! You're my best friend and so is she. We're family and we're all good together. I don't want us to mess that up. So at some point you're going to need to trust me."

"I do trust you."

"Really? Because it didn't look that way."

"I had a moment, okay? It's no big thing. But I trust you. And I trust her."

Both allowed a moment of silence to fill the air around them. Alexander knew that if he had to explain to anyone why he'd suddenly felt envious of his twin and his girl when he'd seen the two so close together, he wouldn't have been able to find the words. In that moment, though, he'd been haunted by their past, the hurt of it rising again like a phoenix from the ashes. And then he'd seen the joy and love on his brother's face, and on Sarai's, what they felt for him blinding. And just like that the past was gone; done and finished forever.

He changed the subject. "Are you ready for this damn fight?"

Zachary grinned. "Did she tell you that I had Cheerios for breakfast?"

"The breakfast of champions!" they both exclaimed together, a fond memory from when they'd been boys.

"A, I've got this," Zachary said. "No one is taking my title!"

Sarai suddenly peered back into the room. "Is everything okay? Everyone is starting to worry."

Alexander cut an eye in her direction, catching her gaze as she eyed the two of them. He smiled. "Yeah, baby, it's all good," he said as he pulled his twin into a one-armed hug. "It's all good!"

Minutes later the room was just shy of being too crowded. Their parents sat off to the side, not wanting to be in the way. Gamon, Sarai, Zachary's personal physician, his cut man, two of his sparring partners, his corner guy, UFC officials, an arena official, and a producer and cameraman with HBO rounded out the group.

Zachary stood in the center of the room warming up. Gamon held up cushioned sparring pads that he was throwing light punches and kicks at. He needed to work up a sweat to get his muscles warm and loose. In that moment he was as fight ready as he was ever going to be.

Thirty minutes later arena officials announced

fight time. With his clipboard and ink pen in hand, their official handler verified everyone's passes, then gestured for them to follow. At the door Zachary took the lead. Alexander, Gamon, and Westley fell in after him. The rest of the team followed, and Sarai and Mama Lynn brought up the rear. Everyone wore their Revolution T-shirts, the bright blue emblem on the lime-green shirts showcasing the gym's logo.

Weaving their way through the back tunnels of the arena, they could hear the crowd chanting Zachary's name. Repetitions of "Hammer! Hammer! Hammer!" resounded through the air. Their guide lifted up his hand and held them in place for a brief second, awaiting the signal to have the current world champion step into view. And then the sound system blasted Zachary's selected theme song to announce his entrance.

When the 1990s rap song "U Can't Touch This," by MC Hammer, sounded out of the speakers, Zachary tossed his brother a look over his shoulder and grinned. Alexander laughed heartily. Zachary stepped through the curtained entrance and moved out into view. The crowd erupted, their loud cheers vibrating through the space. Cameras snapped photographs, fans screamed, and people standing near the path they took reached out to try to touch him. As they neared the infamous octagon cage that the fighters would be locked in, Zachary threw up his arm, pushing his gold championship belt into the air, and he screamed with the music. *Hammer time!*

A Dutch national nicknamed Pit-bull was on the main fight card against Zachary. He was six feet, four inches, and two hundred fifty-nine pounds of rock-hard muscle. Side by side, Zachary made him look like the Pillsbury Doughboy.

The entire match was scheduled for five five-minute rounds. But it was just minutes into the first round when his opponent quickly discovered why Zachary had been nicknamed The Hammer. Zachary *nailed* the man with his first two punches. Hard. Zachary had hit him so hard that blood had spewed from his broken nose, spraying the entire cage. Pit-bull couldn't breathe, and he couldn't see, but he continued to fight. Then he hurt Zachary with a left hook, following up with a series of head kicks, but he couldn't finish him.

The two men went blow for blow, and the crowd roared. Zachary poured it on, nearly finishing the fight in round three. Cornered, with his back to the fence, Pit-bull swung blindly, creating enough space to survive the bell. Zachary went after him again, but by the fourth round he looked like he was running out of steam. From the sidelines Alexander screamed his encouragement. At the end of the round the two fighters glowered at each other, needing to be admonished back to their sides of the ring by the referee.

Then two minutes into the fifth and last round, Zachary nailed Pit-bull in the head again with a spinning hook kick that sent him down to the mat, the man landing with a resounding thud. It was over.

Alexander punched his fists into the air and screamed, acknowledging the results even before the referee declared his twin brother the winner. He scaled the fight ring and jumped down inside, rushing toward Zachary. Sweeping him in his arms, he cheered, months of hard work come to fruition. The battle would go down in the record books as one of the best in history. Both men knew Zachary's performance would have past and potential opponents buzzing. Alexander couldn't have been prouder.

Outside the ring, the Barrett and Montri families both cheered. Tears streamed down Sarai's cheeks, her hands clasped together as if she were still in prayer. Watching the two men in celebration had her heart singing. Days later a photograph of Alexander holding up his brother would grace the cover of every sports page and magazine, but seeing it up close and live would forever be one of her favorite memories.

"My boy did that!" Westley cheered. "That's my son!" His chest was pushed out with pride.

He shoved his way toward the ring, and as he and Gamon made their way inside, Alexander stepped out, rushing to Sarai's side.

Alexander swept her into his arms, hugging her warmly.

"Congratulations!" she whispered. "You both did good!" She pressed her palm to his face, and then she kissed him, not caring who in the world might see.

The celebration party lasted into the early morning hours. With all the fanfare, sneaking away had been easy, and Alexander and Sarai now sat curled against each other. He had kissed and hugged both of his parents, had shaken Gamon's hand, and then had swiped a bottle of champagne from the bartender. Grabbing Sarai, he paused just long enough to whisper into his brother's ear before disappearing back to the suites.

* * *

"Pour me another drink," Zachary said, his teeth chattering. Bruised black and blue, he lay in a tub of ice and water, the ice bath soothing the hurt and reducing the swelling.

"You shouldn't drink," Sarai admonished. "You need to take your anti-inflammatory meds and maybe a pain pill. You know you can't mix them with alcohol."

He tossed her a wide-eyed look, rolling his eyes skyward. Then he shifted his gaze to his brother. "Please tell your woman that I am now free to do everything I haven't been able to do for the last six months. I will drink, eat badly, and tomorrow I'm going to go find a woman to have sex with. I haven't had sex in six months! So I'm having sex and I might even pay for it!"

Sarai blushed, a hint of red shimmering across her face. "That is not funny," she said, rising from the bench she and Alexander had been sharing. "That is not funny at all."

The two men laughed as she stormed out of the room.

Alexander reached for the champagne bottle and refilled his brother's plastic cup. "It'll be okay," he said. "I'll explain it to her later."

"She gets it. She just doesn't like it. She keeps telling me I need to find someone to settle down with. She doesn't understand the necessity for *casual* relationships."

"Maybe she's right. Have you thought about settling down?"

"Hell, no! I'm the heavyweight champion! Women throw their stuff at me! It's a smorgasbord of free pussy! Why would I want to just give that up?"

Alexander laughed again. "Point well taken! So what's next for you?"

Zachary paused for a moment. He shifted in the ice bath, wincing slightly at the pain that shot through his body. "Well, getting you married is at the top of my list."

"Yeah, there is that! I'm definitely going to need your help making that happen."

"After that I have some promotional things I need to do for the UFC, and for the gym. Then I think I might spend some time in Spain. After that, who knows what I might get into!"

"You can always come back to Boulder."

"I'll definitely get back there a time or two. Someone needs to keep you on your toes!"

The two men talked for another hour. When it became obvious that Sarai wasn't going to return, Alexander stood up to leave.

"You need to get some rest. Do you want some help getting out?" Alexander asked.

Zachary shook his head. "No, I'm good. I'm about to get a hot shower and then I'm going to bed. Just check on me if I'm not up in the next two days because right now I feel like I could sleep forever!"

"Not a problem!" Alexander said, giving him a wave. "And congratulations, Z! You made us all proud!"

Back in his own suite Alexander found Sarai sleeping soundly. Once again she'd made herself comfortable in the king-size bed. Stripping out of his clothes, he tiptoed into the bathroom and turned on the shower. It had been a long day and an even longer night. He was as ready for a hot shower as he imagined his brother was.

The room was soon heated, the hot water misting the air. Stepping into the shower, he eased into the warm spray, allowing the moisture to rain down over his shoulders. It felt good, and he pressed his palms against the marble tile as he dipped his head under the flow.

Losing track of time, he didn't have a clue how long he'd been standing there when Sarai suddenly called out his name.

"Are you well?" she questioned, concern ringing in her tone.

Alexander slid the shower curtain aside. "Hey, baby! I'm good. I didn't mean to wake you."

"I was missing you," she said softly.

"I'm sorry. I didn't mean to stay that long. Zach and I just kept talking and the time flew by."

"That's good," she said. "It's one reason I left so that you two could have some time."

Sarai was eyeing him intently. Alexander had to be the most beautiful man in the whole wide world, she thought. He was solid, every sinewy muscle hardened to perfection. His dark complexion mirrored the chocolates she loved, and his spirit was just as sweet. Seeing him standing there, his skin heated from the hot water, water dripping over every hardened line, suddenly had her feminine spirit quaking with desire. Everything about the two of them together brought her immense joy.

Alexander was watching as she slowly teased the strap of the black lace top she was wearing off her shoulders. A smile crawled across his face, his eyes lifting when she pushed the matching black lace boy-cut shorts down past her knees and stepped out of them.

He stepped back as she moved in his direction, easing herself into the shower to join him. As he wrapped his arms around her, he leaned to capture her mouth beneath his own. Neither said another word, but both knew it was going to be another long and sleepless night.

Chapter Nineteen

They had only been back in Phuket for a few short hours when wedding plans kicked into high gear. With everything that needed to be accomplished before the ceremony that was supposed to take place some four short days later, Alexander was expecting Sarai to shift into bridezilla mode, but she didn't. In fact, she was so incredibly calm and even-tempered that Alexander actually found it disconcerting.

Zachary laughed at him. "She is always like that. The building could be burning down around you and she doesn't even flinch."

The two men were both being fitted for their wedding attire. Alexander stood with his arms stretched outward as the tailor took measurements for the traditional silk *barong* and straight-legged trousers that Sarai had selected for him to wear. His brother's *barong* was almost identical, but the color was a pale gold. Both dress shirts were lightly embroidered, collarless, and striking against their warm skin tones.

"She needs to get a little anxious or something because it scares me!" Alexander laughed as the tailor gestured for him to put his own clothes back on. "It's not normal!"

"What's not normal?" Sarai suddenly asked. Neither man had noticed her moving back into the store.

"You!" Zachary said, giving her a wink of his eye.

She shook her head, fanning a hand in his direction. "Are you two almost finished?" she asked. "We all need to talk."

Alexander stepped back into the space. "That sounds serious. What's up?"

She held up an index finger as she communicated with the store clerk.

When he heard the word *baht,* Alexander passed the man his Black Card.

Minutes later when Sarai was confident their suits would be ready for pickup the next day, she suggested they stop for a moment to enjoy some lunch. They headed to the Green Tamarind Kitchen. Taking seats on the outside patio, they ordered burgers, fries, and drinks.

"So what's so serious, baby?" Alexander questioned, taking a sip of the lager beer that he and his brother had ordered.

"Nothing bad. I've called Dan."

"My Dan?"

She nodded. "Nike has put a sponsorship offer on the table for the two of you. What they're proposing is an athletic line that will revolve around you both. It would be a joint venture. I know Dan has been instrumental in negotiating some of your other deals so I thought he should be in on this from the start."

"Wow!" Zachary exclaimed. "That might be pretty cool!"

Alexander voiced his agreement.

Sarai smiled. "They're going to fax over the initial offers and then we'll take a meeting with them to see where it goes."

Zachary extended his hand in a high five. "You done good, girl!"

Alexander winked his eye at her, allowing his leg to gently brush up against hers.

"Which brings me to my next idea," she continued. "Champs and Revolution. You both have incredible athletic facilities and I was thinking that since you two work so well together you should develop a partnership arrangement where you cross-train at each other's property.

"We have kids and men here in Thailand who would love to learn how to play basketball, and Alex, you could do something like your summer camp programs in the US. And since you don't have a fully developed mixed martial arts program, Zachary could help get that set up and be a guest trainer. There would be some back and forth on both your parts but it could really be a great thing." She looked anxiously from one to the other.

The twins both exchanged a look, reflecting on her suggestion. Although both had thought about what their relationship would be like once Alexander and Sarai flew back to Boulder, neither had considered anything past that.

"I like it," both said, speaking at the same time. Then they laughed, giving each other a high five. "We like it a lot!"

Sarai grinned. "Good. We have some details to work out but I think it'll be a good thing."

"How are you working and planning our wedding and not freaking out?" Alexander asked.

Her laugh was a sweet vibration through the warm afternoon air. "The very bossy, very controlling aunties are doing most of the wedding work. And I am freaking out! I'm just keeping busy so it doesn't show."

Alexander brushed the hair from her face with his fingers. The smile he blessed her with was filled with adoration.

"Oh, and one more thing," she said, casting her gaze on Zachary. "The two of you have gotten half a dozen requests for exclusive interviews. I've spoken to all the media outlets and I've narrowed it down to *Sports Illustrated International*. It will be an eight-page spread, color photos, and will coordinate with a sixty-minute prime-time TV special. I just need both of you to agree and I need your permission to give their journalist access to Revolution and to Champs."

"Define access!" Alexander said, sitting a little straighter in his seat.

"They'd be able to come and go without interruption, and also interview staff and members at their discretion. They will also do an extensive interview with the two of you. They would not be allowed to see your financials or client records. It's strictly a public-interest piece to allow their readers and fans an inside look on how you both operate. And you both have final refusal if you don't like what they write or what they film."

"And how long would we have to put up with this person being in our way?" Zachary asked.

Sarai giggled. "One month. Maybe less, maybe more."

The two men stared at each other.

"Do you think this is a good thing for us to do?" Alexander asked.

"Yes," Sarai answered. "I think it'll be very good, especially if you do a joint venture. It'll be great advertisement to promote both gyms and the two of you individually."

Zachary nodded. He looked at his brother as he gestured with his head in Sarai's direction. "You trust her judgment?"

Alexander shrugged his shoulders slightly. "Do you?"

Sarai playfully punched them both in the shoulder. "Really!"

The twins burst out laughing.

"So what do we need to do, baby?" Alexander asked, still chuckling.

"I have some contracts that you both need to execute. Dan has already had your attorney review them. Zach, your attorney has looked them over as well, and now you both just need to sign on the dotted line."

Alexander picked up his burger with both hands, the massive sandwich overflowing with salad, caramelized onions, crispy bacon slices, and chunks of blue cheese. "I can see why you're not freaking out about our wedding ceremony. You've been too busy to think about marrying me!" he said jovially.

"Oh, I've been thinking about you," she said. "In fact, after we eat, you and I have to go do *pa-alam*."

Zachary burst out laughing, practically choking on the food he'd been ready to swallow. She patted him against his back as he coughed to catch his breath.

"Why am I suddenly scared?" Alexander questioned, looking from one to the other.

His brother was still laughing. "Be afraid, A! Be very afraid!"

* * *

For the rest of the afternoon Alexander and Sarai visited the homes of her relatives, most of them elderly, to announce her marriage plans and deliver the formal wedding invitation that had been printed earlier that morning. The senior citizens in the family tree saw the longtime custom as a sign of respect, and it quickly became apparent to him that the gesture was also much appreciated.

Alexander enjoyed the experience. He was in awe of the many family members Sarai had, most especially since both his parents had been only children and he and his brother had never experienced aunts, uncles, and cousins. He also enjoyed the opportunity to practice the language, his hello greeting, *Wai,* spoken with much exuberance.

As with many of the Thai people he met, he was welcomed warmly, everyone kind and accepting. A few were excited, knowing who he was and his connection to the famous Muay Thai fighter with the successful business. It was obvious that many felt Sarai was marrying well and they were happy for her. Those who were surprised asked a ton of questions, wanting to know how they'd met, what he did, and who his parents were. By the end of their *pa-alam,* he felt accepted and overwhelmingly loved.

From her great-uncle's home, they decided to stroll the length of Rawai Beach. Offering a unique local feel, the beach was home to long-established fishermen who made their living from their daily catches, boat chartering, and selling the exquisite shells found in the warm oceanic waters. The area was known as Gypsy Village, and along the right side of the bay, the shoreline hosted dozens of longtail boats, canoes, and speedboats.

The number of seafood restaurants that lined the beach couldn't be counted on two hands. Families were enjoying their evening meal under the shade trees as children danced in the bright blue waters. The views were beautiful, and the atmosphere was peaceful.

As they walked the sandy shoreline, Sarai reached for Alexander's hand, entwining her fingers between his. The look on his face reflected his surprise. "Is this acceptable?" he asked, glancing around to see if anyone was eyeing them.

She smiled and nodded. "We are official. Hand-holding is okay, but nothing more. Not in public."

He nodded. "I like Thailand. I love Phuket, but I'll be glad when we go back to Colorado. I hate not being able to touch you when I want to. I sometimes want to wrap my arms around you and hold you, kiss your lips, give you a light tap on the backside, and it really pisses me off when I can't."

"I'm sorry."

"It's nothing for you to apologize for, baby! I understand that you and your father don't want people looking at you badly. Hell, I don't want people to get the wrong impression about you. You're my fiancée. But I can't help but think that some of the thinking is just a little antiquated."

Sarai squeezed his fingers and nodded. "Next week we'll be back in Colorado and you can tap my backside anytime you want!"

Alexander laughed. "I'll probably embarrass myself not being able to keep my hands off you!"

She laughed with him. "We won't be doing *that* kind of touching in public!"

* * *

Mama Lynn and Westley sat in Zachary's soaking pool, the warm waters easing the day's stress away. Westley had spent most of the day with Gamon, discovering all the man did around the property for his son. When Zachary and Alexander had disappeared to run wedding errands, he and Gamon had snuck into Phuket Town to watch the go-go dancers and share a beer.

Mama Lynn had gone shopping, venturing out to the shops and markets to explore all on her own. The experience had her feeling all out of sorts, and she was venting as they tried to relax in the warming waters.

"She asked me why I was fat!" Mama Lynn exclaimed. "Just came right out and said, 'Why you so fat!' And then she jiggled me!"

Alexander and Zachary both stifled their laughter, fighting not to show their amusement.

"It wasn't personal!" Westley exclaimed. "Thai people don't see questions like that insulting. They just ask about what they see or want to know. It's just full disclosure as far as they're concerned."

"Well, it's rude! Just downright rude. And then another one asked me about my birth control! Do I look like I need some birth control?"

With that the twins lost it, both cackling heartily. Tears were streaming down their faces. Sarai shook her head. "It takes some getting used to, Mama Lynn, but they really didn't mean any harm."

"Humph!" the matriarch scoffed, sucking her teeth in annoyance. "Tch!"

"So how'd your day go, Pop?" Zachary asked, changing the subject.

"Had me a good time. Gamon showed me the ins
and outs around here. It was a really good time!"

The twins exchanged a look, Sarai's cousin Sing
having already gossiped about the good time the two
men had enjoyed. Both bit down on their lips, trying
to contain their emotion. Alexander laughed, the
sound abrupt, and his brother gave him a push.
When Westley turned to stare, they both burst out
again, the laughter gut deep.

Sarai moved onto her feet. "I really need to be
going," she said, waving her hand at her future in-laws.

"You be safe, baby!" Mama Lynn exclaimed.

"Drive safe," Westley chimed in.

Alexander walked her to the door. "Are you excited?" he asked, wrapping his arms around her.

She nodded. "I'm excited that I will be your wife
tomorrow."

"Me, too," he said, leaning to kiss her lips. "You can
still change your mind, you know."

She smiled and shook her head. "Never."

They stood together for a few more minutes, trading easy caresses in the dim light that reflected out of
the cottage window. Their kisses were gentle and
sweet as they whispered words of endearment into
each other's ears. And then he helped her into her
car, kissing her one last time before she pulled out
of sight.

As he stood in the doorway, watching until her tail-
lights disappeared from view, Zachary joined him,
leaning his large body against the doorframe.

"This is your last night as a free man! You ready?"

Alexander turned to look at his brother. He pushed
his hands deep into his pockets. "I'm scared to death,
Z. Ready, excited, and scared to death!"

* * *

The entire property at Revolution had been transformed for the wedding ceremony. Hours before the sun rose, a team of party planners and caterers had arrived to ensure everything was in order. Covered tables and chairs and large floral arrangements decorated the courtyard and the large dining hall. It was as if Xanadu had fallen from the skies while everyone slept.

Up bright and early, the family was dressed and ready to go shortly after the breakfast hour. With his brother leading the way, Zachary and his parents walked across the property to meet Sarai and her father and the aunties, who had helped make everything happen.

Gamon greeted them in the building's foyer. With his prayer hands held in front of his face, Alexander wished him a good morning, then announced his intent to pay the bride price that they had negotiated to compensate him for the loss of his beloved daughter. Bowing slightly, he handed the patriarch a basket of money, the sum total of one million baht, or just under thirty thousand dollars. There were hushed whispers around the room, the Montri family nodding their approval.

As the money was spread in a circle atop a table, Sarai entered the room. Alexander was awed, his mouth dropping open as he stared. She was stunning. She wore a traditional Thai wedding gown, the rich silk fabric a deep shade of gold with a lace overlay and white embroidery accents. One shouldered, it featured a tailored, ankle-length skirt and fit her petite frame to perfection. Her thick hair had been tamed into a chignon that featured a gold headpiece.

From across the room, the two locked gazes and were barely able to take their eyes off each other for the rest of the day.

The family led them into the main hall, where nine orange-robed Buddhist monks had been invited to perform the blessing ceremony. Facing the monks, everyone sat behind Alexander and Sarai, who knelt close together with their hands clasped in prayer, signaling their respect and supplication. After the blessing, the couple presented the monks with gifts and a small donation and then were prayed over a second time.

When the blessing ceremony was complete, Mama Lynn and the aunties offered the monks a morning meal that was served by Sarai's uncles. Everyone else exited the room until they'd finished eating, no one else was allowed to dine. Before the monks departed, they prayed and chanted over the couple a third time, applying a powdered incense to their foreheads.

With the bride and groom kneeling side by side on a special pedestal, the guests were given an opportunity to bestow their individual blessings and good wishes upon the couple. One by one, each poured water over Alexander and Sarai's hands, the moisture passing into a flower-filled bowl.

Every aspect of the wedding continued with a series of traditional ceremonies. There was the candle ceremony, where two candles were lit for Alexander and Sarai to use to light a single candle that symbolized the joining of their two families and to invoke the light of a higher power into their married life.

There was the veil ceremony, where a white veil was draped over the bride's head and the groom's shoulders to symbolize two people being clothed as one. The cord ceremony had a family member draping a decorative silk cord in a figure-eight shape over their shoulders to symbolize everlasting fidelity. Then Alexander gave Sarai thirteen coins blessed by a priest as a sign of his dedication to her and the children they would one day have.

Everyone was surprised when the couple added their own ceremonial touches to their uniting. Mama Lynn clapped excitedly when Alexander dropped down onto one knee and pulled a small black velvet box from his inner pocket. Inside, a five-carat diamond ring shimmered in a platinum setting. He slid it and a diamond-encrusted wedding band onto her ring finger. They concluded the ceremony with the Western tradition of jumping the broom to honor Alexander's parents and his heritage.

The party afterward was truly a party. The food was abundant, and everyone was having a wonderful time. Alexander and Sarai moved from table to table to pay their respects to their guests. It was hours later when they finally sat back with Zachary and their parents.

Alexander grabbed Sarai's hand and kissed the back of her fingers. He held up her fingers, waving her new ring for them to see. "I'se married now, Pa!" he said with a deep laugh. "I'se married now!"

Mama Lynn laughed at his mocking the infamous line from the movie *The Color Purple*. "This was something," she said, her face flushed. "I have never seen anything like this before. It was a beautiful wedding!"

Zachary nodded in agreement. "Your wife is amazing. I hope you realize that," he said to his twin. He gestured with his hands, pointing out everything around him. "How she managed to pull this off in one week is beyond me."

Sarai laughed. "I'm good at everything I do. You should know that by now, brother!"

Zachary cringed. "She called me brother!" he teased, feigning annoyance. "Now I have a sister!"

Alexander wrapped his arm around her shoulder. "You've always had a sister."

His brother smiled.

Westley cleared his throat. "Okay, these folks are big on tradition around here. So you know your mama and I couldn't let you get married and not give you something . . ." He paused, reaching into the pocket of his suit for an envelope that he slid across the table to Alexander.

"What's this?" Alexander looked from her to him and back.

Mama Lynn grinned. "Sarai's aunts were telling me that in the old days there would be a wedding chamber ceremony where an older married couple would prepare the wedding bed for the newlyweds."

Sarai giggled, cutting an eye at Alexander.

Westley nodded. "That's right. I told Mama that was a bit much so we thought we'd just help get your honeymoon started," he said.

Alexander peeked into the envelope and grinned, pulling a hotel room key from inside.

The Shore at Katathani was a luxury beachfront villa resort in the southern end of Phuket. The luxurious property boasted boundless space and seclusion, the honeymoon villa featuring a private infinity pool, ocean views, and a garden-enclosed patio for sunbathing. It was extraordinarily beautiful.

Still dressed in their wedding clothes, Alexander and Sarai moved from the entrance through the living room, into the bedroom, eagerly inspecting the space.

She came to an abrupt halt at the foot of the king-size bed, tears suddenly misting her eyes.

"What's wrong?" Alexander asked, concern vibrating in his tone. He moved to her side, a large hand caressing her back.

She shook her head, gesturing to the bed top. A large gold platter rested in the center. The platter held an assortment of fresh fruit and other tokens that she explained. "They symbolize fertility, good luck, and prosperity. Your parents have honored us with good fortune."

"They're your parents now, too!"

She pressed a hand to his chest. "All of you make me very happy!" she said, sniffling slightly.

Alexander pulled her into his arms and kissed her, their tongues coming together. His mouth danced atop hers with easy abandon. It felt like an eternity before he came up for air, voicing the thought that had been on his mind. "The minute you are unhappy, you tell me and I will do everything in my power to bring you back your joy," he whispered, and then he kissed her one more time.

Chapter Twenty

For two days Alexander and Sarai made love over and over again. When they weren't making love they slept, showered together, played in the pool, and just enjoyed holding each other. For hours on end they exchanged the sweetest kisses and traded teasing caresses.

Sarai had just stepped out of the shower, an oversized white towel wrapped around her. Alexander stood at the foot of the bed, staring at her, when he felt his warm cock growing into a thick erection.

The lights in the room were dimmed, and music played out of speakers built into the walls. An interlude of flutes and violins resounded through the air. Alexander crooked his index finger and gestured for her to come to him. As she moved to his side, Sarai let the towel fall to the floor beneath her feet.

She pressed her palms to his bare chest, rising on her toes to kiss his lips. Her tongue danced against his, exploring, teasing, entwining, and she tasted like mint and fruit, sweet and fresh against his tongue. Blood surged, coursing through his veins as he wrapped himself around her, his hands skating the length of her torso.

Reaching between them, Sarai took him into her hand, stroking him gently as his dick hardened against her palm. She lifted her gaze, losing herself in his blue eyes as he smiled down on her. He shivered with excitement, and the slightest smile pulled at her lips, satisfaction gleaming from her stare.

Disengaging herself from his embrace, she dropped to her knees. His erection was magnificent, and it jutted proudly from his tangled bush. Alexander marveled at how days of practice had made her so proficient, her mouth a talent as Sarai eagerly pleasured his dick with her tongue. She licked and sucked at the head before taking every inch of him quickly and easily down her throat. Her lips would lock tightly around his shaft as she withdrew; then she would roll her tongue all around the head again. The sensations were amazing!

When she turned her attention to the underside, teasing that sensitive spot behind the glans, he almost lost it. And then she went back to sucking him, over and over, as he matched her rhythm, slowly pushing himself in and out of her mouth.

"You are so good at that . . ." he whispered excitedly as he put his hands on the back of head, urging her on.

Sarai suddenly pulled herself from him, moving back onto her feet. Her gaze danced over his face as she backed her way onto the bed, spreading herself open, her legs parting as she drew her knees to her chest. The invitation was unspoken; no words needed to say what she wanted.

Alexander eased his body against hers, plunging himself into her in one swift motion. Sarai gasped, her ecstatic wail the sweetest sound imaginable. Turning her head so that she could see him in the mirrored closet door sent currents of electricity sweeping through her. She held her legs high in the air, engrossed as his ass pumped furiously in and out of her. Turning back to him, she moaned into his open mouth, latching her lips back to his.

He suddenly rolled, turning onto his back as he pulled her above him. Sarai was no weight at all in his arms as she rolled easily with him, straddling her body over his. As she dropped herself down hard against him, Alexander slid his hand along the crack of her ass, then slipped a finger into the warm, dark tunnel, no part of her off-limits to him.

It was sexual heaven for them both as he filled her, teased her, then flooded her with an overwhelming sensual warmth. Pushing the limits of their loving, she was in complete control as she lifted her body from his and lowered herself again, his thickness nuzzling the snug rosebud that his fingers had just teased. He smiled, sucking on his bottom lip as she slowly let her weight settle on him, the sensation delightful as his cock opened and filled her.

He blew a low hiss of air as his body slipped into the tight, velvety confines of her rectum. Gripping her thighs, he held her as she impaled herself over and over again. Then he thrust his fingers between her legs, thumbing her swollen clit. They settled into a natural lusty rhythm, the intimate coupling raw and animalistic. It was pain and pleasure as she watched his climax building in his handsome face, his hips thrusting urgently, wanting more, and wanting it deeper and harder.

Alexander suddenly tensed, his whole body erupting into orgasmic bliss. He gripped her tighter, pushing his hips higher, thrusting himself deep into her ass, and then he cursed, screaming his pleasure as every nerve ending erupted. As he spilled into her, the sexual electricity through her cunt vibrated, and she fell off the edge of pleasure with him. Every muscle in her body quaked as she dropped into the throes of her sexual ecstasy.

Hours later they would lay side by side, her body pressed tight to his, savoring another sweet session of lovemaking. They would share how much love they had for each other and whisper their dreams and secrets to each other. They would be awed by the trust and the thirst that they had for each other. It was sheer bliss.

"Fuck!"

Zachary and Alexander both turned abruptly, unaccustomed to hearing such foul language from any woman in Thailand. But the young woman coming through the door of the main office wasn't Thai. Or at least Zachary didn't think so.

Her complexion was honey, a deep, rich, sweet coloration that paid homage to her African heritage. But her features were Asian, almond-shaped eyes, forest-thick lashes, and chiseled cheekbones. Her hair was a definite melding of the two cultures; thick, voluminous curls that fell past her shoulders. Her body was a contradiction, her petite stature boasting a small waist and voluptuous curves. She had a full, lush bustline and a bubble-shaped ass that could easily make a strong man weep.

She cussed again, fighting with a large, oversized suitcase with a broken handle that she was struggling to get through the office door.

He watched with amusement as she pushed and pulled at the garment bag, unable to get any kind of a grip on the container. She suddenly gave up, spinning herself into the room. She jumped, startled to find him staring at her. They both eyed each other warily.

Sarai suddenly spoke up from the desk she'd been sitting behind. "May I help you?" she asked as she rose from her seat and moved to the front counter.

The young woman shot Zachary one last look before turning her attention toward the woman offering her some assistance. "Yes. I'm looking for Sarah Montri. They said I could find her here."

"It's Sarai . . . *Suh-rye.* Sarai Barrett. I just got married! You must be Kenzie Monroe."

"I am. It's nice to meet you, Sarai Barrett. And congratulations on that marriage thing!"

"Thank you and welcome to Revolution. Let's get you checked in to your cottage."

"I really appreciate that. I had a miserable flight. Some bald, toothless guy kept trying to grope me."

"That's not good," Sarai said, skewing her face.

"I wanted to tase him. Then I remembered they wouldn't let me fly with my Taser! I had to elbow drop him in the crotch instead."

Zachary laughed, shooting Sarai and the young woman a look. Amusement painted his expression. The look on Alexander's face said the twins had read each other's minds.

Sarai shook her head, but before she could comment Kenzie shifted her attention.

"Congratulations on your win, Mr. Barrett. It was an impressive fight. And it's nice to meet you as well," she said, shooting a look at Alexander.

Zachary nodded, his head bowing ever so slightly.

"Thank you." He extended his hand to shake hers. "And you are?"

"Kenzie Monroe. I'm with *Sports Illustrated International.*"

"Kenzie is here to do the article on you and Alex," Sarai interjected.

Zachary's gaze shifted between the two women, then settled back on the newcomer. "Where are you from, Ms. Monroe?"

"Please, call me Kenzie. And I was born here in Thailand, in Bangkok. But I was raised in New York."

"So your mother is Thai?"

"No, my father," she said, her eyes fastened tight to his. "My mother was black."

Zachary stared at the woman, his expression shifting into something Sarai didn't recognize. The moment suddenly turned awkward. She looked to Alexander for assistance, but he'd turned his attention to an incoming call on his cell phone.

She cleared her throat. "Zachary, will you please help Ms. Monroe with her luggage?"

He turned, giving his new sister-in-law a look. "Find Sing. Have him take care of it."

"But you . . ." Sarai started.

He stalled her comment, snapping rudely. He spoke in Thai, the exchange meant to be between the two of them. "Get Sing. Then call that magazine and tell them this isn't going to work. I have something I need to handle."

Both women watched as he suddenly turned and stormed from the room. Turning her attention back to Kenzie, Sarai looked embarrassed, her face flushed.

Kenzie was thoroughly entertained. She spoke in Thai. "It looks like things are going to get quite interesting around here!"

**Don't miss the next book
in the Bad Boys of Boulder series,**

Perfect Pleasures

On sale in November 2016!

World famous MMA champion Zachary Barrett
has returned to his home in Phuket, Thailand,
and his elite training camp, Revolution.
Thanks to his twin brother, a renowned pro trainer
in Colorado, Zachary is primed and ready for his
next title bout—but his toughest match may be with
the sports journalist assigned to write an exposé
on him. Not only is she gorgeous, she's after a
well-guarded secret that Zach soon realizes
makes her off limits in every way . . .

It's true that Kenzie Monroe has an ulterior motive
for pursuing Zachary. The half-Asian beauty
believes he's connected to her estranged father,
a former MMA fighter who disappeared years ago.
And the more Zachary avoids her, the more
determined she is—and the hotter their game
of cat and mouse becomes . . . until they both
surrender. But as lust, love, and friendship
combine, Zachary knows he has to answer all of
Kenzie's questions—because outside of the ring,
the heart makes the rules . . .